DREAMING DEATH

HEATHER GRAHAM

DREAMING DEATH

mira

ISBN-13: 978-0-7783-1010-5

Dreaming Death

Mira
22 Adelaide St. West, 40th Floor
Toronto, Ontario M5H 4E3, Canada
BookClubbish.com

Printed in U.S.A.

A special thanks to friends who have always helped with crazy ideas, from Writers for New Orleans to B-con and more.

Rebecca Barrett
Pat Walker
Patty Harrison
Cindy Kremple
Cindy Walker
Kristen Moum
Sharon Murphy
Ginger and Larry McSween
Janice and Thomas Jones
Susan and Kevin Cella
Kristi and Brian Ahlers

You give so much!

DREAMING
DEATH

PROLOGUE

A monster had come.

His eyes burned like twin globes of fire.

He was big and moved with purpose. All she could see was the red of his eyes and the bright red and pitch black of his demon face.

She'd seen him before...seen his face.

Somehow, she realized he wasn't a demon. He was wearing a mask, dark shirt and pants, a long jacket...and there was a bulge at his hip.

She thought he was carrying a gun.

She was grateful to realize he couldn't see her. She was hidden, looking out. She couldn't fathom her hiding spot, but he couldn't see her. She knew because she was looking right at him, watching him, but he couldn't see her.

He was in her father's office, tearing things apart, jerking drawers from the desk, letting them crash to the floor. He rifled through the papers that fell from them, searching with the urgency of desperation.

Yes, she'd seen this as well...the demon-man tearing the place apart.

He went to the computer, swearing when he found it was

password protected, sending the keyboard flying to the floor as well.

Then she heard her father's voice. He was talking to someone. Her mother.

The man with the burning red eyes went still, and he drew his gun, aiming it at the door.

This was new; this she hadn't seen before.

It was then she started to scream. She had to warn them. She had to stop them from coming.

Her voice rose with urgency.

But the demon didn't hear her. Her parents didn't hear her.

The door began to open.

"Stacey! Stacey, sweetheart! Wake up!"

Her mother was holding her. Her father was beside them. While her mom comforted her, her dad smoothed back her hair.

"Baby, it's a nightmare," he said.

Her mother looked at him anxiously. "David, this is the third time. We've got to do something. We've got to get help."

"Stacey, stop shaking! It's a nightmare. Just a dream," her father said firmly.

"No. No, Daddy, it's a man, and he's coming, he's coming, and—"

"Yes, sweetheart, I know you're seeing something. The devil, a demon, whatever." Her mother took a deep breath. "We're… well, we're going to get someone to help you. I know someone. A nice doctor who can talk you through this. She works with many people—young and old—who are troubled with nightmares. There's something you're afraid of, and if we can just find out what it is…" Her mom trailed off at a look from her father. Then she asked, "Will you be able to sleep? Do you want me to stay in here with you?"

"Judith," her dad murmured.

Stacey didn't want to cause trouble between them. She was

frightened. Bone-chilling scared. But it wasn't for her own safety. She saw what was going to happen from a distant place.

She was terrified for her parents.

Her father thought himself a capable man. He was a private investigator. He'd been in the military. He consulted and investigated for the police and other law-enforcement agencies. He was a man who knew that life could be very dangerous.

He knew how to use a gun, but he didn't always carry one. When he worked at home, it was kept locked in his gun safe. She'd heard her parents talk about it. Her mom didn't like guns, so even though she admitted that at the age of twelve, Stacey was unlikely to disobey them and go grab her dad's gun, the weapon was to always be locked up in the house. It was one of the few arguments she'd ever heard them have.

Her parents were special people. A true love-match. She was their only child. That was because her dad had been sixty when she'd been born, her mother nearly forty. People—well-meaning people, friends and family—had thought the age difference might be too much.

Some had thought her mother was after his money. Rather silly, since she was an important banker and made way more than him.

Her father was such a cool man: he thought it important for a girl to learn everything. He cooked as often as her mom. If her mom made dinner—even if it was icky fish sticks—her father said thank you and told her what a wonderful meal it had been.

He even did dishes.

She'd heard someone ask him once if for his so-called one shot, he was sorry he hadn't gotten a boy.

He had shrugged and said, "We were thrilled with a happy baby. And a girl? Well, heck, she can do anything a boy can do!"

She adored him.

She loved her mom, too.

And she didn't want them fighting.

"No, Mommy, no, you're right. It was just a nightmare. And it's over."

"See?" her father said proudly. "Judith, she's smart as a whip."

"We still have to do something about…whatever it is!" her mom said.

"We will," her father promised.

They kissed her good-night.

"Leave the hallway light on?" she asked.

"Yes, sweetie," her mom promised.

They left her, she fell back to sleep, and the dream didn't come again.

Not that night.

Her name was Dr. Patricia Blair, and she was very nice. Stacey liked her just fine. She had worked with her dad and David Hanson Investigations before.

Dr. Patricia encouraged Stacey to talk, and she listened and didn't mock. Stacey might have been twelve, but she'd spent a lot of her time with grown-ups, and she knew how to deal with them. She never resorted to tears or dramatics. She tried, in a calm and even voice, to explain the way the dream had come.

First, just the burning eyes.

Then, the demon face.

Then, the man in her father's study…

The good doctor did everything a psychiatrist was supposed to do, Stacey knew. She asked if Stacey was having any problems at school. Was she, perhaps, being bullied?

No. She loved school. She liked her friends. She was in a magnet school for music. Nerds did not bully nerds. They were all…nerds.

She was surprised when the doctor asked her to describe the nightmares in more detail. And equally surprised by the way the woman listened to her. The doctor then asked her mom if she might have a friend speak with Stacey as well.

Was he another doctor?

No, just an amazing man with incredible insight.

He seemed old; tall and thin with white hair and a face that was somehow beautiful.

Stacey liked him. People around her were calling him Mr. Harrison, but he told her his name was Adam, and he liked being called that.

He also asked her to go over the details of the nightmare. He listened to her so intently, and his nod was sincere as she finished.

"Someone is going to kill my dad...and my mom, I think. But they don't believe me. Everyone just thinks I'm a kid with crazy nightmares. Well, I am a kid with crazy nightmares, but I'm still so scared!"

"Let me talk to your parents," he told her. "They'll listen to me, I hope."

Adam did talk to them, but they were in another room, and she could only catch parts of the conversation.

"I don't think my family is in danger, but I guess the most worrisome case I've been on is the McCarron case," her father told Adam Harrison. "And what I have strongly suggests something far more nefarious than money laundering and even his illegal drug running from within his company. I have pictures of McCarron himself going into the hospital the night Dr. Vargas and Mr. Anderson died in the stairwell—and it sure as hell looks like he's carrying a gun of some kind in a holster—his jacket moved while he was walking."

"You think McCarron forced them down the stairs?" Adam asked.

"I don't have any solid proof. Proving anything on this... Well, the prosecutors need more. I think McCarron and his pharmaceutical empire are guilty in many cases of 'accidental' or 'natural' death, but I don't know if what I have is enough. I've kept gathering, but not everything has gone to the police yet.

Obviously, I go through what I have and try to sort the wheat from the chaff. That's what I do."

"But you have pictures of McCarron entering the Anderson Building thirty minutes before Richard Anderson and Dr. Vargas were found dead next to each other on the landing at the foot of the stairs," Adam said.

"Anderson and Vargas were found by one of Dr. Vargas's associates, Dr. Henry Lawrence, and Lawrence was so upset at finding his beloved mentor that he moved the body and tried every conceivable medical maneuver to bring him back, but Anderson was gone."

"Yes," Adam said. "I've read all the reports. Richard Anderson's was supposedly a natural death—a heart attack at the top of the stairwell, causing him to fall all the way down. That's what the ME said. And Dr. Vargas supposedly tripped on the same steps in his haste and died trying to reach Anderson to help him. So the scene made it appear. It was tragic, everyone said, so there wasn't much of a police investigation."

"Here's why I'm involved. Sally Anderson didn't believe it. She said she'd heard her husband arguing with someone a week before his death. All he would ever say to her was there was nothing she needed to worry about. She'd hired me at that point to investigate the situation. Supposedly, Anderson was a good guy; he gave a lot to philanthropies. He was a major supporter of organ-transplant research and more. Anyway, I already had him under surveillance on the day of his death. Yes, I have pictures. But I don't have pictures of McCarron doing anything to Anderson. We did have a video that somehow magically disappeared. One of my investigators filmed McCarron going into Anderson's office. The video was the best possible proof. To the best of my knowledge, after I turned it over, someone managed to delete it from the prosecutor's files. Of course, the defense also said it was gone," her dad told Adam.

"You and I both know," Adam said, "that the prosecution has

worked hard on this. Another doctor and a nurse are planning to appear as witnesses for the prosecution to swear they heard McCarron threatening Dr. Vargas. But Vargas wasn't afraid; he dismissed McCarron's words later, saying he was just a bunch of bluster when he didn't get his way."

"What I've dug up," said her father, "is that it seems McCarron thinks his family didn't get a fair shot—his brother died, in need of a kidney transplant. But he hadn't come up on the list yet. And Vargas was the best of the best at kidney transplants. By all accounts, Vargas was a straight shooter—he always followed hospital criteria and couldn't be bought. I think that McCarron had tried just that—to bribe both Anderson and Vargas— and when it didn't work, well… I guess he thought that anyone could be bought. We just need a bit of physical proof. We know McCarron's criminal activities go far beyond insider trading and money laundering. The man rules through fear. He's managed to bribe cops, buy off witnesses, and slip through the justice system time and time again."

Adam was silent for a few moments and then said, "You're a danger to this man. You brought in the first proof against him, and he probably knows there is more you might have obtained."

"I was a Marine, for God's sake! I can protect myself—"

"No one man can protect themselves against the kind of killer that might be sent in against you," Adam said. "Think of your wife and child."

That was it. Her father was a capable man, but he'd also been quick to say no man was an island.

And when it came to his wife and his child, he wasn't taking chances.

Adam made the arrangements. Agents discreetly came to the house. Then it became a tense waiting game.

Four nights after Stacey first met Adam Harrison, it happened. She learned about it later.

Stacey and her mother had gone to stay with an aunt. Her father was at home with the agents when a man wearing a demon mask broke into her father's home office.

The agents stopped him before he could fire at her father. Under arrest, he confessed that he'd been hired by McCarron.

Later, Adam was in the courtroom when the work David Hanson, her father, had done for the local police proved to be invaluable, as several exceptionally malicious and devious criminals were brought to trial and, in the end, brought to justice.

Stacey watched it all on TV. She saw McCarron and the man who had tried to kill her father, as well as those who went on the witness stand and cried and said McCarron was a wonderful man. Several of them were women who were somehow in love with him.

Had he paid those women to swear that he was a good man? The man who had intended to kill her father—and possibly her mother and her—had sworn under oath that McCarron had hired him to do the killing.

"Money can do powerful things!" her mother had muttered. She hadn't gone to court, either. She'd stayed with Stacey, but she hadn't kept her daughter from watching the trial.

Stacey saw the widows of Dr. Vargas and Mr. Anderson try to be brave but break down on the witness stand.

Dr. Henry Lawrence's testimony might have been the saddest of all: crying on the stand, he said that not only had he lost a friend and mentor, the entire world had lost out on a great man.

McCarron was remarkable on the stand. He also broke into tears, denying all charges.

Despite his Oscar-worthy performance, he was convicted and sent down.

So, the McCarron trial was over.

But Stacey's father didn't think that was the end of it. She heard him telling Adam that even though McCarron went down, he was pretty sure there was someone higher up the chain or, at the least, in place to take over.

But McCarron didn't talk, and those they found who he'd hired for certain of his deeds, such as the attack on Stacey's father, thought he'd been the top dog.

"I'm telling you, there was someone there. Someone else who was really pulling the strings," her father said.

"Maybe," Adam said. "And that's just how life goes—'Meet the new boss, same as the old boss.' There will be someone out there to take McCarron's place. But we'll be there, too. We'll just keep going after the bad guys."

Adam Harrison and his agents saw it all the way through. Then it was time for them to move on.

Stacey was so grateful to them.

She hero-worshipped her parents, and now she also felt that way about Adam Harrison. When they talked next, she was no longer having the nightmare. She was grateful, telling him he had saved her parents—and her.

"No, Stacey, you saved them," he told her.

"I want to be a PI like my dad!" she said. Then she frowned. "What's your job?"

"Me? Uh, I don't do anything special. Well, maybe I do. I find people—the right people," he told her.

"Am I a *right* person?" she asked him.

He knelt by her, giving her a hug. She wasn't sure how such a cool man could also seem like the world's sweetest grandfather.

"You sure were this time!" he told her. "But you're only twelve years old. Let's see where life takes you. You have high school, college…a lot of living to do. But when you're older, if you want to see me…well, I will definitely want to see you again!" He gave her a business card with his name and phone number on it. It felt very grown-up to her, and she beamed.

She hugged him tightly; she knew he was leaving. She hoped she'd see him again.

But it wouldn't be soon.

Her mother insisted they move away from Georgetown and Washington, DC.

Their new home was situated on a beautiful hill in Harpers Ferry, West Virginia. It was still easy access to the country's capital but distant enough so Stacey's mom felt they had a quiet and normal life.

Her mother left her job to teach, and her father retired.

Life was pretty good. Despite her mom not being particularly fond of anything that had to do with guns or law enforcement, Stacey joined a young-citizens watch group in high school. And through local police programs she learned a great deal about averting and investigating crimes and how officers and forensic investigators often solved crimes together. Legwork, the art of interrogation, and science.

She also spent many an hour watching the ID channel, learning all about crimes, both past and present, and the way they were solved.

Sometimes—just now and then—she'd have strange little dreams. One time, she had a vivid dream about a broken zipper on her parka, and it seemed almost silly.

Yet, putting on her parka the next day, the zipper broke.

Then she dreamed that the underdog—Charlie Waters, worst player on the school's team—scored the winning touchdown for the school's football team.

The following Friday night, remarkably, Charlie did just that.

But it wasn't until she was almost eighteen that she had a frightening dream again, one that really mattered—a piece of life and *death* she had to hope she could change.

And that time it had to do with a friend, Kevin Waverly.

Kevin was a running back for the high-school football team. He was well-liked, did decently in all his classes and planned on either professional ball or, if he didn't quite cut it as pro, going into coaching or therapy for sports injuries.

Then he fell in love with Elaine Gregory, who was sweet and beautiful. But easily manipulated.

Elaine met an older boy who introduced her to cocaine. Soon, Elaine and Kevin were missing classes, and Coach was threatening to kick Kevin off the team. It wasn't a large school, and Stacey had heard the gossip.

Stacey's dream started with her walking through the night. She was walking in a cemetery. She knew, somehow, it wasn't the historic Harper Cemetery with the fantastic view that was a must for any tourist—no. It was the almost-forgotten Miller Cemetery just a bit to the south toward Port Royal. It offered no view except by night, when the fog rolled in and the trees seemed to drip eerie fingers of moss, and the greatest danger was tripping over a broken headstone or footstone.

Only one angel stood guard over the place, and sadly her wings were both chipped, and her face was eternally muddied. There were a few above-ground tombs and obelisks scattered between the overgrown grasses, shrubs and trees.

It was a perfect place for teenagers to come.

To drink, or to sell drugs, or to do drugs.

The first time the dream came, Stacey just saw herself walking through the cemetery.

The next time, she saw Kevin and Elaine and a shadowy figure were by the broken angel, and the three were arguing.

The third time she heard a gunshot.

She told her father about her dream. He didn't want to listen at first; then Stacey reminded him about Adam Harrison's faith in her, and he did. He told the local police he believed drug deals were going down in the cemetery. The police ignored him. The officer on the phone told him that yes, they watched the cemetery. They didn't have the manpower to watch it day and night. But they thanked him, saying they were forewarned.

The dream came again, night after night. But this time as she walked through the broken stones in the eerie darkness punctuated by the light of the moon, someone touched her shoulder. She turned and trembled and tried to scream but could not.

It was Chastity Miller: she knew that from pictures. Chastity Miller had been one of Washington's spies during the Revolutionary War. She had been beautiful and charming and part of an elite group that became known as the Culper Spy Ring, set up by Major Benjamin Tallmadge under Washington's orders. It was said he kept the identities of those in the ring so secret that not even Washington knew all their names. In 1778, Chastity worked in British-occupied New York, bringing valuable information to the table. She could charm any British officer with her facade of sweet innocence.

She had, however, been found out. Her body had been discovered hanging from a tree outside the city, but it was taken down secretly at night and returned to her family in the Harpers Ferry area. Her tombstone had long ago disappeared. It was believed she did rest in the Miller Cemetery.

Except in Stacey's dream, she didn't rest. She stood there as if she was *real*.

Terrified at first, in her sleep Stacey struggled to remind herself it was a dream.

"It's coming. You must do something. You can do something. It's coming," Chastity Miller said.

"I know. I've told them!" Stacey managed to say at last. "I've tried!"

"It's coming soon. You must try harder!" Chastity said. "You can, and you must!"

Stacey spoke to her father again; he wearily reminded her he'd spoken to the police. They were dismissive of a man telling them something bad was about to happen. They wanted to know how he knew. Was he selling drugs himself?

"Call Mr. Harrison," she told him.

"Stacey, for the love of God..." He walked away, distraught.

That night she had the dream again. She saw Chastity Miller

again, beckoning her to follow and hide. And she heard the conversation. Kevin wanted the shadowy figure to leave Elaine alone. Elaine was addicted. Either it stopped or Kevin would go to the police.

The shadowy figure had a gun. He drew it…

She forced herself to wake up.

Stacey remembered Adam Harrison had left her with his card. That had been years before, but maybe, just maybe, she still had it somewhere.

She searched through her drawers, her little jewelry boxes, every nook and cranny of her room.

She finally found the card slipped into pages of a diary she'd kept when she was twelve.

She dialed the number before she could think too hard about it, and he answered. Since she'd seen him last, it seemed he'd upped his game. He was now an assistant director, working for the Federal Bureau of Investigation.

Adam came out with two agents: one named Jackson, and the other a very tall young man with sandy hair and striking dark eyes, Special Agent Someone or Other. She didn't really talk to him. He had to be new because of his age, and because of the way he deferred to the other men. She figured he'd be a really cool agent one day because he sure as hell looked the part.

They listened to her, and the agents went to check out Miller Cemetery.

Adam stayed with Stacey. She asked him why it was he believed her so easily. And he smiled and said, "My son. He was very much like you."

"And he's…gone?"

Adam Harrison's smile grew broader. "Oh, sometimes, I believe, he's very much still with me."

It took three nights. Then it happened. Kevin and Elaine slipped into the cemetery. The drug dealer was there. He listened to Kevin; he drew his gun to kill him. Kevin screamed and begged for his life and a shot went off...

But Kevin hadn't been shot.

One of the agents had fired first, with amazing aim. He shot the gun right out of the drug dealer's hand.

It turned out to be the first domino to fall in a major chain of busts. The dealer had been selling across several states and in DC. He had many connections, and eventually a whole network was brought down.

Because many deaths could be linked to him, the dealer had gone for a plea deal to avert the federal death penalty. He had, as she had heard said, *sung like a canary.*

Adam Harrison was careful to keep any mention of Stacey from the news. According to all sources, the FBI had received an anonymous tip.

Stacey had to go to the Miller Cemetery, not in a dream but in person. She went the next day when it wasn't spooky, just derelict and sad. Crime-scene tape remained in the one section, drooping with the night's rain and as sad as the rest of the cemetery. But the crime-scene investigators were gone.

As she walked, she felt a touch on her shoulder. She turned, and Chastity Miller was standing there. It wasn't a dream.

Stacey would have been terrified, except she felt a strange sense that was both chilling and warming as the young woman hugged her.

"I knew you could do it," the ghost said.

"I—I was so afraid! I don't know, I can't—"

"You could and you did. Fear is something important; you need to know fear. It will help you behave intelligently, keep you from being rash. We have all known fear. The thing of it is to learn how to deal with that fear and meet it so you are stronger than it, and stronger than those who would create it in others."

"But you—"

"I made mistakes. I know. But I wouldn't have changed what

I could do for my country. And I will do my best, always, to see the dream of our country remains strong." She smiled. "Whatever the challenge, we fight. We fight for what is right, whenever there is a right that must be upheld. You can do it!"

Her last words were spoken softly. She smiled and dissolved into the sunlit air.

Adam Harrison was still in Harpers Ferry, but he was leaving shortly.

This time when they said goodbye, Stacey told him she'd see him soon. "I'll be working for you next," she assured him.

"I don't doubt it. Just be sure it's what you want," he told her.

She passionately assured him, "I owe you—for believing in me!"

"College," he told her.

"Oh, you bet. The University of Maryland. They offer great courses. I'll do it, all right, Adam. But there's nothing else I want to do. Please... I won't be able to stand my life without... without coming to work for you."

"You'll need to apply to the FBI Academy."

"Oh, I will," she promised. Her smile deepened. "And I will kick ass! I promise you."

Her parents weren't happy with her choice. "We've spent our lives trying to shield you from danger!" her mother told her.

She adored her parents. But she knew what she was doing.

"I need to learn how to use what I have," she told them.

They let her choose her way.

Soon after her twenty-fourth birthday, she graduated from the FBI Academy at Quantico.

And walked straight into the offices of Adam Harrison and his Krewe of Hunters.

CHAPTER ONE

Keenan Wallace's phone rang at 5:00 a.m.; it wasn't the alarm, it was a call. Before he looked at the caller ID, he knew who it was.

Not many people would call this early.

"Jackson?" he said, after he'd groped around on his nightstand to find the phone.

"We're going to be assigned."

"The mutilation murders?"

"Yep. You'll need to get to the Lafayette Square area."

"All right. Is there another victim?"

"I don't know. If you can get there around six thirty, that would be perfect."

"I can be there sooner."

"No."

"No?"

"The body hasn't been discovered yet. It will be, just after six. I'm sure they'll have Fred Crandall on the case for DC local law enforcement. He called me after the second victim was found in Alexandria. But give him a few minutes to get there once the police have received the 9-1-1."

For a moment, Keenan pulled the phone away from his ear to stare at it, a frown furrowing his features.

Keenan understood that information gained via the Krewe of Hunters network was unusual; they had sources who had special insight. And while Keenan himself had the special talent—or bad luck, as he sometimes felt it was—to communicate with many a deceased soul, he'd yet to know a ghost who could use a phone to call in a tip.

"Jackson—"

"Trust me. She simply hasn't been discovered. No, I don't know who the killer is. I want you on this one. You know Fred, and you work especially well with him." Jackson seemed to hesitate just a moment, then added, "You'll also be working with a new partner."

Keenan had worked with a number of other agents—top-notch all of them. This case was as high profile as they came: when prostitutes were being found dead and mutilated in the nation's capital, it was bound to attract major attention.

"Who is it?" he asked.

"She's new."

"A rookie?"

"This will be her first Krewe case, yes. She's just out of the academy."

"Wait, wait. These are some of the most heinous murders imaginable, and you're giving me a rookie—a new agent? One I don't even know yet?"

"Special Agent Stacey Hanson. She'll find you at the crime scene."

The name was vaguely familiar to him.

"This is happening in our backyard," Jackson continued. "You'll have the full force of the Krewe behind you."

Still. A rookie?

"Okay, wait," Keenan said. "I want to make sure I understand the situation. There's another victim—ostensibly murdered by

the killer who struck in DC once and Virginia once already—
but she hasn't been discovered yet. And I shouldn't get to Lafayette Square until six thirty. Fred Crandall will be our local
contact…and I'm working with a partner I've never met, who
has never worked a case before?"

"That's it."

"And this new agent will find me there?"

"Exactly."

"Jackson, I know you're right on top of everything, but I'm
just saying. This is going to wind up being high profile, and
I'm not sure a rookie—"

"The rookie is the reason we know a body will soon be discovered, Keenan. You'll do fine. Work with her. Yes, it's going
to be high profile. And I know you know what you're doing.
Trust me on this, Keenan. You were a rookie once, and I trusted
you." He paused just briefly. "This new agent will be invaluable. Catch me up on everything you discover today as soon as
you can."

Keenan started to reply, but Jackson had already rung off.

Groaning, he dragged himself up and to the shower.

Trust me, Jackson had said.

He did trust Jackson Crow. There was no better man, personally or professionally.

He let the water run long and hot.

Work with the rookie. Well, he would try.

It had been coming. The dreams always started off with something innocuous and then led to the dangerous and deadly.

Life had taught Stacey that few people would ever believe
her. It was more likely they would lock her away, since, by all
appearances, her knowledge would mean she'd had something
to do with the violence.

The dreams had been building for the past few weeks.

A walk, early morning, sun just rising, through Lafayette

Square. And then the sight of feet sticking out from behind the base of a statue.

One foot with a shoe, one without.

Last night, she had seen the body.

Anyone with a television, a laptop, a phone, or even eyes had to know about the two recent murders that had been committed in DC and Alexandria. The gruesome details screamed from every media site and newspaper and magazine in the country.

So, Stacey had called in what she knew—straight to Jackson Crow.

Stacey had become an agent very recently and hadn't expected to be put out in the field so quickly, and certainly not on such a case. She had wanted to give the Krewe a heads-up, grateful there were people out there who believed her. She'd only had a jump on the discovery of the body.

She couldn't help but wonder just what good that was. She hadn't prevented anything.

"I've got a seasoned agent heading to the scene you described," Jackson Crow told her over the phone. "He'll go in after the 9-1-1 call. We have to be cautious, or it won't go over well with local law enforcement—because you understand explaining dreams to those who are unaccustomed to the unusual is not an effort that succeeds."

"Of course, sir," Stacey assured her direct superior. "Show up at the scene at approximately seven fifteen. Give Special Agent Keenan Wallace a bit of time to do his own initial investigation. Then, get in there."

She inhaled a long breath. "I'll recognize him because he'll be by the body?" she asked.

"Yes, well…that and you can't miss him. Keenan is almost six-five." Jackson paused. "He's got sandy hair and makes an impression. You've actually met him before. He was the other agent with me and Adam when you called about your friends being in danger in the Miller Cemetery. Anyway, he stands out in a crowd. Yes, he'll be by the body. If not, trust me, you won't miss him."

"Okay, thank you, sir." Biting her lip, she rose and walked to her window. She was back in Georgetown. She loved the neighborhood, the old buildings on the street, the cherry trees here and there…

And it was strange.

It was where she'd first experienced her bizarre nightmares. There were other places to live. She'd made the choice, however, to take an apartment in Georgetown when she'd graduated and come to the Krewe.

She wondered if Georgetown wasn't somehow special to her.

She realized she was nervous. Her first case. Shower, dress, get to work. It was time.

Before now, she'd never been able to tell others what she saw. Now she was going to turn nightmares to good use.

Yes, it was time to prove herself.

"She was…oh, my God, she was just lying there," the young woman told Keenan. "I'm a nurse—on my way to the day shift—and I know… I *know* the smell of blood!"

Keenan nodded sympathetically. He adjusted the blanket around the woman's shoulders. The morning was warm, but she sat shivering in the rear of an ambulance.

The woman who'd found the body, one Jennifer Maples, was in her early twenties, dressed in scrubs, eyes damp with fear, huge green pools in a face the shade of ash. He understood.

"They'll take you to work or home, whichever you wish," he said. "It was just six when you passed by the statue, right? And saw the victim there?"

She nodded. "Yes, sir, I know it was just about ten after. I work three twelve-hour shifts a week, and I am a creature of habit. My shift starts at seven, but I like to get in a bit early for coffee and charts. I walk this way to the metro… Did you see her? Oh, my God!"

She covered her mouth again, as if trying to prevent herself from spewing the bile that was rising within.

"It's all right."

"I'm a nurse. I'm not squeamish. But that—"

"It's all right," Keenan repeated softly.

Yes, he'd seen her—the victim.

"Did you see or hear anyone near you—cars moving out, anyone running, anyone behaving suspiciously in any way?"

She shook her head. "The square was quiet. I think I saw a few people pass on the other side of the statue, but you can't see her unless…you're on this side of it. No one was running or behaving oddly," she said wryly. "There were cars out on the road, but I didn't see any of them speeding by, no running lights or anything like that… There was nothing unusual," she said earnestly. "There was just her—that poor woman!"

He nodded, silent for a minute.

She looked at him. "I've heard about this killer, this man they're calling the Yankee Ripper. He's killed twice already, right? The media has been subtle and not so subtle about warning sex workers he's on the prowl. I don't care what she did for a living. She might have been down and out. She might have been the nicest person in the world—or not. No one—oh, God, no one should have happen to them what happened to her!"

"Of course not. Every life is sacred," Keenan said.

"And you'll find whoever did this, right? You won't just figure someone is killing sex workers and who cares?"

"As yet, we don't know who she was, or what she did for a living. But that won't matter," Keenan promised. "I assure you, we will seek this man with all our resources."

She looked baffled for a minute. "Who are you? You're not in uniform. The other man I talked to first—"

"Detective Fred Crandall. He's DC police," Keenan told her.

"And you're—"

"FBI," he said. He offered her a grim smile. "We're all on this, Miss Maples. We will find this person, and we will stop these killings."

Her eyes widened suddenly. "I'm not in any danger, am I?"

"I don't believe you're in danger, but you should always take care. You know that, of course. Lock your doors, watch your surroundings. Be wary. But I think you already are, and will be, as soon as you have a second to get some strength back. You're smart and savvy," he assured her with a smile. "Miss Maples, thank you so much. If you'd like to go home, we can speak with your employers. You've suffered a truly traumatic experience, and you reacted with a speed that has certainly helped us."

"I couldn't bear the thought of a child coming across…that," she whispered.

She'd had the presence of mind to dial 9-1-1 immediately and get the call through despite what must have been a serious trembling in her fingers.

She was still shaking.

"I—I don't want to go home. I live in an apartment alone. I don't want to be alone."

Understandable. But Keenan had to get over to see the victim; the medical examiner was waiting for him along with Fred Crandall.

He leaned out the back of the ambulance and beckoned to a uniformed officer to come and watch over their distraught witness, see that she was helped. Then he stepped down and headed for the crime scene. Passing by two DC officers with a nod, he ducked under the yellow tape.

And reached the body.

Fred Crandall was standing next to Dr. Beau Simpson, who was on his knees by the body, still doing his initial inspection.

Crandall was in his early forties, a longtime cop who had seen a hell of a lot. Washington, DC, could be beautiful beyond belief, beloved by natives to the city and by tourists who came from all regions. It was also a political hotbed where many a strange crime took place.

Fred was a veteran of many of those crimes and a damned good detective. Medium in height, he was still built with the wiry strength of a tiger. He was bald and had sharp blue eyes, the kind that could intimidate many a perpetrator.

Dr. Simpson was also a seasoned man. Fiftysomething with salt-and-pepper, close-cropped hair, he was impressively cool, calm and stoic, always.

Simpson had once told Keenan that it came from living in DC—the heart of the Union—and having been named Beauregard after the Confederate general P. G. T. Beauregard by a mother from South Carolina. He'd seen so many lifted eyebrows and smirks that he could maintain a totally blank expression at any time.

The three of them had worked together before. Keenan was glad Beau seemed to be the Washington medical examiner on the case. Along with giving investigators his findings on any case, he always told them how he determined every detail he found.

"To the best of our educated reckoning, she's number three," Dr. Simpson said, not looking up.

"Cause and method of death?" Keenan asked.

"No way like the old Whitechapel Ripper, as the rumors have been saying," Simpson told him. "Or maybe a little. That killer possibly strangled his victims for silence before slashing their throats. No slashed throat here—she was strangled. And the removal of her internal parts...somewhere else."

"The organs are missing?"

"The organs are missing," Simpson said. He added, "Just like before."

"Do we have an ID?" he asked Fred.

Fred shook his head. "No, but—"

"This is different. We know the first two were sex workers. Of the lowest and saddest variety, I'm sorry to say. On initial inspection, I'd say this woman is different. Doesn't mean she wasn't in the world's oldest business, but she wasn't out on the streets working. If it proves that she was a sex worker," Beau Simpson went on, answering before Fred could say more. "Her hands. Look at the manicure she's got. Yes, she could be a good manicurist herself, but she's also wearing a diamond I judge to be an expensive one, and her hands are soft as a baby's—she'd not doing dishes or laundry or any kind of manual labor. Well, that depends on your definition of manual labor." He winced and let out a long sigh. "That was not an attempt at humor. I'm merely saying I don't think this woman has ever washed a dish or even scraped one for the dishwasher."

"Clothing looks designer," Keenan said, hunkering down by the ME.

While much of what the woman was wearing had been shredded by the killer's knife, Keenan could see that the skirt-suit had originally been impeccably fitted. He believed the material was a silk mix—even torn-up it looked expensive.

"I only have what I've gotten from the Virginia folks on the second victim," Fred told Keenan, "but I'm sure you know that. The first victim, though, I saw her. Just like this. Belly ripped out and the guts gone. But her nails sure weren't manicured. Her clothing was clean enough, but cheap. Turned out she was a working girl, cruising our most dangerous streets. Now, you don't want to think the murder of anyone is a common thing, but we did think maybe she picked up the wrong john, maybe she didn't follow through, she tried to rip him off… Something. I came on because of the violence of the crime. Because…well, because we don't find that many murder victims missing all their organs. Naturally, once I compared notes with the lead detective in Alexandria, we talked to the Feds, and here you are, and we have our third victim."

Keenan nodded. "I'll be playing catchup," he said. "Obviously, I know something about what has gone on, but not all the details. Doc Beau, you were called to the scene of the first murder, right?"

Dr. Beau Simpson was still staring at the current victim, taking in every little detail. Police photographers had moved off; crime-scene investigators were prowling the area, but Lafayette Square was traveled constantly by tourists as well as locals like their witness, Miss Maples. While no one ever knew what amazing forensic find might prove to be an invaluable clue, Keenan doubted they'd find this killer had been careless about what he left behind.

"They're calling this monster the Yankee Ripper," Beau said, shaking his head. He looked at Keenan. "First murder was Jess Marlborough. Yes, ripped to shreds. Strangled, face slashed… but her throat was not slit. And none of her organs—those cut from the body—were left behind or displayed. Kidneys gone, uterus gone, liver gone. The woman was just about hollowed out. I'd never seen anything like it before. The killing did not take place where she was found—police have yet to discover where she was killed."

"Jess Marlborough worked rough streets. She did quickies in alleys and cars, according to her friends or…coworkers," Fred said. "From what I could get. No one wanted to talk to the police. They split and ran. They might be terrified of the killer, but they're just as afraid of police. As far as I know, she lived in that alley. The last address she had on file with anyone anywhere was in Baltimore."

"The second victim—in Virginia—all the details were similar?" Keenan asked.

"According to Jean Channing, yes," Fred said. Detective Jean Channing, who worked Alexandria, was an excellent investigator. She wouldn't miss anything, and she wouldn't make mistakes. "And she's even more frustrated, trying to get info on the victim. When you live in the underbelly of any city, you keep low. That girl kept low, too."

"I didn't autopsy the second victim," Beau offered. "Alexandria folks were on that call. The methods and cause of death being so close, we were in touch. And yeah, from what I've read and discussed, it was very much the same. Enough so that we're looking at one killer—at least, in my humble, but well-educated, opinion."

"On Jess," Fred said, looking frustrated, "all I managed to get from any of the girls I found near the dump site was that Jess worked a second back alley that we've raided over and over again. I don't get it. They should want to talk. Does little good to stay silent."

"Andrea Simon was the second victim—that's the name we got on her. And since we don't know of any other murders similar to what we're dealing with here, we believe she was the second victim of the same killer," Fred said tonelessly. "Detective Channing and I shared reports. She was hollowed out, too. And like Jess Marlborough, she worked rough streets, back alleys, hotels that rent rooms by the hour, cars. Jean can't find an address on Andrea, either. Last known for her was someplace in Nevada."

"Homeless, down-and-out women," Keenan muttered.

"Well, they may have had homes, but no one is talking. The girls and women working those streets, they have pimps. And they're often more scared of them than even a butchering murderer. The murderer getting them is a risk. A pimp beating the hell out of them or worse is a sure thing."

"This could be a game changer, though," Keenan said. "Interesting. I believe this woman will put a new spin on the victimology." He rose.

"The slashes to her face..." Beau said, pointing to the cruel marks that tore apart what had once been a face

"…those strikes were hard and sure. Not hesitant." He was quiet a minute. "Inflicted before death, I'd say."

"The other two victims had their faces slashed as well," Fred offered.

"No hesitation there, either. I've compared notes with Dr. Bowen over on the Virginia side," he said. He looked up at Keenan. "I suppose you have every detail on a report somewhere in your office. You couldn't have had much time yet to absorb it all, but it's pretty straightforward. Three victims. All disemboweled—with body parts gone."

"And no, uh, pieces sent to the media or anything like that—not that we know about. Not yet," Fred told him.

Doc Beau sighed deeply and then reached to grab Keenan's hand for an aid as he came to his feet. "I'm going to get her back to the morgue. Photographers are done, and I won't know more until I have her on the table. She has no pockets, so we won't find an ID that way. I don't believe any of our people have come up with a tossed handbag or anything like that. Again, though, she wasn't killed here. She was dead—and disemboweled—before she was dumped here. Gentlemen, I'll have my assistants get her moving, if you'll kindly step back."

As Keenan turned to go, he saw a young woman in a blue pantsuit showing her credentials to one of the officers by the crime tape.

"We have company," Fred said.

His new partner? Keenan wondered.

She ducked under the tape with ease, a smooth swoop beneath it. Her hair was as close to jet as he'd ever seen, and she was obviously young, early twenties, tops.

He groaned inwardly. Great. He'd been given a pretty kid.

He frowned, watching her approach. There was something familiar about her.

She hurried over to greet him, a hand outstretched. "Sir, I'm Stacey Hanson. Field Director Crow asked me to find you here."

She offered a nod of acknowledgement to Beau and Fred along with a grim smile.

"Special Agent Hanson?" Fred asked, smiling and offering her a hand as well. "Detective Frederick Crandall, and Dr. Beauregard Simpson. Pleased to make your acquaintance, and happy to have you on what will now surely be a task force."

"Thank you, sir," she said. "Though the circumstances are quite tragic. May I?" she asked, indicating that she'd like to take a closer look at the corpse.

"Of course," Dr. Simpson said. "I have finished my initial inspection. The absence of so many of her organs makes an exact time of death difficult at this point. But due to several factors, I believe she was killed in the wee hours of the morning, possibly no more than an hour before she was brought here. The murder site being elsewhere and unknown at this time."

"What organs are missing?" she asked.

"Liver, kidneys, uterus and heart. Ribs were cracked and broken for the removal of the heart," Simpson told her.

Stacey looked at the victim, not turning away and not showing distress. She wasn't without emotion, though: she seemed to look upon the dead woman with empathy and sorrow.

"Same as the first two victims," Fred told her. Keenan saw Fred was intrigued by Special Agent Hanson. He was interested himself; she was young to have not only made it through the academy but into the Krewe. She was certainly striking with her coal-dark hair, silver-gray eyes and fine features. She had full lips, a lean face and defined cheekbones. She was dead serious as she studied the corpse, paying heed to every word spoken by Beau Simpson.

Again, Keenan had the feeling he recognized her. Maybe they had passed on the street, or in the hallways at FBI Headquarters.

"And no idea of who she might have been?" she asked.

"None yet," Fred replied.

Stacey stood easily in a clean, coordinated movement. She

looked at Keenan. She said nothing, just waited for his instruction, acknowledging his senior position.

"When's the autopsy?" Keenan asked the ME.

Usually, a body needing autopsy for whatever reason came in and was catalogued, and the procedure was done the next day.

"This afternoon," Beau said. "There's not much to work with. I think I want to move this along as quickly as possible."

"That's greatly appreciated," Keenan told him, and Fred nodded his agreement.

Beau called out softly to his assistants. "Shall we?"

Keenan, Fred and Stacey moved away so the morgue workers could do their jobs. Keenan looked at Fred. "You've had officers out trying to find eyewitnesses, I'm sure."

Fred nodded. "Nothing's come from it, as far as I know. They are doing door-to-door questioning, but…she had to have been dumped around four thirty. Not many people are out around here at that time, barely anything open. They'll try and obviously let us know if there's a hint of someone who may know something. Anyway, I'm heading in, and we'll hope Doc Beau can get us an ID. Check with Missing Persons, fingerprints, every possibility."

"All right. We'll see you at autopsy."

Fred gave them a wave and headed off. As he made his way through the gathering crowd of onlookers and journalists, he lifted his hands, palms out in a calming gesture, and stated, "Folks, no comment until we have something definitive to say!"

Keenan's new partner stayed silent, respectfully waiting his orders.

He was silent, looking past the crime-scene tape to the crowd and around the square.

"Sir? Should we be reading every detail—"

"Soon. We need to take a walk," he said. "Or, perhaps you would rather head in and start—"

"A walk is fine, sir."

He gritted his teeth. She was doing her best; he didn't know why he was irritated. Possibly because she was the reason he'd got out here so soon—and he didn't know why.

He studied her for a moment. Yes, he knew her. She was the kind of woman a man didn't easily forget. But where was it that he knew her from?

"You knew about this?" he asked quietly as they made their way around behind the waiting morgue vehicle where there weren't so many people. Even then, it took a bit to move out of the immediate area.

"Yes," she said.

"How?"

She was silent a minute. "Um…a dream. A nightmare."

"Oh?"

"Yes."

Simple. Direct. She didn't seem inclined to elaborate. "You've been partnered with me. That means you share information."

"A nightmare. I don't know what else to say," she told him. "I have strange dreams. They begin innocuously enough. And sometimes my dreams are just that—dreams, and they don't come again. Sometimes, they repeat, longer each time, and pointing to something."

He paused. Looking ahead, he could see a handsome man, slight in build, wearing a loose bow tie and long jacket, and sporting a slightly drooping mustache, leaning against the wall of one the buildings that edged the square. They were just off Sixteenth Street.

"Excuse me," he told his partner.

He moved ahead, but she followed. She could move damned quickly on legs that were nowhere nearly as long as his.

"This is right by the area where General Sickles gunned down Philip Barton Key II," she said. "Poor man. They say he begged for his life, but Sickles was furious over an affair Key was having with his wife and shot Key three times. Key was unarmed. And through legal machinations—the first time, I believe—the *not guilty on the reason of temporary insanity* plea was instigated. Sickles got out of it and went on to serve in the Civil War, causing not great things at Gettysburg, getting his leg shot off, giving it to medical science or a museum or some such thing. And that's Philip Barton Key II, son of Francis Scott Key, the man who wrote the poem that became 'The Star-Spangled Banner'!"

He cast a glance her way. She seemed to be in awe. But it was clear—she did see the dead. Well, he could have assumed, she *was* in the Krewe.

"Yeah, I know who he is," Keenan said. "And you need to learn to be more discreet. If you gush out loud over a ghost, you'll put all our credibility in jeopardy."

She didn't reply. She stepped ahead of him and leaned against the wall, then turned as if she was speaking to him.

"Sir! What a pleasure."

The ghost of the slain man smiled slowly, turning to look at Stacey Hanson, and apparently appreciating what he saw.

The man *had* been gunned down for having had an affair with another man's wife.

Keenan leaned against the wall and gestured as if he was showing Stacey something across the street. "We need help," he told the ghost.

"Indeed, you do. Ghastly, perfectly ghastly business going on," the ghost of Philip Key agreed sympathetically.

"What do you know about it?" Keenan asked. "If you've got anything, Philip, please share. Anything at all."

"I didn't see the woman being left there. I do wander about, you know. There are some lively venues for entertainment in the area. Well, that's neither here nor there. What I did see was a sedan. A black sedan. I believe it drove by me and must have been on the street near the statue at the appropriate time. I did hear the young woman screaming when she discovered the body, and then I rushed to the scene. Lingered at the back of the crowd a bit." He offered Stacey a rueful shrug. "I eavesdrop on some of the finest law-enforcement officers—other than Mr. Wallace's Krewe of Hunters, of course. They say a killer often returns to the scene of a crime, reveling in the reaction. Or some types of killers. My ill luck was to be murdered by an attorney. No need for him to stick around and watch the blood dry! Sorry, I digress. I'm afraid I saw no one acting in any way salacious. No one who appeared anything other than horrified and grim." He hesitated, shaking his head. "I haven't seen Bram yet this morning. He and some of the others might have been about. I'll certainly speak to them, and so should you. My dear, what is your name?" he asked Stacey.

"Special Agent Stacey Hanson," she told him.

"A pretty thing, aren't you? Do forgive me, but you are quite lovely."

"Thank you. And I'm…sorry about your…loss," she sputtered somewhat awkwardly.

"Time brings about forgiveness," the ghost told her. "And a new passion—that others do not suffer so. Keenan! What a lucky man. Such a charming partner."

"Yes, well, we don't always need charm—" Keenan began.

"And sometimes we do," Key said sagely.

"All right, thank you," Keenan said, ready to move on. Competent crime-scene investigators were working the area. Until the autopsy was done, it seemed the most efficient use of their time would be reviewing the case files.

"It's been a pleasure," Stacey told the ghost.

Keenan gritted his teeth. Saying nothing more, he started walking to his car.

She followed, hurrying after him.

"Who is Bram?" she asked.

"My great-grandfather," he said curtly.

"Does he work around here?"

"You could say so."

"Oh? What does he do?"

He paused and stared at her. "He investigates. He joined the FBI in 1920, and moved out to Chicago to work with Eliot Ness."

"And he's still—"

"He's dead. He's just...he still investigates, okay? But I didn't see him anywhere. May we get in the car and drive, please?"

She hopped into the passenger's seat. They drove in silence for a minute.

Then she blurted out, "Do we have a problem here? Or rather, do you have a problem with me?"

Surprised, he glanced quickly her way.

"I don't have a problem with you."

"Then?"

He shook his head. "You're...inexperienced. And this case..."

She turned to him. "Don't think I don't know what we're up against, or that I can't follow orders, or that I don't know my way around a crime. Don't ever underestimate me. Field Director Jackson Crow personally assigned me to this case, so I'd appreciate it if you'd quit treating me like an unwanted puppy tagging along!" She might be half his size, but she was fierce.

Her vehemence almost made him smile. She was hardly a shy, wilting flower. She had balls. And maybe there would be times ahead when it would help to have a drop-dead stunning, kick-ass new partner.

"Well?" she demanded.

He smiled.

"I'll do my best," he promised.

CHAPTER TWO

"After the second murder, they started calling the killer the Yan-kee Ripper," Stacey said quietly. "Named by the press, I imag-ine. There have been no notes to the media, though. I think Ripperologists believe only one note received was from the real killer back then. This killer didn't name himself, but he could be trying to reenact the past."

"There's always someone out there who wants to be bigger and badder," Keenan told her absently, poring over the notes on his desk. The Krewe had handled a similar case in New York City years ago. "There's a difference with this victim, com-pared to the last two. The condition of the bodies troubles me, though."

"Because the organs have completely disappeared?" Stacey suggested. "I know the Victorian Ripper removed organs… but he liked to drape the intestines around the body. He didn't just…make all the organs disappear." She winced, looking at Keenan. "Do you think it could be cannibalism?"

He shrugged. "I'm reading the notes from both detectives and both medical examiners on the other victims. No clues were found. Certainly, none of the obvious clues—fibers, hairs, fingerprints, saliva. He's wearing gloves, taking precautions."

"He dumps his victims in public places, wanting them to be found and seen," Stacey said.

She looked at Keenan again. His head was bent, attention on the text he was reading. He replied when she spoke, but she was certain that he wasn't really paying attention to anything that she said.

"He *wants* us to compare him to the Ripper, but he's killing for another reason," she suggested.

He gave her his full attention at last. "Did you dream that?" he asked. She thought there was skepticism in his voice.

"I'm being mocked by the man who sometimes works with his dead great-grandfather?" she asked.

He didn't blink; he didn't betray a speck of emotion.

"You wouldn't be here if you didn't have your special talents for communication," he said.

"So, why do you doubt me? You know they're real—my dreams are real," she said, angry with herself because she was beginning to sound desperate. "You were there. You were one of the agents who came to Harpers Ferry when my friends were nearly killed. So, you know what I saw was real. And this morning…yes, I dreamed of the body. Bits and fragments leading up to an event, and then…"

"Then a corpse," he said quietly. "Yes, I was in Harpers Ferry. It's been driving me crazy—I knew I'd seen you somewhere before. Adam didn't say much about you at the time. You were a kid, and he wanted you kept out of it."

"So…why are you so dismissive of me?" she demanded.

He was silent for a minute, head bent over his files again, and then he looked up and met her eyes, stared at her hard. "I'm not dismissive of you. I'm afraid for us both. This is going to get worse before it gets better." He hesitated. "You're just out

of the academy. Your talents are very real. But they aren't...
field talents."

"I see. You're afraid I won't have your back if there's a dangerous situation."

"You haven't been in the field. And I'm sorry, but that means
something. We really don't get many car chases, but you may
wind up in a situation with a shooter. In a crowd."

"I did go through all the proper training."

"Yes, and you can take scuba lessons in a pool, but it's—nowhere near the same thing as being in the ocean."

She forced a smile. "By the way, should we need to jump in
the river, I'm an excellent swimmer and a certified diver."

He stared back at her.

"Well, apparently, there are others here with more faith," she
said curtly. She wanted to stand up and walk out. She wanted to
strut into Jackson Crow's office and tell him she was sorry, she
wanted to be a Krewe agent, it was all-important to her really,
but Keenan Wallace was insufferable.

She managed not to leave. She lowered her head and gritted
her teeth, and then she continued her own study of the notes
that had been taken on the first and second murders.

They kept working in uneasy silence. Stacey had her computer open as well, and she went back and forth reading up on
the case notes and researching.

She hadn't realized she was shaking her head until Keenan
spoke.

"What?" he asked.

She looked up, startled. She hesitated, afraid that he'd mock
anything she had to say.

But she had been partnered with him. And it would be wrong
not to share.

"I... I mean, she was torn to pieces, but I felt like I'd seen
our victim before."

"Maybe you passed by her in a store, or just walking down the street?"

Stacey shook her head. "No, um, nothing recent. And I didn't know her. I just have a memory of her that I can't quite grasp. I'm sorry. Never mind. Back to the killer. If he's gone from street girls to a more refined escort, or so it appears—"

Keenan's phone rang; he lifted his hand to interrupt her and answered the call, speaking briefly with "Yes" and "Got it" and "Thank you."

He ended the call and looked at her. "We don't need to assume anymore. The fingerprint ID came in. The victim was a woman named Billie Bingham."

"Billie Bingham? I know that name."

"Yes. She was in the news—a scandal. Involving some politicians and the escort service she ran. She managed to elude every legal inquiry. It's a tight-knit group that plays around her business. Bingham's clients and workers are tight-lipped and all swear the business is on the up-and-up. Last year, though, the wife of a junior congressman started a social-media campaign against the Bingham Company that got a lot of traction. She fell silent when it seemed there was no proof of anything illegal going on."

"I think I remember. The angry wife was threatened with a lawsuit."

He nodded. "The junior congressman is out—and the marriage is over. I haven't heard anything since."

Stacey quickly keyed in a search on her computer. "Cindy Hardy, ex-wife of J. J. Hardy." She went to another site and one more. "She didn't go back to their home state of Arizona, though. She's living in Northern Virginia. We need to speak with her! I mean, she surely believes Billie Bingham ruined her life. Maybe our Jack the Ripper is a Jill."

"It's possible. Except I believe whoever is doing this has a certain amount of strength. They carried a body to the statue.

If memory serves me, from the few times I saw her on a television screen, Cindy Hardy is about five-three and can't weigh more than a hundred pounds."

"But—"

"We should definitely interview her," he said, "and now we know why you recognized the victim—despite the condition of the corpse."

She gave him a dry glance. "You're suggesting I was a client of hers?"

He laughed. "No, just that you might have seen her in the papers."

"No. Haven't you ever had something tease in your mind, but you don't know why?" she asked him. "That's not any special talent—everyone has that, I imagine."

"Yes, and hopefully you'll figure it out in time. Whether it has bearing on the case or not, it will probably drive you to distraction until you do figure it out," he said. He rose and reached for his jacket. "It's time to head to the morgue."

"So quickly? They've barely had time to catalogue the body and start on prep."

"For this case, full speed ahead. We're going to try to move quickly. The media is going to be all over this. And we are looking at DC. There's no way out of the fact many people are going to be deeply concerned. We were obviously committed to finding the killer from the start—all life is equally valuable—but now someone has been murdered who might bring all kinds of unwanted publicity, really shining a light on those who might have seen the street girls as unfortunates who got what they deserved. Whether we like it or not, Billie Bingham's murder is a game changer. Let's move."

Dr. Simpson stood next to the corpse that lay on the stainless steel table.

"Too bad we didn't have today's technology back in the day

of the original Ripper," Dr. Simpson said. "They'd have caught that sucker and ruined many a moviemaker's dream. The thing is, there was speculation he might have been a doctor or someone medically trained. Others thought that was reaching too high, and that a butcher might have just as easily performed some of the mutilations, the removal of body parts."

"And what are you seeing here?" Keenan asked him.

Stacey stood next to Keenan. Fred Crandall was on the other side of the autopsy table. The three of them had been quiet as Simpson had gone through a few of the formalities, explaining that, minus so many of her organs, there would be little he could tell them about her last meal or time of death due to digestion.

Beau Simpson looked at Keenan, pursing his lips and shaking his head. "Could be someone who knows basic anatomy or could be someone with real medical training. I've asked some of my colleagues to assess the removal of the internal organs and tell me what they thought. We are leaning toward someone with certain medical knowledge. How much? I don't think the killer is necessarily a surgeon. You can learn almost anything online these days. And as in yesteryear, anyone working in a butcher shop would have some experience with the placement of organs. Like it or not, we're not that different from the animals we kill for food."

"What do you think he's doing with the organs? Not leaving them at the scene," Keenan said.

"I haven't the slightest idea. If he's pulling a Ripper ploy, a piece of a kidney will be delivered to the police, along with a letter."

"Jack the Ripper claimed to have eaten a piece of the kidney he sent to the police," Stacey said quietly.

She was looking at the body on the table. It was barely recognizable as human. There were slashes that marred the face and cut through one eye. The flesh on the chest and breast had been ripped away—as had that in the abdominal area. Loose flesh, torn and red, hung limply over an empty cavity. It was hard not to turn away, not to feel a tightening in every muscle, seeing what could be done to a human being.

Stacey's face was drawn, grim and slightly gray. But she held her ground.

"We'll be expecting a letter," Fred Crandall said.

Stacey looked at Beau Simpson and said, "From what you see here, is it possible the organs were removed...intact?"

"You're thinking transplants?" Beau asked her.

She looked around at Fred, then Beau, and then Keenan. "Why not send cops and the FBI out after a maniac—while stealing human organs? There's huge money in it."

They all considered it for a minute. "It's certainly possible. Doc, what about the first victim?" Keenan asked.

"Very similar."

"Same organs taken?"

"Yes," Beau said.

"Removed elsewhere, and the body brought to the dump site?"

Fred cleared his throat. "Yes. Very little blood found at the site."

"But the organs were cleanly removed. Possibly kept in usable shape?" Keenan asked.

Beau Simpson nodded gravely. "Um, Jess Marlborough's body is still here," he said quietly. "There's been no one to claim her. And we've stalled...hoping someone might show up."

"She did look just like this," Fred said.

"May we see her?" Keenan asked.

Beau nodded gravely. He nodded to his assistant to cover up the remains of Billie Bingham and led them from the autopsy room to another that held a wall of small freezers. Beau headed straight to one whose location he appeared to know well. He pulled out the drawer and gently removed the sheet that covered her.

Jess Marlborough's face hadn't been as badly slashed as Billie Bingham's. She had been young, only twenty-eight, Keenan knew from the notes he had studied. All traces of makeup were gone, and it was easy to see at some point she had been a pretty young woman with rich, curling black hair. Her mouth—despite the slash that ran through it—had probably easily turned to a smile, he thought. She was a bit haggard—the cost of life on the streets—but somehow, no matter what she'd been doing, he had the sense that she had been hopeful.

From the neck down, she did look much the same as Billie Bingham. Torn apart, organs removed so that all that remained was a strange shell of flesh and cracked bone.

He thought he heard Stacey make a little sound. The contrast between the still-pretty face and the destroyed body was somehow more shocking than the previous corpse they'd seen. Not that any one death was any more or less heinous than another, but because even after such butchery, it was obvious the victim had been young and full of life, and time should have stretched before her.

They were done here, Keenan determined. They had learned all they could.

They thanked Beau and headed out.

"We're going to Fairfax to attempt a meeting with Cindy Hardy," Keenan told Fred. "You remember the case?"

"Sure, I remember the case. Wife of a slimy politician. Wronged and then threatened with a lawsuit. I thought she left this area long ago. But you know the news here. Something more outrageous each day, and thus even the outrageous is forgotten. I should have thought of her after the identification was made on Billie Bingham. But I don't see a woman, a tiny woman, managing all this. Unless she had help."

"Always possible. You're welcome to come with us. And I'll notify your counterpart in Virginia, Jean Channing," Keenan said. "We all need to be sharing information."

Fred nodded. "I'll let you take this on. I'm going to follow up on Jess Marlborough."

Stacey nodded. "Her friends, coworkers…someone has to know something."

"There is already fear on the streets," Fred noted. "After this, it may be hard to get anyone to talk to us."

"Jess Marlborough. Twenties," Stacey said, looking to them both. They stared back at her. She sighed with a bit of exasperation, Keenan thought. "Young. In good health. She was just down and out. She wasn't an addict. She'd offer good organs."

Fred nodded gravely. "You're right. But the media has named the man, and everyone is hooked on the notion we have a psycho on the loose. Well, sorry, whether there's an agenda here or not, anyone who can do that to another human being is a psycho to me. But we'll investigate known associates. I'll get you a list. Seems like she crashed at an apartment with some other girls in a rough section of town. But I'll also list local convenience stores and such."

"Thanks. We'll get out there by tonight or tomorrow. Fairfax isn't far. And we could hit a wall with Cindy Hardy. We'll be back soon. Thanks, Fred."

"No, thank you," Fred said. "This thing… Man, it's got to be solved—fast."

He started out; they turned and headed for their own company vehicle.

"Why are they always black SUVs?" Stacey muttered, sliding into the passenger's seat.

He was surprised that he smiled. "This is DC. I'm not sure you're allowed to drive anything other than a black SUV or sedan with tinted windows."

She smiled and nodded, not looking his way as they moved out in the traffic.

"And the ghost of Philip Key saw a black sedan," she said after a moment.

"Of course. Couldn't have been a pink hatchback or anything like that," he said.

She didn't reply. He glanced her way and then hit a button on the dash and said, "Call Angela."

"Calling Angela," a robotic voice replied.

In a few moments, Special Agent Angela Hawkins came on the line. Married to Jackson, Angela was among the first six agents to join the Krewe. Her expertise was in determining where members' special talents might be most useful, and managing their tech teams for searches, logistics and more. "Special Agent Wallace—along with Special Agent Hanson, I presume," Angela said.

"Yes, I'm here," Stacey said.

"Angie, we're going to head to Fairfax. Stacey found an address there for Cindy Hardy. You know today's victim was identified as Billie Bingham."

"Yes. Of course. Do you want me to tell her you're coming—or just make sure she's really at that address?"

"I'm afraid she'll refuse to speak with us. Can you find out if she's home, if she's working and leaves during the day, the situation with the children…"

"Got it. I'll get right back to you." Angela ended the call.

Keenan drove for a while. At a red light, he looked over at Stacey with curiosity. "I knew I wanted law enforcement from the time I was a kid. My family tree is filled with various types of law enforcement, back to the Pinkerton who haunts Lafayette Square. You're barely out of college—"

"I'm twenty-four," she told him with dignity. "My dad was a private investigator."

"But you've got a major in criminology, I'd bet. And then—straight to the academy?"

"Yes. And no experience in the field."

"But you feel you have a good sense of what's going on?"

"Are you mocking me again?" she asked, turning to stare at him.

"I'm not. I'm trying to determine what makes you tick." He navigated to the I-66.

"Why?"

"Because I'm working with you. And I'm on this case because you had a dream about a corpse."

She inhaled a long breath, then spoke evenly. "I'm an agent because I found out early in life that I wanted very badly to stop people from doing horrible things to other people. I studied hard—I don't just dream. And there are lots of bad things out there that I won't have the luck of dreaming in advance. I'm good at what I do, and I add everything in my arsenal to try to save lives and bring about justice—and stop future, horrible events from happening. All right?"

He lowered his head, and she thought that he might be smiling.

"All right?" she repeated.

"Yes. Fine. You've definitely got lots of passion, and, as you said, you've worked to get here. And you dream. Let's hope that putting it all together really helps us."

She glared at him. "Okay. So can we get back to business? No organs. Taken. There's a huge market in illegal trafficking of human organs."

"Or this guy is a cannibal. Or keeps the innards as trophies."

She shrugged. "I think the murders are planned. I don't believe the victims were random. Jess Marlborough was young and healthy."

"Billie Bingham was in her forties," Keenan countered.

"Still, that's not old. And to manage her empire, she probably kept her wits about her. Kept herself healthy and fit. No addictions. Which would certainly make her organs viable."

"True. And if what you're saying is right, then we are looking for someone with medical expertise. And the victims are being killed where the organs can be safely harvested."

"But right now we're still driving out to see the angry ex-wife of a congressman?" Stacey asked.

He glanced her way. "Cindy Hardy is one lead. You may be on to something with this new organ-harvesting theory. You may not. We cover all our bases."

"And that's something I would have known—if I was an experienced field agent."

He let out a long sigh of exasperation.

"Once the press gets word of Billie Bingham's death, everyone and their brother will be looking at Cindy Hardy. We need the jump on it. We need to know if she was clearly not involved, if we can rule her out. Or if there is concern for further inquiry."

"You think that Cindy might have murdered two street workers in a Ripperesque manner in order to get away with killing Billie Bingham?"

"Bizarre, but possible."

She winced slightly. "Yes. Possible."

The car phone rang, and he spoke aloud to answer it.

"Angela," he said.

"Cindy Hardy is indeed living in a gated community in Fairfax. Her children are attending one of the local Catholic schools. She received a decent settlement in the divorce and is working part-time on specialty costume-design pieces from her house. She's dating. Her social-media pages have her as in a relationship, and there are several pictures of her with a friendly-looking bald guy. He's a local plumber."

"Thanks. When you say *gated community*—"

"I already called her to make an appointment with her for you, so they'll let you in. I assured her you were the nicest people in the world, trying to get her cleared before there was another media frenzy. Of course, she suggested her ex-husband could be the killer. Nothing amiable about that divorce. But I guess he wasn't all that into his marriage—or his children. He's back in Arizona. Gets his kids for two weeks in the summer. Naturally, I checked on him. He was camping near Sedona and has a friend who verifies that they were together. Fishing."

"Thanks, Angela. We'll be there soon."

"Stacey?" Angela said.

"Hi, I'm here," Stacey said.

"You doing okay?"

Stacey smiled. "I'm doing fine. Feeling determined. Thanks."

"Be decent, Keenan," Angela said a bit loudly.

"I'm always decent," he said tersely.

"Yes, that's true. Let me rephrase. Be gentle. Remember being a rookie yourself."

"Yes, ma'am. On it," he said, then he cut the call.

Stacey was smiling more broadly. "So, you're always a hard-ass?"

"Hey now!"

"Sorry, that was out of line."

He found that he was laughing. "No. Not always. Just some-times," he told her. They had reached the high-arched gates that led to the Havenwood housing development where Cindy Hardy was now living with her children.

Keenan pressed a button on the call box. A female voice, toneless, answered. He swung the car around and into the long drive that led to the conclave of upper-income homes.

Cindy's was a two-story colonial surrounded by a white picket fence. She stood on the porch waiting for them as they pulled into the driveway.

She was an attractive woman of about forty, medium in height, with shoulder-length, wavy hair. She was dressed in tennis whites. They were apparently holding up her schedule.

She offered a hand as they walked up the two wooden steps to the porch. "The FBI," she said dryly. "As if the whole thing with that horrible woman hasn't already caused me enough grief."

"Special Agents Wallace and Hanson," Keenan said, introduc-ing himself and Stacey. "And, ma'am, that woman is dead now."

She nodded. "It's all over the news—along with my name again! I tried to call her out on what she was doing, and what did I get for it? First, she convinced my husband he needed to give me anything as long as he got rid of me. Then, when she was sure she had the upper hand, she threatened to sue me! I'm sorry, where are my manners? I'm just so distressed over all of this—not that she's dead. I'm glad she's dead, even if that makes me a horrible person. Please, come in. Would you like some coffee or ice tea perhaps?"

"We're fine, thanks," Keenan assured her.

She led them in to a handsome, and predictable, parlor. Sofa, large-screen TV, a few wingback chairs, and a mahogany coffee table.

She indicated they were welcome to take a seat.

"Isn't it a serial killer?" she asked, perching at the edge of the sofa. "The Yankee Ripper, or whatever they're calling him?"

"We believe it is the same killer who has now struck three times," Stacey said.

"Right, so...why are people looking at me? What could I have against those other girls?" Cindy asked. She seemed to be truly perplexed.

"Well, because now it's Billie Bingham. And everyone knew how much you despised her. Your fight was very public," Keenan said.

"We just need to know where you were last night," Stacey told her. "And the last time you spoke with or had any dealings with Billie Bingham."

"Last night I was here, in bed. I still have a fourteen-year-old girl and a sixteen-year-old boy. They think they're adults, but I'm still in charge. Just because their father bailed. He was a decent man until he met that woman. She twisted him to pieces. Personally, I don't think she was that attractive. Although from what I've heard, she was...talented. But just how special that—

that box of hers might have been, I can't even imagine. Oh, I'm sorry. I was raised better than this!"

"It's all right. So, you were here all night?" Keenan asked.

Cindy nodded vigorously. "I have the kids and live-in help. Maria will vouch for me."

"That's good, thank you. Now, with everything that went on, did you meet anyone else who might have wanted Ms. Bingham dead?" Stacey asked.

"Oh, hell yes! Dozens of people. Men and women—of all orientations. Billie Bingham was happy to supply anyone with anything. She solicited people. And don't get me wrong, believe it or not, there are a lot of decent—sincerely decent—people in Washington. But anyone can become a victim of power. Billie knew how to solicit people, and how to bribe them…and also blackmail them. She was horrible! So sure, half the wives in Washington and maybe a quarter of the husbands would love to kill her as well." She sighed deeply. "My kids are going to go through this all over again, too."

"Where are your children?" Stacey asked. "Dinnertime, isn't it?"

"Harris has football and Christy is in chorus tonight. They won't be home until about eight," Cindy said. "This will mean more trips to the therapist!" She shook her head and then looked at them. "Are you sure I can't get you anything? Maria makes a delicious Arnold Palmer. Squeezes the lemons herself and brews tea leaves. She's wonderful. She's the best thing I got out of the damned divorce and eighteen years of marriage."

"Hmm, sure, then. I'd love an Arnold Palmer. How about you, Stacey?" Keenan asked.

"An Arnold Palmer. Sure. How nice."

The way Stacey looked at him, he realized they'd been going all day. They'd never even stopped for a meal break.

He returned her look with one he hoped said *Sorry!*

Cindy called for Maria. A smiling woman in sweats with

dark eyes and very dark hair hurried into the room from what Keenan thought had to be the kitchen and dining areas.

"Hello, hello!" she said, nodding in greeting to Keenan and Stacey. Then she looked at her employer.

"Maria, they'd love to try your Arnold Palmers, please," Cindy said.

"Ah!" Maria said, beaming. "Yes, right away!"

She started to walk into the kitchen. Stacey said, "Let me give you a hand," and leaped up to follow.

"Oh, she's fine," Cindy said.

But Stacey was already gone.

Keenan turned and smiled at Cindy. "She seems lovely. And such a help, I'm sure. Raising two teens on your own can't be easy."

"Oh no, the trials and tribulations of youth," Cindy said and added bitterly, "All enhanced by scandal their father created!"

"I am so sorry for what you've been through."

"Well, I know murder is horrible. But in the case of Billie Bingham...well, maybe it will save a lot of people in the future. Marriages. Families."

"Is there anyone you remember specifically who might have wanted to hurt her?"

"Specifically? No. I told you, dozens of people might have wanted to hurt her. But she was surely killed by that crazy guy. I'm sorry for the other two—how terrifying. How tragic. But... if he was going to kill someone else, at least he picked a deserving victim."

"When was the last time you were in contact with her?" Keenan asked again.

"I was never in contact with her. Her law firm is Dickens and Dillard. You can call them. They'll have the details. It's been nearly two years since she threatened to sue me, since my divorce was final. I just shut up and decided I was going to have a life— without my husband. And I've done it. I've created a good life here. Maybe I should have left town. But I didn't know where to go. I'm originally from Mississippi. I went to school out west and met my husband there. Years ago. I didn't want to go back west, and I didn't want to go back to Mississippi. Anyway… Call the attorneys. They'll have records of what went on. But as I said, we're talking a few years now."

Stacey and Maria returned bearing glasses of ice-tea lemon-ade drinks.

"I've sipped already!" Stacey said. "Delicious."

"Truly delicious," Keenan said, swallowing down most of his glass in a gulp. Cindy was looking at her watch. They were delaying her tennis match.

He rose. Stacey followed suit.

"Thank you," he told Cindy. "And, Maria, thank you. We won't take up any more of your time. If we need you…"

"You know where to find me," Cindy said with forced cheer.

They waved as Cindy stood on the porch to see them off.

When they were in the car, he started the ignition and turned to Stacey.

"What did you get from her? Was she prepared?"

"Oh, yes. I asked Maria if Mrs. Hardy was home all night last night. Maria immediately became very nervous. But she did say yes, repeatedly, no matter how I pressed."

"Hmm. So, you think she was lying?"

"I don't just think she was lying. I'm certain she was lying."

Keenan studied his new partner. She was very confident.

He suddenly found himself intrigued. Yes, she was a rookie. But she'd done all right through the day. She'd held up at the autopsy, and she was ready to bring forward theories, be they right or wrong. And any theory was important, though the proving was what came next. And now, at the moment, they had little to go on.

"Where do we go from here?" she asked.

"We have tech see if we can confirm Mrs. Hardy left the

complex at night. She has a key card to flash when she comes in or goes out. Tech can hopefully find out for us. We check toll booths and see if we can find her. We delve deeper into her doings and talk to that law firm. She didn't deny hating the woman. She's glad Billie's dead. Maybe she was too honest. We'll find out. There'll be a task force meeting in the morning, and Jackson will give a press conference. He'll put out a warning. He can't do much more at this point. There will be speculation about dozens of politicians. Jackson will have seen to it that a forensic team has been to Billie Bingham's place to search for her little black book—be it physical or digital. But I'd also like to—"

"You think we might learn more through the first victims?" she finished.

He studied her a moment longer. He smiled. "We might just get through this," he told her.

"Thanks," she said dryly.

"Especially," he added, "if you can dream us the face of a killer."

She sighed softly. "It just doesn't work that way."

"Of course not. That would be way too easy."

CHAPTER THREE

The day was almost over. Stacey was glad.

She was right where she wanted to be—doing the work she had wanted to do since she was a child. She hadn't really expected everyone to greet her with open arms, but she hadn't been prepared for Keenan Wallace.

By the end of the day, he was beginning to seem okay. They might just make it through it all.

What was his story?

Every Krewe member had one. For each agent in the Krewe, there had to be a time when they had realized they were a bit different from others. For some, discovering their talents to speak with the dead came very early. For some, it came later.

And then, she knew there were others like her. Who had different strange talents.

Keenan Wallace wasn't one of them—she didn't think. She found herself wondering about his great-grandfather, who had worked with Eliot Ness. And there was a Pinkerton in his background. Intriguing to wonder if he'd felt he had to live up to the past.

"Another theory?"

"Pardon?"

"You've been silent. Any new ideas?"

"What? Sorry. No. Just thinking."

"Want to see what's nearby?" he asked.

"Pardon?"

"For food. A drive-through."

"Oh! Yes, certainly."

"And then where do I take you?"

"Georgetown," she said.

"Oh. That's convenient."

"It is?"

"I'm in Georgetown, too," Keenan said.

"Great."

"So, what do you want to eat?"

While the day had been long, it was still early enough for almost everything to be open. Stacey asked Google to list nearby restaurants. There was a drive-through place right on the way, and that seemed to be fine with Keenan Wallace.

He ordered chicken nuggets and fries—easy to consume while driving, she figured. She went with the hamburger.

Soon after, he had her at her door.

"Have you been taking the subway in?" he asked her. "Sorry. I was in Maine on a case and had a few days off. I don't even know when you started."

"Four days ago," she told him. "Yes, I've been taking the subway."

"I'll get you at seven thirty," he told her.

"Fine," she said, hopping out of the car in front of her apartment building.

"Be right here."

"Yes, sir!" she said, and closing the door, she started up the cobblestone path to her apartment complex.

Her home had once been a single-family mansion, but those days were long gone. Years ago, the old house had been converted into condos, and she rented hers from an old friend of her dad's who had retired and now spent much of his time working with children in war-torn areas of the world.

He was a great landlord—charging her half of what was usual for the area.

There were six families living in the complex, and they all met once every few weeks to air any grievances or see that repairs were done. She found the association a bit petty, but when she couldn't be at the meetings, she apologized ahead of time. And Marty Givens, her next-door neighbor on the ground floor, was great at taking notes and carefully reported to her.

Sometimes Stacey smiled and nodded while listening to Marty when her mind was really just about anywhere else. The college professor meant well, but the woman had a habit of going on and on and not getting to the point.

The front door could only be opened with two keys. Stacey turned one, then the other.

On entering, she was startled by Marty, who had been hovering just behind the front door.

"Hey!" Stacey said. "Marty, are you all right?"

"Oh, yes, just nervous. There's a horrible murderer out on the streets. But you know that. You're with the FBI, aren't you? Still… Billie Bingham! Oh, the scandal that will rip through this town. I mean, that's one thing. But…oh, my God! She was so horribly murdered. And after the other two. I'm scared. Just to think someone so sick is out there!"

"Is that why you were looking out the front door?" Stacey asked.

"Well, Myrna and Joseph Martin are in already, as are Cory and Amy Wang and their little boy. I suppose I was waiting for you to come home."

"There's an alarm system on the door," Stacey reminded her. "I think that when it's all locked up at night, you'll be just fine."

"Easy for you to say. You do guns and all that. I'm a single woman who barely knows how to swat flies."

Marty was what one might have called an old-maid schoolteacher in previous centuries. She was in her midfifties and far tougher than she imagined. Her students were in awe of her. She could control a college classroom with a single look, so Stacey had been told.

"You always keep your phone near you. And trust in our system and our police."

"And you, when you're home. Which is almost never."

"I'm a rookie, Marty. I have to put in my hours."

"Of course, of course, I know that. But tonight, tell me that man was a date. Such a face—oh, my God! I'd never be afraid of anything with him around. Handsome, yes, but fierce…and yet I'll bet he can smile, too. Right? Date? You must have some free time."

"I'm sorry, Marty, no, that was not a date. He's my partner. For now."

"Oh! Well, I am sorry."

"So am I," Stacey muttered dryly.

"Oh, are you not allowed to date?"

"That's not what I meant… Never mind. Marty, we're locked in. Alarm is set. And I'm here. You can reach me in two seconds. I'm so sorry. I have to get some rest. I have an early morning."

"Oh, of course, dear. I am so, so sorry!"

"No, you don't need to be sorry. But I do need to go in now."

"Yes, of course! Good night!" She went to her apartment.

Stacey walked down the hallway to her door.

She'd seen the old floor plans. Her part of the house had once been the music room, dining room and pantry. The original kitchen had been outside. It was long gone, as were the old stables and smokehouse. There was only a small yard behind the building now, backed by another, newer building that offered more modern condos.

There was only one door to her section of the house. The pantry had been turned into a small kitchen, the dining room into her bedroom, and the music room into her parlor. Though only three rooms with a small bath created out of a section that snaked out into the hallway, it was about fifteen hundred square feet and very comfortable as far as Stacey was concerned.

It was still a little strange to be on her own. She'd gone from home to a dorm to an apartment she'd shared with three other girls, and then she'd gone into the academy where she'd also had a roommate. She loved living alone…and she hated it.

There was no one here. Well, she could have kept chatting with Marty in the hallway. She liked Marty. She just wasn't in the mood to deal with the woman's nervousness. Though, that made her feel bad, and she hoped she had assured Marty.

She really didn't think Marty was in any danger.

Her organs weren't as viable as those belonging to a younger woman.

"I could be wrong. I could be way off base, going in this direction because of the investigation Dad was involved in years and years ago," she said aloud to a small Victorian mirror on the wall by the entry.

She groaned, still staring at herself. "A cat! I need to get a cat. Even a parakeet or a hamster," she told herself. "Then I wouldn't be talking to myself."

But not tonight. It had been a long day. She wanted to shower and get in bed—and pray she could fall asleep quickly. She thought she had done okay on her first day in the field—even dealing with the hostility of her first Krewe partner. She supposed it was natural he'd want to work with someone he knew. An old friend. Someone he trusted in the field.

"He was still a jerk," she told the bathroom mirror.

But Jackson Crow had been right about one thing: Keenan Wallace wasn't a man you could miss. His height, of course, was enough. Because of his height he appeared lean, but he was solidly built. She had a feeling he frequented the agency gym. His eyes were the darkest shade of blue she had ever seen.

Why the hell was she remembering his eyes and the way they focused on someone?

She gave herself a shake. He was impressive in his appearance. Though he didn't behave arrogantly—he didn't have to. All he had to do was walk into someone's view.

Still…some of his behavior could improve.

Twenty minutes later she'd showered, having washed her hair as well. She'd felt like she smelled of the morgue.

And then she went to bed. She needed to sleep. She could usually find a movie on cable she really wanted to see. That guaranteed she'd fall asleep in about twenty minutes.

Instead, she found herself searching for documentaries on Jack the Ripper.

She found several. She chose the one that looked to be the most scholarly, curled up with her pillow, and started to watch, certain she'd be asleep in minutes.

But they were discussing notes from the medical examiner on the first acknowledged Ripper murder, that of Mary Ann Nichols.

The murder had taken place right where she had been found.

"And a copycat would know that," she said aloud. She groaned to herself.

Details of the Ripper killings kept coming. The victims— Mary Ann Nichols, Annie Chapman, Elizabeth Stride, Catherine Eddowes and Mary Kelly. On the double-murder night, he killed Elizabeth Stride and Catherine Eddowes, apparently interrupted before disemboweling Stride and carrying out his grisly work just hours later, making good with his customary technique of mutilating Catherine Eddowes.

It wasn't really bedtime fare. But somewhere in there, she did fall asleep.

And the next morning at 7:26, she went out to wait for Keenan Wallace, who somehow managed to arrive at exactly seven thirty.

The room was filled with people. Representatives from the DC police, the Maryland State Police, the Virginia State Police, and FBI agents from the DC bureau as well as the Krewe of Hunters had gathered into the large conference room.

Jackson spoke to the gathered officers, warning them the killings had sparked an atmosphere of fear that might necessitate them responding to dozens of calls, many of which would mean nothing, all of which must be addressed. He filled them in on what was known, which wasn't much. He informed the assembled officers of the steps being taken, including investigations into the lives and activities of the younger victims and into everything regarding Billie Bingham and her business enterprises.

Detective Crandall spoke, telling the crowd his observations regarding the first and third murders. Detective Jean Channing from Alexandria spoke at length about the second victim. And then it was Keenan's turn to go up. He expressed the various theories they were working on: they had a vicious, mentally disturbed individual on their hands who had admired the work of Jack the Ripper, or the killings were to hide the identity of someone who specifically wanted Billie Bingham out of the way.

Before he continued, he found himself looking across the room at his new partner. Stacey was standing next to Detective Channing. The two had met and spoken briefly at the top of the day. He noted, too, that Stacey knew several of the Krewe members here: when they had arrived, she'd been greeted with friendly smiles.

He'd realized she wasn't just attractive, she was a beautiful young woman who downplayed her looks. She wasn't attempting to be *ugly,* but she kept her raven-dark hair pulled tightly back and wore minimal makeup. She was dressed in a white cotton tailored shirt and a dark blue pantsuit—common apparel for an agent.

She wore it well.

Stacey was still, watching him, listening to him. He nodded slightly in her direction.

"Or...there's the possibility we're looking for something entirely different. Someone who isn't depraved and doesn't get a sexual pleasure from this form of mutilation and murder. The killer—or killers—may have a devious plan going on. We have noted Ripperesque removal of the victims' organs, but none have been left with the bodies. We could be looking for a businessman—or a business cooperative. These murders could be taking place specifically for the removal and sale of those organs. Naturally, all specifics are to be kept from the press, lest the media trip us up when we are moving in the proper direction."

"What about that congressman's wife? The one who created all the hoopla over Billie Bingham and her husband, forcing him to resign?" an officer asked. "That's motive for murder."

"Yes. We're investigating along those lines. The point is, the killer is out there. We need the officers working the streets to warn the women they know to be sex workers. Everyone needs to be vigilant. There will be dozens of people who need to be questioned, and we'll be asking for help in all directions. I know in this room we're all aware that these are particularly heinous murders and we must find the killer—or killers—quickly."

Jackson took the floor again, and Keenan stepped back. Soon enough, the meeting ended. He noted Stacey, Jean and Fred were talking together. He couldn't get to the group right away because he was greeted by longtime friends who had just come in from the field and a few others who were heading out to other states.

He was stopped by Will Chan, one of the six original members of the Krewe of Hunters and a fascinating man. Will had worked as a magician, and those talents still stood them well at times when they were investigating.

Will knew how to work a crowd.

"I just wanted to let you know that the Krewe has faced something similar before. Way back, Whitney Tremont worked with then-detective Jude Crosby on a case in New York City. Bodies being left in shreds. Jude and Whitney are finishing up some work out in Seattle right now, but I've let them know we're looking at a similar case. I don't think the details are quite the same, but they might have some insight. I personally think your theory on the organs just might be right."

"Thanks," Keenan told him. "I'll look forward to their take on what we've got here. And it was Stacey Hanson who brought forward the idea that the killings might be for organ harvesting."

He'd been anxious to get to Stacey, Fred and Jean, and it seemed they'd been as eager to talk to him. The room was thinning out, and the three came over to him.

Stacey hadn't met Will yet; Fred had, but Jean hadn't, either. Intros went around.

Keenan looked at the detectives. "Later, I want to cruise the streets where Jess Marlborough was working. Find some of her friends, see if they know anything. We'll do the same with Andrea Simon. Stacey, the CSI crews have finished up at Billie Bingham's residence. We should have a look there."

She nodded, told Jean and Will it had been a pleasure to meet them, and followed Keenan to the door. Jackson was standing there.

He was studying Stacey as they prepared to leave. He glanced at Keenan, nodded to him grimly, and looked at Stacey again.

"Anything new?" he asked her.

It took a second for her to realize that he was asking if she'd dreamed any more details. "I'm sorry, no," she said.

"We get what we get," he assured her. "Going to the Bingham place?" he asked Keenan.

"Right now. We'll just keep going from there," he told Jackson.

"We're working it here," Jackson said. "I'll call you with any-thing at all."

Keenan nodded.

As they left the building and headed to the company SUV, Keenan asked Stacey, "He thinks you can dream an answer?"

He'd grown up being taught to be polite, so automatically, he opened the passenger's side door for her.

She just murmured a *thank-you* and slid in.

He went around and took the driver's seat, revving the igni-tion and starting out. She hadn't answered him yet.

"Stacey?"

She swung to look at him. "He's hoping the dream will come again—and go further. When my dad—well, my whole fam-ily, really—was in danger, I saw a little more bit by bit. The same with the situation you were called in on. When you were a rookie. The dreams develop with more and more informa-tion each time."

He thought about that, wondering what it must be like. Be-fore he had a chance to ask more about how it worked, Stacey spoke up again.

"So, you know about me. I know nothing about you. What brought you into this? I don't know a lot about people like...like us. Those who see the dead. I didn't know anyone else who had this talent until Adam told me about the Krewe, and I finally came here and joined. Everyone I've met all have something in the past that brought them to the Krewe. Then, there's you—a seasoned agent having a hard time believing in me. So, what's your story? Because if you want anything more on me, you'd best start sharing, too!" Her tone had hardened with every word.

He supposed she had the right to question him, and she couldn't possibly know what his answer would be.

"A murder," he said tightly. "My girlfriend."

She gasped. "Oh, God! I'm so, so sorry," she said and fell silent.

It was long ago now. Most of the time, the pain was on the

back burner, along with the helplessness he had felt when it had happened. Yes, he'd been involved with finding the killer. But that didn't change the fact that he hadn't been able to stop it— and Allison had paid the price.

"Even as a kid, with my family's past, I knew I wanted to be a cop, a detective, or an agent. The tales in my family are intriguing. My great—I don't know how many *greats*—grandfather guarded Lincoln at that time. And my great-grandfather worked on some of the most notorious cases. He helped bring down a lot of mobsters. So, hearing all that as a kid, yes, I wanted to follow the path." He paused, shrugging. "With Allison…well, I knew where I wanted to go and what I wanted to be. It wouldn't bring her back, but I knew that it mattered that we find her killer. And after that…well, I guess I was like you. I became passionate about stopping what I could—and about finding and stopping killers before they could kill again."

"I'm so sorry," she murmured again.

"We all came from something, like you said," he told her.

There was a pause between them. He felt closer to Stacey, and incredibly awkward at the same time.

Then he purposefully changed the subject. "So. At the Bingham house—CSIs have been through. They're working on what they've gathered. I'm afraid what we need isn't going to be on any kind of a list. And I doubt anyone is going to be able to trace much through credit cards. We're looking for what others don't see, right?"

"Right," she said.

They arrived at the Bingham house—or estate. In an area where homes might be grand but land limited, there were gates and a drive that led to the imposing Victorian manse.

Stacey stared at the arched iron gates, manned by two officers in uniform, one of whom quickly pressed a button that sent the arched iron gears in motion, and then at the house they approached.

"Whoever thought there could be this much money in sex!" she said.

He glanced her way, smiling. "My dear Miss Hanson, they do call it the oldest profession. Now, this is an escort service, you know. Billie Bingham would have had you believe she merely supplied handsome people to link arms with the high-and-mighty when they were supposed to make appearances at galas or balls."

"Yeah, right, whatever," Stacey said, shaking her head and still staring at the house. "I just wonder..."

"What?"

She shook her head, wincing.

"What is it? Tell me?"

"I... I was just wondering how good you have to be to make this kind of money! Wow, sorry, that was embarrassing."

He laughed. "Good, I imagine, is in the mind of the...client. Which again makes you wonder about the massive difference between Billie Bingham and unfortunate girls like Jess Marlborough and Andrea Simon. I guess wealthy clients can pay more. And Bingham ran it like a business. She was the boss."

They pulled behind a police car at the curve in the driveway. Keenan got out, flipping his wallet and ID out for the officer at the door of the house.

"CSI is done, but we were told to hold guard here for today," the officer told him and Stacey. "We'll be out here, should you need us for anything."

"I'm sure she had live-in help," Stacey said.

"All told to leave," the officer said. "The house is empty."

"What about heirs to the estate?" Stacey asked. "Did anyone attempt to stop searches or gain entry?"

"She was apparently queen of her own castle," the officer said. "Her secretary was terrified when she learned about the mur-der—ready to do anything the cops said. Forensic Accounting is going through Bingham's books. There were two live-in maids, and they were eager as hell to get out and away. This killer…the brutality… People are scared. There's not a protest to be found."

Keenan thanked him. They went in.

"I'm sure there are plenty of protests," Keenan said. He glanced at Stacey. "From scandal mags and media, I'm willing to bet that there are many high and powerful men—and women—who would have loved to have gotten in here first."

"Definitely. But they'd have no power to stop a search."

"Exactly."

The entry was grand, with marble floors, high ceilings, a curving stairway to the second floor, a finely carved mantelpiece over a fireplace, and red velvet sofas and love seats with carved wood end tables for whatever libation someone might need to set down.

"They had parties?" Stacey said.

He laughed. "Hey, I don't know. I was never here. Above my pay grade," he said.

She looked at him.

"Joking."

She smiled weakly. "Above my pay grade, too," she said. Then she grew serious, shaking her head. "I don't get the murder of this woman. As we were saying before, if he's kind of copying Jack the Ripper, there's a lot off. No slashed throats. The victims killed elsewhere, and their bodies dumped. And something else. The Ripper—according to most detectives, then and now, and scholars who have studied the case—started with Mary Ann Nichols and then killed Annie Chapman. But his third victim was Elizabeth Stride, found with just her throat slashed. He killed two women that same night—the next being Catherine Eddowes, who was ripped to shreds. So, our guy is off already—if he even is trying to be the Ripper. It still makes no sense."

"Maybe he wants to be his own kind of Ripper. Maybe it's a

loose inspiration, and he doesn't even know all the details. The media came up with the name, after all."

"Yeah, but…something else is up."

"I told you, I think your theory is solid."

"So…what now?" she asked.

"Let's see if we can discover anything here. Find her bedroom. That's probably where she'll have anything meant to be hidden," he said. "I'll do a cursory search down here, see if CSI left anything unturned. I doubt it. They're good. You take the bedrooms and the attic. I believe her live-in help, the two maids, had tiny rooms up there. But find Billie's bedroom first. Think outside the box. You have instinct—use it."

"Aye, aye, Captain," she said.

He grinned. "I am the senior partner."

She glanced back at him. "As I said, aye, aye, Captain!"

She started up the stairs, her movements slightly slow as she studied the artwork lining the walls. There were no nudes or anything that could be even slightly suggestive. Billie Bingham's place was above the tawdry and obvious.

Keenan started his search.

He slid on his back to look under chairs and sofas. Finished with the grand entry and parlor, he moved on to the dining room. Handsome hutches contained plates and service items.

He picked them up one by one, went under the tables and chairs, moved the furniture to see if there was anything behind it, lifted picture frames. She might have a safe in the wall somewhere.

But not here.

The kitchen took him longer. He went through all the cabinets, looked over and under dozens of dishes and containers.

And then, he noticed the tapestry that hung from the far side of the wall, away from appliances and the large island in the center of the state-of-the-art kitchen.

It was an odd place for a tapestry, even in such a residence.

Walking over to it, he studied it for a minute. It was of a medieval domestic scene, women working at the hearth, men talking in the background with one holding a pheasant, a recent kill.

Right for the kitchen, but still…

A tapestry in the kitchen.

He reached out, tapping it. Sounded like a wall. He kept tapping, and the sound changed. He'd hit wood.

A door. To a basement? But why cover it up? Had Billie Bingham hidden something there? Had she just considered the door an eyesore?

He moved the tapestry and found an old-fashioned latch opening to the door. The space was dark, but he found a switch. The light that came on was still weak, but he could see down. It was a basement—and seemed to be used as such. He had half expected to find an exotic cave with a hot tub and feather fans over a plush daybed.

He could see containers of cleaning fluids, yard tools and a huge pile of wood along with a wood-burning stove. He almost closed the door.

He walked down the wooden steps, shining his powerful penlight over the place as well.

At the woodpile, he froze for a moment and then moved forward.

Billie hadn't been keeping her basement as a secret rendezvous haven. She hadn't been hiding anything down here.

But the killer had been.

The grand house had five bedrooms, all beautifully appointed, and each themed. There were even little plaques to designate the rooms. The first she entered was labeled *The Jungle*. The walls were painted with lush scenes of vegetation. Ropes—imitating vines that Tarzan might use—were suspended from the ceiling over the bed. In all, it looked like a charming little tree house.

Not Billie's room, Stacey was certain.

The next room had a plaque that read *Animal Kingdom*, with the bed a giant platform that might have been in the center of a circus ring. The walls were painted with lions, tigers and bears. Various whips rested on a table by the door.

The third room she came to was labeled *The Bird's Nest*. Naturally the walls were painted with images of various birds in flight. The bed was big and puffy and covered with a comforter that had scenes of a cloudy sky.

"For her tamer visitors," Stacey said aloud.

But not Billie's room.

Two left: she tried the door opposite. A small plaque designated it as the entrance to *The Dungeon*.

It was definitely designed for a different clientele. This one had a bed with black sheets, and the scarlet walls were covered with hooks that held handcuffs and leather straps and various other implements for bondage.

She felt a little shudder rip through her. Some of the things on the wall…

Well, they weren't appealing to her.

Only one room left; it had to be Billie's.

The room was handsomely appointed with the walls simply painted a light mauve. The bed had a comforter that was a bit darker than the walls. There was a full-length, swiveling mirror to the side of the bed before a balcony, and a large and impressive dressing table.

The closet door stood open. She was sure CSI had been there, and they had gone through every drawer in the dressing table and in the dresser that stood against the opposite wall.

She went into the closet. Shoes neatly aligned; the woman had at least forty pairs.

And the clothes filled the racks in a horseshoe shape within the walk-in closet.

It would take forever, Stacey thought, drawing her thin gloves on more securely, to go through every outfit. And yet, that might be what was left to do.

She started with the right side, methodically going from elegant gowns to business apparel, designer dresses, pants, tailored shirts, feminine blouses.

Then she stopped. If Billie had been keeping any special assignations a secret, they wouldn't be in her cell phone—too easily seized and tracked if a search warrant was issued at any time—nor would she keep it stuffed away in the pocket of a designer gown.

It might well be in a robe.

The woman kept five of them, from flashy satin to cozy terry.

She reached for the terry robe, a simple garment in dark red with a belt and two pockets.

Reaching into the right pocket, she found a small notebook.

"Yes!" she murmured out loud, dropping the robe and flipping open the pages of the notebook as she moved into the hall.

There were names in the book. Dates! And references to the various rooms. She flipped, anxious to find what had been written for a day and a half ago, for the night—or early morning—when she had been killed.

"Stacey!"

She heard Keenan calling to her from below and she hurried to the stairway. "Keenan, I've found something!"

"I have, too," he told her.

"Her little notebook, Keenan. Names and dates and..."

She ran down the stairs and stood before him. There was something about his face.

"Excellent," he said. "We're really going to need it. To follow everything within it."

"I was just getting to the date she was killed. She uses nicknames or pet names. Obviously—you've got to see some of these rooms—even in her notes, she's careful to hide the identities of her clientele." She paused. "What did you find?" she asked him.

"Your Elizabeth Stride," he said quietly.

"Elizabeth Stride," she murmured.

"A body. In the basement. Throat slit on this one. And when the medical examiner looks at her, I'm willing to bet he'll find she was killed before Billie Bingham. She hasn't been disemboweled. She was left, as if he was interrupted in his work, as the police back in the day believed with Elizabeth Stride. Stacey, he is doing it in order."

She stared at him. "Then, it isn't over."

CHAPTER FOUR

Ben Wimberly, head of the forensics team who had searched Billie Bingham's home, was mortified. "I swear, my team is good. We are excellent at details, fingerprints, fibers, the tiniest speck of blood or any kind of body fluid... I even walked down the basement stairs and...wow. Maybe I should resign."

"Ben, it's all right. I would have concentrated on the rest of the house. You weren't looking for a body; you were looking for records. For her last movements," Keenan told him. Well, the man had missed a body. But it was true, too, that their assignment had been to discover Billie's life—not another death.

He thought as well that the body had been meant to be more easily discovered than it was—the killer hadn't planned for the weight of the wood in the pile to shift and fall.

"Do you trust me to even be here?" Ben asked him glumly.

Keenan smiled. "Yeah. Get to it."

Jackson Crow and Detective Fred Crandall had arrived. Jackson stood back, watching while the CSI team began working. Dr. Beau Simpson was doing his preliminary exam of the body.

Keenan had been careful not to touch anything—not even the fallen logs around the body—until Beau had arrived. But he had observed that little had been done to the woman as far as torture went.

She'd been killed swiftly. The massive spill of blood on the bricks, the floor, and the victim's face, body and clothing showed that she had been killed here—in the basement.

Jackson walked up to him. "I imagine she was one of Billie's escorts," Keenan said to the assistant director.

"But what was she doing in the basement? I can see her outfit—designer pantsuit. She didn't come down here looking for more firewood," Jackson said dryly.

Beau looked up at them. "The house was occupied until the police came and executed the warrant. Whoever did this did it with Billie's secretary and the two live-in maids here."

"Stacey and I have another lead," Keenan said. "She found a little notebook in one of Billie's robes. We're going to do our best to decipher who the nicknames in it might be for—and who she might have been planning to meet the night she was killed. We'll get on that while they track down the secretary and the maids."

"The case that keeps on giving," Jackson said.

Beau stood up then, his salt-and-pepper hair a bit awry, like that of a mad scientist.

"I'll do the full autopsy immediately. But I can tell you now— she didn't have a chance to fight back. Stacey, if you would?"

Stacey had been watching Beau work in silence. She stepped forward, allowing Beau to use her to show how the woman had been killed. "Swift and sweet. The killer stood behind her, used a very sharp blade. She was choking on her own blood before she ever knew what happened. This is different—notably different—from the other murders. Billie Bingham was strangled. The others were strangled. And then the organs removed. No ID on her that I can find, but I'm estimating late twenties. No mutilation of the body."

"Elizabeth Stride," Keenan said.

Beau frowned, looking at him.

"The third victim," Stacey said, moving away from Beau and his imaginary blade. "Jack the Ripper. According to historians, he killed five women. Two mutilated—the third, they believe, wasn't mutilated because someone came by or he was otherwise interrupted. He went on from Elizabeth Stride to Catherine Eddowes that same night—ripping her to shreds."

"And a piece of her kidney was sent to the police," Keenan said.

"I don't think our police are going to receive a bit of kidney, and if they do, it won't have belonged to Billie Bingham," Stacey said. "That kidney is too valuable on the black market."

"Yes," Keenan found himself agreeing. "This is all a sham. Beau, when you're working on our unidentified woman here, please check if she has any health issues that aren't obvious. I mean, from what we can see, she was young and fit."

"But there's going to be some issue," Stacey said, looking at Keenan. She seemed grateful for his support on her theory.

"You want to start with the maids or the secretary?" Fred asked Keenan.

"Secretary. You have info?"

"Angela just called it into me," Jackson said. "The secretary's name is Tania Holt. I'll forward the exact address. It's an apartment complex near the Smithsonian. Fred, can you get an officer to see that she's there and stays until my agents arrive?"

"Will do," Fred said, studying his own smartphone. "And I'll check out Miranda Lopez and Greta Gunderson, the housekeepers. We've got them at a small hotel near here—neither had family or a place to go, so we decided to put them up and keep them near in case we needed them." He shrugged. "And to let them get on their feet. They'll obviously be needing new employment."

"Stacey?" Keenan said.

"Ready," she assured him.

They headed out. Jackson would be overseeing the removal of the corpse. Beau would make the autopsy top priority. DC would be in an even greater frenzy when news of another murder—this one at Billie's infamous mansion—reached the media.

They were soon in the car, the address of Tania Holt in Keenan's phone. Her hands still gloved, Stacey was at his side, studying the little diary she'd found in Billie Bingham's robe.

"Her last notation was on the evening before she was killed. Assuming that Dr. Simpson was right, and she was murdered between, say, three and five in the morning. Well, it's her last entry. She has written here, *Sigh. Guess I'm going to be meeting with Coffee Boy myself. I had thought he'd want to come to the mansion. Ugh. God knows what is up. Maybe just a business meeting. That would be preferable to all else. But must keep businessmen remembering the rewards of business.*"

"We need to know who Coffee Boy might be. The CSI team might have missed a dead body in the basement, but they have Billie's computers and other datebooks and notebooks. We'll have to start a process of elimination. But we need to find out what went on at the house—and who the body in the basement belonged to. We'll know that soon enough. How she was murdered with no one seeing anything is beyond me."

"Maybe not so strange. I did notice there were no cameras around. Billie's clientele would not want to be recorded. Though, I'm surprised she wasn't doing some filming in secret. Maybe she was, but I didn't see any cameras. And that basement... I guess the tapestry was to cover anything as menial and mundane as a basement."

"I'm not sure how she always stayed ahead of the law, but she did. She was always on the pages of the scandal magazines, dragging down a lot of names—and I'm not talking about any particular political party. Billie was a businesswoman. She had no party loyalty," Keenan said. He glanced at Stacey, who was studying him curiously. He laughed. "Trust me. I never knew

her. I just knew that at times, there were going to be investigations, but no one—other than Cindy Hardy—ever tried to bring
her down. Her clients were close-lipped. We can go through old
magazines and find out who she was pictured with. And Cindy
will remain in our suspect pool."

She smiled. "I don't imagine you've ever had to pay for a
date."

He smiled.

A compliment—of sorts—at last.

"You'd be surprised. There are people who really hire others just as escorts. Individuals who just don't want to show up
somewhere alone but don't want any involvements. Male—and
female."

"I know. I'm not judging—I just don't imagine you… Never
mind. Let's focus on Coffee Boy. Someone who likes coffee, I
take it."

"Or someone with an interest in a coffee company," Keenan
said.

"Maybe both!"

"Maybe." He slowed the car. "That's the building, with the—
cop car out front. I'll slide in behind it."

"Can we park here?"

"With the medallion on this car? Yes."

As they got out of the car, an officer approached them, assur-
ing them that, to the best of their knowledge, Tania Holt was
in her apartment.

They headed up in the elevator. Billie's secretary had apparently been well-paid. The apartment complex was new, taking
the place of a building from the 1920s that had been condemned.

The place was all chrome and glass and was very clean. The
elevator plaque informed them that the spa, pool and gym were
all on the penthouse level.

Keenan knocked on the door of Tania Holt's apartment. There
was no answer. He knocked harder.

"FBI, Miss Holt. Please open the door."

Still nothing.

Stacey glanced at him and knocked again. "Miss Holt? Let us in. Under the circumstances, if you don't answer, we'll have to break the door down and make sure you're not in danger."

The door flew open.

Tania Holt stood there in a flowery silk robe that would have done her boss proud. She looked at them with fear, auburn hair a mess around her face. She was an attractive woman, probably in her midthirties.

"FBI?" she said, stepping back. "Really? Show me your badges!"

They flipped out their ID.

"Perhaps you'd like to sit down," Keenan said gently.

"Yes, I should. I...um, should offer you something. I have tea. I have stronger stuff."

"We're fine, thank you," Stacey said.

With a jerky movement, Tania indicated her living-room couch.

"Thank you," Keenan told her, taking her arm and leading her to the sofa. She suddenly fell against him, sobbing.

He winced, balancing her until he could get her sitting down. Stacey looked around for tissue and found some.

"Oh, what was done to Billie!" Tania cried.

Stacey was looking at him. They both knew that her grief was real.

"I'm so sorry to tell you this, but another woman was found dead at Billie's house," Keenan said quietly.

"What? No! Who? Oh, my God! No!" Tania cried. Then she began to babble. "But...that's impossible. We were there when we found out, when the police came. You can't come in unless someone opens the gate. Billie said no cameras—because of all the high-powered people who came—but she had an alarm system, and she had the gates, and...and there was no one there

that day after she left, just me and Miranda and Greta. Oh, no—
please, please, tell me that it wasn't Miranda or Greta!" she said,
staring at them.

"I don't believe it could be one of the maids," Stacey said.

"Why?"

"The way the victim was dressed," Stacey said.

Keenan quickly put in, "Honestly, Ms. Holt, she's right. The
clothing, the look… I don't believe that it will prove to be either of them."

He hesitated. He remembered he had a picture of the dead
woman on his cell phone.

Tania was talking again, worried. "They are such sweet
women, so good. New to the country—such hard workers. Billie helped them and insisted on work permits. She wasn't going
to get caught hiring anyone illegal. She kept it all so…clean."

"Her escort service, you mean?" Keenan asked softly.

"Yes, of course. Her business. And I know the reputation, but
Billie wasn't a horrible person. No one ever had to do anything
they didn't want to do. I came to her, thinking that I wanted
to be an escort. But I wasn't right for it. She needed someone,
though, to keep her straight. I'm very organized. Sometimes,
she'd act as an escort herself, but only for certain people. We
paid taxes. We did it all…the American way?" she asked, sobbing again. "Who would do that to her?" Then suddenly she
was angry. "There's a lunatic on the street! A psycho would-be
Jack the Ripper. And you're here… Billie's killer is out there,
and you're harassing me!"

"We're certainly not trying to harass you. Billie isn't the only
victim," Keenan reminded her. "We need to find out about the
woman in the basement."

That caused Tania to pause and then to shake her head with
something like desperation. "It's not possible!"

"When did you leave the house after Billie went out—the
night before she was killed?" Keenan asked.

"About seven. I said good-night to Miranda and Greta, and I drove home. Oh, no, I stopped. I stopped at the diner on the corner and picked up a to-go order, and then I came here. There was no one at the house except Miranda and Greta when I left. There had been no one there since earlier in the day, and then..."

Her voice trailed.

Keenan pulled out his phone and said softly, "I'm sorry to show this to you. But I believe that it's important and may, at least, show you that the dead woman isn't one of the maids."

Tania stared at him wide-eyed and nodded, then slowly moved her eyes down to look at the picture.

She gasped.

"Do you know—" Stacey began.

"Lindsey! She came to work for Billie not long ago. Lindsey Green. I—I don't know her well. I—I—didn't know her well. I don't know anything about her. I...oh!"

Tania sobbed for a minute, and then Stacey gently urged her on. "You said that there had been no one there earlier in the day, but then?"

"Someone came. Who was it?" asked Keenan.

"I can't say. I really can't say. We work on anonymity."

"I'm afraid you're going to have to say. No one is working—not for Billie Bingham, not anymore," Keenan told her. "Who was there?"

She paled. "Smith."

Keenan and Stacey glanced at one another. "Smith?" Stacey repeated. And then she said, keeping her voice level, "Congressman Colin Smith?"

Tania had a look of pure desperation on her face.

"Tania, it's all right," Keenan said softly. "Billie is dead. No one can hurt her anymore."

"But...all those people. All those powerful people. And those women. Dead. Horribly." She shook her head. "But I'm safe. I'm careful. I don't open my door. I watch what I'm doing...

I'm lying. I'm scared silly. The woman in the basement…to get into the mansion, she had to be one of our girls."

"Most probably. Tania, as you know the police and crime-scene units have been through the house. No one will know that you ever said anything to anyone," Keenan assured her. "If you fear immediate danger, call 9-1-1. We'll leave you our cards. If you're suspicious of anyone, don't hesitate to call us."

He produced his card, and Stacey handed over one of her own.

As Stacey caught Tania's gaze, she asked, "Who is Coffee Boy?"

"Coffee Boy?" Tania repeated, sounding strangled.

"Does that refer to Colin Smith?" Stacey pressed gently.

Tania nodded. "The congressman really likes coffee," she said.

"Where did the two of them meet—if not at the house?" Keenan asked.

"He almost never came to the house," Tania said. "Billie would meet him. At the old Victory Inn, out on the Beltway. I honestly don't know quite what their business was. I think that he had her encouraging investors for a clothing line. Yes, she made all the tabloids, physical and online, but Billie was stylish, and she held a lot of sway." She looked at Stacey. "I'm sure you don't approve. But Billie was honestly a nice person."

"Tania, I'm not going to judge her—we're going to try to find her killer," Stacey said.

"And whoever killed the woman in the basement," Tania said, burying her face in her hands. "What if… Oh! It could have been me!"

Stacey reached out and touched her hands, gently leading them from her face. "Tania, it wasn't you. And this is painful and horrible. But if you're afraid, dial 9-1-1 immediately. And if you think of anything, if you're worried about someone try-ing to contact you or see you…call one of us. Okay?"

She nodded. "I'm scared."

"That's understandable. You'll be very careful," Keenan said.

Again, Tania nodded. "I won't leave. I'll send out for groceries. Just groceries—no other deliveries. And I'll have a friend in the building be with me."

"Smart. Very smart," Keenan told her.

Her eyes widened. "You'll catch him fast, right? I won't be a prisoner forever?"

"We'll do our best," Keenan promised.

Stacey smiled weakly. They rose to leave. Stacey stretched out a hand to Tania. "You call if you need us," she reminded her.

Keenan stretched out a hand, too. Tania didn't take his hand; she threw her arms around him again, holding so tightly he had to disentangle himself.

He managed to eventually get out the door with Stacey behind him.

She was smirking.

He groaned as they entered the elevator. "Don't!" he warned her.

"Hey. You're a big, strong guy. You make her feel safe…" He gave her a warning glare. She was still grinning. "You can't help being a stud, Special Agent Wallace."

He stopped, hands on his hips, amused and ready to turn the tables. "Jealous, Special Agent Hanson?"

"She's a pretty woman," Stacey countered. "But not my gender of choice."

"Uh, I meant jealous that she was all over me."

"Sure. Because you're so charming and good to me."

"Well, you did just call me a stud."

"You're tall. Being tall can go a long way for a man." She strode out of the elevator and across the lobby.

He realized they were both grinning. In the midst of it all. And yet, he knew that if you didn't take time out to smile and laugh and appreciate things—and people—in this vocation, you would end up burning out.

"Hmm, if only you weren't such a warty little thing," he said, keeping pace with her.

"Little?" she protested. "Five-five is quite respectable. And come on, I try to hide the warts."

"You know that you're beautiful," he told her, surprising even himself with the serious tone he had taken. "You don't play against it, though you don't play it up."

She arched a brow slowly. He wondered why he had lost the teasing banter, and now he didn't know where to go from here. They had stopped walking and were standing close. And it was occurring to him that his words were true: she was beautiful—and electric, and smart as a whip. He forced a broad smile and turned to the car.

His phone rang.

It was Jackson.

"Dr. Simpson says you might want to get into the autopsy," Jackson said.

"We might have an ID," Keenan told him. "Lindsey Green. It's the name the woman was going by, at any rate."

"Lindsey Green. Hopefully, we'll verify. Dr. Simpson is starting his autopsy."

"Autopsy? Do they even have the body at the morgue?"

"They took the body right after you left. Under the circumstances, Beau put the autopsy as top priority. You might want to join him."

Stacey was looking at him.

"Autopsy," he said.

"Tomorrow?" she asked. "Later today?"

"Now."

"But that's—"

"For this case? Apparently, it's not just possible. It's happening."

The morgue was kept spotlessly clean—antiseptically clean. And yet, despite the multitude of products used to keep germs and bacteria at bay, Stacey felt as though the smell of death some-how seemed to permeate the place, from the autopsy rooms to the reception and the hallways.

It didn't, really; Stacey simply knew that she was in the morgue. She supposed that now she associated the specific smell of the place with death.

Ashes to ashes, dust to dust. Death, she knew, was a part of life. Part of the natural world. But sometimes, life was stolen. And that was why she so passionately wanted to be right where she was, seeking to stop those who would steal life.

Beau had really moved swiftly, pulling out all stops, sailing through paperwork and getting the job done. The body was lying on the autopsy table when they arrived; the Y incision had been made. Beau was speaking into the microphone above the body, clearly stating details for his recording of the autopsy.

Jackson was already in the room, observing. He caught Stacey's arm as they entered, stopping her and Keenan.

"Your source was right. Her name is Lindsey Green," Jackson told them quietly. "She worked for Billie Bingham. Positive fingerprint match came in quickly; she was arrested three years ago for soliciting close to the Smithsonian. The DC police have her on file. Apparently, Billie found her after her release and taught her how to ply her trade legitimately."

They both nodded. Beau Simpson was in the process of re-moving the organs.

"Liver, enlarged. The damage has caused injury to the spleen as well. Other organs most likely bearing an effect as well."

It seemed to Stacey that the autopsy went on forever. She wanted very badly to escape it.

"Any sense of anything?" Jackson whispered softly to Stacey.

She looked up at him, frowning, and then she knew what he meant.

In her experience, she'd never seen ghosts at an autopsy. But then, she'd never been at an autopsy before she'd joined the bureau. Ever since her second dream, she had seen the spirits of the dead, sometimes in a cemetery, more often where there was life, music, sunshine—things they might have enjoyed in life. But here, now... She blinked, cringing at the thought that the dead might return and witness something so horrible as the autopsy of their own body.

She saw that Keenan was shaking his head. He was frowning and moved closer, ostensibly listening to Beau, leaning forward—and touching the victim's arm lightly—while asking a question.

Nothing.

Finally, it ended, and Beau left the sewing of the body to his assistant, stepping out to speak with the three of them.

"I'm sorry to call you in. I know you have the living to question. But this seemed important. No one would have stolen this woman's organs. I suspected when I initially examined the body. She was suffering from cirrhosis. I have a feeling that they might have charged her for drunk and disorderly behavior as well as solicitation, but someone kindly forgot about that charge. For Billie, it wouldn't have mattered. Lindsey might have made a fun drunk."

"Thank you, Beau," Keenan told him. He was anxious to move on. He looked at Jackson. "Whether the killer is trying a sham with a mask of the Ripper to steal organs, or if he's really just a Jack-the-Ripper wannabe, he's got the pattern down."

"If he's following the pattern, the next murder will be indoors—and it will be horrendous," Stacey said. "All murder is horrendous, but according to most who have studied the case, law enforcement and others—"

"Mary Kelly was the last, murdered in her home, viciously torn apart. Yes," Jackson said. "I talked to Fred Crandall. He was interviewing the maids. I'm going to join him back at the house with the CSI team. I have a hard time believing that Billie Bingham didn't have a hidden camera somewhere. What's your plan from here?"

Keenan looked at Stacey. It was getting late. They would have to rest at some point. There were other agents who could be called in.

"I want to figure out a way to, er, *diplomatically* speak with Congressman Colin Smith. If we go in too hard too fast, we'll have ourselves and the bureau in trouble, and might be shut out when we need to be in. Until then, I want to speak with Fred quickly and then hit the streets. Someone had to have been friends with Jess Marlborough. Just a...hunch, I guess. We need to go back to the beginning."

Jackson nodded.

Stacey didn't protest. But she addressed Jackson. "Sir, with recent discoveries, I'm worried about Tania Holt. She's terrified. I don't think she was lying to us—she was stunned to find out that a woman had been murdered in the basement and is scared that she might be next. Is there any way we could put an FBI protection detail on her?"

"Do you think she's so terrified because she knows something?" Jackson asked.

"No," Stacey said.

"There's always the possibility that she knows something that she doesn't realize she knows," Keenan said. "I don't think it would hurt, if we could spare the resources."

Jackson nodded gravely. "I'll find a few agents just in from the field. Guard duty calls for vigilance but also allows for a little rest and relaxation. I'll see to it. Go on."

"Thank you," Stacey said.

They walked out the door of the autopsy room, removing their masks and ripping off their gowns. Stacey was surprised when she felt Keenan's hand on her shoulder. Surprised by his touch and the little electric jolt that seemed to pass through her.

The look in his eyes, too. Honesty. Deep blue honesty.

"Stacey, that was brilliant. It occurred to me how right you are—Tania might be in danger. Not just because she could be a target for this killer, but she could be a target if someone thought that she might know too much. Tania just might be in real danger."

She swallowed. "I...um...thanks." She grinned, trying for humor. "I wouldn't want your girl hurt." She grimaced once she said the words. "Sorry. That was...dumb."

"Hey, don't worry. Sometimes we have to try to joke in this business, right?"

As they left, Keenan called Fred Crandall, asking about the area where Jess had worked. He kept the phone on speaker so that Stacey could hear.

"She was found right near her usual corner. Rough neighborhood. Be careful even questioning people. The girls there have rough pimps. No one works those streets without protection. Make sure you watch out for your partner."

"She's right here, Fred. And after getting to know her better, I think the bad guys better be watching out for her."

"Thanks, Fred," Stacey said. "We'll watch out for each other."

"Well, sure, watch the giant's back," Fred said.

They ended the call and headed out to the car.

As they drove, Stacey asked him, "Keenan, do you think that the killer *might* be planning on getting to Tania for his last attack?"

He turned to her and asked dryly, "Do you think that there is going to be a 'last' attack? If you're right, and these killings are to steal organs, they're not going to stop. Jack the Ripper lives in infamy because of the horror of his attacks, and because he remains a mystery. But there have been other mutilation murders in history. Unfortunately, many of them. I'm afraid that if we don't stop this lunatic—or businessman—now, this will just go on and on. Maybe in a different city. I do know that we have to stop this." He hesitated. "Brutal hours, lousy food, little sleep. You okay with that?"

She smiled. "I'm just fine with it."

"Here we are. I'm going to park. We'll do a little cruising on foot and see what we can find out."

They were, beyond a doubt, on the wrong side of town. Keenan had pulled over at a corner with broken parking meters—new ones, but smashed, nonetheless. The building they'd parked in front of was a liquor store with bars covering the glass windows. Next to it was a dark alley, where graffiti covered the walls.

A haze seemed to linger over the area. Steam rose from the subway below and combined with the smoke from various greasy restaurants to coat the figures walking casually along.

Women in short-shorts and spiked heels, slinky dresses, halter tops.

"Jess Marlborough was found just ahead, about fifty feet. The alley is a known thoroughfare for working girls and those seeking their business," Keenan told her. He shrugged with a grimace. "Be careful out here. You may find that you're getting some pretty good offers."

"In this alley? I doubt it!" she told him.

"Shall we?"

"They may all bolt the minute they see us. We look like cops." She indicated her dark suit. Stacey hesitated and then said, "Think you ought to let me go first? I'll stay where you can see me."

When he didn't answer right away, she spoke again quickly. "Keenan, I'm sure your size comes in handy for lots of things. But it's also intimidating. I'm a little overdressed for this, but I'm not half as intimidating as you. Especially to women who might be scared of guys they don't know right now."

After a moment, he nodded. "I'll get out after you do and

lounge on the wall there. Stay in sight. I don't want anything happening to you."

"Ah, so you do care!"

"Jackson would kill me if I lost a new partner right off," he said.

She smiled and stepped out of the car.

She headed down the alley, aware that he exited the car soon after her and did as he said, walking to the side of the building facing the alley and leaning casually against the wall, his hands in his pockets.

The figures moving through the haze stopped to stare as Stacey approached, walking at an even pace toward them.

"Well, lookie what we have here!" a voice exclaimed.

She found herself facing a tall woman with an elaborate bouffant hairdo. She was wearing a sequined skirt and bra top. She was probably in her late twenties or early thirties but appeared to be older. She looked tired.

"You in the market for a good time, cutie? Hey, girls, this one is a cutie! One of us could pay her!" She chortled with laughter.

At that, a group of five women slowly appeared out of the haze, coming closer.

Curious.

"I'm not on the market or in the market," she said. "I've come here for your help."

"Cop." A dark-haired woman sniffed. "You can smell 'em a mile away. Look at that suit."

"I'm FBI. And I'm here because I need your help."

"Our help?" a sandy-haired girl—who seemed so young—asked skeptically.

"There's a killer on the streets," she said. "Targeting women who—"

"Targeting whores!" the woman with the bouffant snapped.

"Yes," Stacey said simply. "Your friend was mercilessly butchered and left here to be seen by all—and you all have to know you're in danger."

"I told you!" the young, fair-haired girl said. "Nan, I told you that it was too dangerous for us to be out here. Someone else is going to get killed. I heard on a news thing that there's another woman dead, too!"

"Great. And what about us?" the woman with the bouffant, the one the younger girl had called Nan, replied. "What about surviving? I don't know about you, honey, but I like food in my mouth and a roof over my head, wretched as that roof is. And again, I don't know about you, but I'm just as scared of…other people," she said, glancing Stacey's way.

"Your pimp?" Stacey asked flatly.

It was at that moment that she heard the footsteps behind her. She spun around, hand on her holster.

There was a man behind her; he'd moved up quickly. He was dressed in jeans and a hoodie but had several thick, gold chains at his neck, and a shiny watch flashed at his wrist. And she could see that he had a knife in his hand.

Well, he'd brought a knife to a gunfight.

He had almost reached her.

"Stop right there, asshole!" a male voice called out.

The man froze and dropped the knife; his hands went up.

Keenan was right behind him, the nose of his Glock pressed against the man's back.

"Officer. Hey, man, I just came on back here to see why this woman was harassing these fine ladies."

"Right." Keenan had reached into the man's jacket pocket for his ID. "So, Mr. Rafael Sabatini—entrepreneur. One way to call it. Well, you can explain at headquarters. Oh, I'm not an officer—I'm an agent. Small detail. But there is an officer on the way. Sorry to mess up your night, but you threatened a federal agent."

"What? No, man! I was just going to chat—"

"With a knife. Sorry," Keenan said.

They heard the sirens then; flashing lights showed at the end of the alley.

For a moment, Rafael Sabatini looked as if he meant to flee— but Keenan was like a brick house in front of him, and when he turned, Stacey had her Glock aimed at him as well.

"Bastard and bitch!" he muttered. "I'll be out before you know it. And these streets aren't safe, you know. Not for bastards and bitches. You mark my words. You beware. I'll be calling my lawyer. This is a setup! You'll be facing the charges, not me!"

"We'll have some paperwork to do now," Keenan told Stacey, regret in his voice. "But that's okay. I'll get Fred's guys to take it slow until we have a chance to chat here."

Police officers in uniform came walking down the alley.

The girls shied back several steps, as if they could disappear in the haze.

"It's all right. No one is after you," Keenan said, turning then to speak more loudly as the officers approached. "It's this man— he threatened a federal agent with a knife!"

"We'll meet you down at headquarters," one of the officers, a stocky man with a buzzed cut to his hair, said. "Why, Jimmy," he said to his partner, "if it isn't *Rafael Sabatini*, better known as Harold Johnson down at the station. Why, goodness, Harry, I think we have you on something with proof at last!"

The man was handcuffed and taken away, protesting all the while.

"I'll see you to the car," Keenan told the officers, glancing at Stacey with a nod as he followed the officers and the pimp.

Stacey watched him go, then turned as the women came out of the haze, forming a half circle around her.

The sandy-haired girl let out a sigh, staring after Keenan long-ingly, a sigh worthy of the finest princess in an animated film.

Stacey forced a smile. Work. Whatever managed to get these women to trust them was worth it.

"Not to worry, he'll be back," she said. "But for now, please, help me. Your lives might depend on it!"

CHAPTER FIVE

"Candy can help you most," a big blousy woman in a glittery dress was saying as Keenan returned to the alley.

"Candy?" Stacey asked.

They were now surrounding her as if she were the head cheerleader and a school game was about to begin.

She'd been right; they had her trust. And he supposed they might trust him now, too, because he had come up at the right moment.

"Yeah, and it's my real name," a young woman with ash-blond hair said. "Well, Candace. And I loved Jess. She was truly a kind person. We're out here trying to survive, and she'd still run in and buy food for Dave, the homeless guy on the other corner. She was a good person—a really good person, though I'll bet more than half the world would never see her that way," she finished bitterly.

"Hey, we all do what we have to do. And we can only ever do what we think is right—or necessary—when we do it, right?" Stacey asked.

The girl flushed. "Yeah. I guess we do."

"So, can you help us?" Stacey asked.

The bouffant woman moved in again. "Why, honey, if we could nail the bastard, we would. You see the group of us here? We live together, about a block away. And we do our best to look after one another." She hesitated and seemed pained. We didn't talk to the cops before because we didn't want them at our place. It's a dump, but it's all we've got. Cops might have got us evicted or the whole building condemned. So we said we all lived on the streets or took rooms when we could. We were also worried about the place where we slept getting out, just in case. You have to be so careful who you trust. Cops coming to our place couldn't help Jess. Anyway. We tried to look after Jess. Candy can best tell you her story."

"She was excited," Candy said. "She wouldn't tell me any particulars, but she was so excited. She said that she finally hit the big time, and she was going to be able to help us all. She took her time getting dressed, and she wore her low heels. It's not like she looked like a schoolmarm or anything, but…"

"She looked classy," one of the others put in.

"Did you see her leave?" Keenan asked. "Was she picked up in a car?"

Candy shook her head thoughtfully. "I didn't see… She was picked up in front of our place, though. I heard the car. We're on the ground floor."

"Rain seeps in all the time," another muttered.

"Well, it is a bona fide hovel," Candy said dryly.

"But the car—it stopped right in front of your place?" Keenan asked.

Candy nodded, her brows knitting into a frown.

"Would you mind taking us there?" Stacey asked.

"The cops already came," Candy said. "Well, not to the apartment, but here. They wanted to speak with us. They tried to find next of kin for Jess. We're the best thing she had. She doesn't know of any next of kin. She grew up in an orphanage and passed from foster home to foster home."

"And she came out of it nice and kind to others," Stacey said sympathetically. She glanced at Keenan. He knew she meant to find a way to have a respectable funeral for Jess Marlborough.

"But your place—may we see it?" Keenan asked.

"I'm Nan, honey pie," the bouffant-haired woman said, stepping forward. "You've met Candy. We round up with Betty, Zora, Tiffany and Gia. And not one of us wants to work tonight, if you're sure that prick Rafael can't get out tonight."

"Trust me, attacking a federal agent is enough to hold him tight for a while," Keenan said.

"Well, then, walk this way!" Nan said.

They walked out of the alley and down the next block. The entry to the apartment—one that looked as if it had been built as part of a low-income housing project—was on the side street, but the women were on the first floor. As they went in, Candy explained how she had been picking things up by the window and that's how she heard a man speaking.

The apartment was spotlessly clean. It couldn't have been more than fifteen hundred square feet, and before Jess's murder, there had been seven women living in it. The furniture was old and worn, and the walls needed painting. In the parlor area, there was a bunk bed.

"There are two bedrooms, but I like it better out here. We really are clean," Tiffany told them. "I mean, neat and tidy and not diseased. We go to the clinic and check on our health all the time," she added.

"Have you eaten?" Keenan asked them.

They all looked at each other.

"I could eat something!" Betty, a tiny brunette, spoke up, looking around as if seeking an okay from her friends.

"You're going to cook?" Nan asked.

"I'm going to call for delivery," Keenan said, taking a seat on the sofa. "So, what's your pleasure?"

Two of the girls burst out laughing.

"Sorry, that's usually our line," Betty said.

"Let me backtrack," Keenan said, smiling at her joke. "What would you like?"

"Anything?" Tiffany asked.

"Anything."

Stacey was standing by the window, looking out. As the women talked among themselves about what kind of food they'd like, Stacey turned to Candy again.

"You heard a man's voice. Did you hear what he said?"

"I—I'm not sure. I think he was rushing her. Trying to get her into the car quickly. As if he was afraid of being seen in this neighborhood. At least, that's what I thought. He was probably a married man. Most of the time, they are. They just get bored. They need some excitement," Candy said.

"Italian?" Nan asked Keenan.

"Italian, it is," Keenan said. "Now, for your orders?"

On his phone, he'd already brought up the webpage for one of the food-delivery companies that the Krewe used frequently—he knew that while they might not be happy about the area, they'd get food there quickly.

"You mean…we can get more than pizza?" Gia asked, wide-eyed. She was a tall girl, dark-haired, dark-eyed and bronze-skinned. Once, he thought, she'd been beautiful. She looked tired.

"Anything you want," he said.

"Hey, you guys have better budgets than the cops—or you're just nicer," Nan said.

"There are nice agents and nice cops," he said. "Maybe the cops just didn't know that you would all enjoy a good meal. So…place your orders."

They did. He filled the order form and sent it through.

He glanced over at Stacey. She shook her head and then her gaze went back around the women and their tiny, shabby home.

He could see that she was touched by the plight of the

women—and that she had taken Candy's words regarding Jess Marlborough to heart.

"Okay, food's on the way," he said, rising. "I'm going to stroll out front and around the building, all right? Be right back."

Nan had taken up a weary position on the sofa. "You won't find Tess's killer out there. Out there, if someone has a beef, they shoot you or stab you straight up. Even the dope dealers— it's just bang-bang."

"I'm not looking for a local," Keenan assured her. He smiled and stepped outside. A minute later, Stacey joined him.

He was on the sidewalk that fronted the window on the side of the apartment where the car had picked up Tess.

He looked her way; she was watching him. "What are you doing?"

"Hoping against hope that there's a security camera of some kind on a building near here," he told her.

"Oh!"

"Unlikely, but I'm ever hopeful."

She stood by his side silently for a few minutes. He found himself distracted. It was amazing; after their long day, she still smelled good.

"Keenan!" she said suddenly. She, apparently, hadn't been distracted.

"Yeah?"

"There, right there. Across the way. There's something on that little store…looks like a pawnshop!" she said excitedly.

"You may be right."

He started across the street. She would have followed him; he stopped her.

"Hey, wait, please, for the food? I can find out—I mean, even if they have one, it may not shoot far enough, though it isn't a big street…"

His words trailed as she nodded and went back inside.

The pawnshop was closed, but it did indeed have a security

camera. He could only hope it surveyed the street—and that the camera was taking footage and wasn't up just for show.

He pulled out his phone and called Fred Crandall, explaining where he was and what he had found. "Figure you might have had a run-in with the proprietor or questioned him at some time, seeing as how he's across the street from where Jess lived."

Fred made an unhappy sound. "We didn't get anyone to talk enough to even tell us where she lived. When the women in the area saw us coming, they scattered. You understand, of course, that sex workers aren't generally pleased when they see the police coming."

"Even when someone has been butchered and they're terrified."

Fred laughed. "My friend, I figured you were on to something when that scuzzball pimp made it on down to the station. Are you coming in for paperwork?"

"You can hold him overnight without it, right? We could have filed federal charges, but the timing wasn't right. Needed to be where I was, and I knew that your guys would be there in seconds."

"Yeah. We can hold him twenty-four hours before charges. And trust me, we will. And I'll have video—if it exists—for you first thing in the a.m."

"Thanks, Fred. Talk to you then."

Keenan headed back across the street and to the apartment.

Stacey was sitting there, handing out various containers and plastic dining implements, chatting all the while, smiling easily, and getting them all to talk.

"By the way," she said, "I know that Jess was being secretive—hoping that things would work out for her, and maybe all of you—so we assume this man she went with had some kind of money and influence."

"Oh, I'm sure!" Candy told her. "I've never seen Jess so... Like a teenager going on a first date! She checked her clothing and her makeup and hair over and over again." She hesitated. "She was so excited. She hugged me so warmly before she left."

"But she didn't say a name?" Stacey asked.

Candy shook her head. She stopped speaking, taking a bite of her Italian food.

"Oh, this is good!" she whispered around the mouthful. She looked up at Keenan and said softly, "Thank you!"

The echo of her words went around.

"My pleasure," he said, glancing over at Stacey.

She arched a brow slowly to him.

Looking at Candy he said slowly, "You said that she was excited about getting dressed, and obviously, that clothing is… gone. But what was she wearing before she started getting ready for her date?"

"Jeans and a shirt."

"Do you still have them?" Stacey asked.

"In the closet. Stacey, if you want to look in there with me?" Candy asked, reluctantly putting down her fork.

"Sure. Thank you."

Stacey followed Candy through to the bedroom, which had a double mattress on the floor and another bunk bed. Because it was an old building, the room also had a fireplace and hearth. The small closet apparently afforded space for all the women's things.

She emerged with a pair of jeans and a T-shirt, handing Keenan the jeans. He went through the pockets as she studied the T-shirt.

The jeans were empty.

He saw Stacey's expression change as she found something in the tiny pocket that was sewn into the chest area of the T-shirt.

It was a tiny scrap of a napkin—torn, as if Jess had meant to discard the entire thing, but that bit had ripped off and remained in her pocket.

It bore just three letters.

I T H

But he knew what they were both thinking.

Smith.

Congressman Colin Smith.

"You've found something!" Nan said breathlessly.

"Not really, just initials," Keenan said easily. "But hey—we will look at absolutely everything. And I swear, we will do everything in our power to find out who did this." He glanced at Stacey. "Ready to go?"

"Yes, yes, of course. And you have our cards," she told the women. "You'll be careful, promise."

"Oh, you bet!" Nan said. "But…"

"Yes?" Stacey asked.

Nan looked at the others.

"He's going to kill again!" Tiffany said.

"And…it could be one of us," Gia put in.

"And we can pray that you're right, that they're going to keep Rafael Sabatini locked up," Candy said. "Once he's out…we'll be back working for him."

Keenan paused, looking at Stacey. "Hang on," he said.

He dialed a number. They could all hear his hurried conversation about protection.

When he finished the call, he turned back to them. "Detective Crandall—he's the main DC cop you talked to before—is a great guy—"

"He was respectful," Candy said.

"Anyway, stay off the street. Detective Crandall is making sure that Rafael is hit with enough charges to keep him in lockup without any kind of bail for several days, at least. And he's going to see to a two-man patrol on the streets out here until we get somewhere."

They gushed around him, thanking him.

He tried to be gracious.

"You still put through calls to us right away if anything happens, if you see anything, anything at all," Stacey told them.

"Yes, yes, yes!"

They grouped around her then.

Stacey hugged them all goodbye. Keenan made a point of getting to the door and waving.

They were back out on the street, heading for the car.

"The security camera?" she asked.

"Fred is on it."

"Great. And that piece of napkin. Keenan, we may have something. I-T-H. Smith. That slimy bastard is involved in this somehow."

He was quiet for a minute. During his time in the Krewe—stationed in Virginia, but in an area that housed much of the government—he'd learned not to believe in a strict adherence to a political party. The modern world had too many issues, and so when he looked at candidates, he looked at their individual stances on issues that mattered to him.

There were good men and women in the government. And there were men—and women—in government who were slimy as hell as well.

He didn't know Colin Smith other than as the world saw him, what was seen on TV and in other media.

He couldn't stand the man's manner or his politics. He had a way of talking that invited hostility between people of different sexes, religions and ethnicities. He seemed to have no sense of common decency and liked to rile up issues that had been nonissues to create a frenzy.

No, he didn't like the man.

He had to put that aside for the investigation, though. And whether he'd really figured how to do it properly or not, it was past time for them to have a good heart-to-heart with the congressman.

"We'll have a full day tomorrow. They've managed to hold

Sabatini, but he's going to be arraigned. We'll have to give our statements. We're going to want to see the security video Fred will have pulled. And then get an interview with Smith somehow. That won't be easy. Jackson—or even Adam—may have to step in."

He suddenly realized that she wasn't answering him.

He glanced her way; she had fallen asleep. Her eyes were closed. Her dark hair was waving an angelic frame around her face. Her lips were just slightly parted, and her breath came softly between them. He smiled to himself. She did give one hundred percent. And he could sleep damned easily himself right now, too. Long days on a case like this.

He was on the Beltway when she started talking. At first, she startled him; he thought that she was speaking to him.

She was not.

Her eyes remained closed. Her face twisted from side to side.

"No, no. Oh, no, no. You can't, no, you can't…don't. Don't. Don't take advantage like that… I know what you're going to do, no, no…"

She was becoming violently fretful, straining against her seat belt. Her hands flew and she fought her sleep-battle, and she whacked him in the face.

While he was on the Beltway.

He quickly exited the busy highway. As he navigated, he tried to wake her, saying her name, to no avail. He touched her shoulder gently, a little more firmly…

Nothing.

His place was close, just off the Beltway. He had the entire ground floor of an old building with a parking spot he could just swing into. He made it there quickly and parked, hopped out of the car and came around to the passenger's seat, unbuckling her while he tried to awaken her.

"Stacey! Stacey! Stop, stop, you're all right, you're all right!" he said.

Her eyes opened. She stared at him. He wasn't sure what she saw.

But she must have trusted him; her eyes closed, and she went dead limp in his arms.

He carried her up the walk and to the porch, glad that the entry to the upstairs apartment was to the side of the house. With a bit of maneuvering, he opened his front door and keyed in his alarm code before walking into the parlor and laying her as gently as he could on his sectional.

He checked her pulse and her breathing.

She seemed to be fine, just…deeply, deeply sleeping.

Perplexed, he hesitated. It had grown late, but he knew that wouldn't matter to the assistant director, so he called Jackson and explained the situation.

"Leave her."

"Just leave her—sleeping on my sofa?"

"She'll be fine, and when she wakes, she may have something for us."

"This dream thing is…unpredictable."

"I've long ceased trying to explain or understand what some people are capable of or why. Or how," Jackson told him. "Stacey's nightmares seem to be a forewarning of what could happen, and when she sees the possibility of what might be, she has a chance to try to change it. I imagine a scientist would say that in the depths of the part of the brain we don't use, there is a fountain of possibilities, and Stacey sees them in dreams. You're both bone-tired, right?"

"Right—it's been a few long days, but then, you know that."

"And they'll get longer. Let her sleep. Did you get anything today?"

"Yes. I called Fred. He's getting his people to reach the owner of a pawnshop that has a video camera. It might have picked up something. And Stacey found a few street girls who would speak with us—Jess Marlborough's roommates. Jess was excited about a date. She didn't suggest it was anyone political, but she did suggest someone with money. Someone who didn't want to be seen in a neighborhood known for being…on the wrong side of the tracks, I guess."

"Interesting," Jackson said. "At least that's something. I spoke with Detective Crandall. He told me that he struck out with the maids. They were just terrified. They had no idea that anyone had been in the house, much less someone killing a woman in the basement."

"Well, in the morning, hopefully, we'll see something on that video."

"Right. I think you and Stacey need to get out to see Colin Smith. I managed to get you an appointment. It wasn't easy. I wanted to ask him to come in to headquarters, but I know something about the political games these guys play, and I'm damned sure he'd refuse."

"We'll speak to him at that meeting. Come hell or high water, somehow. So. All right." Keenan hesitated again. "So…just let her sleep on my sofa. Until she wakes up?"

"That's my suggestion."

"Okay. I guess I'll leave a note for her there that *you* suggested that I not wake her and head to bed myself. Be back with you in the morning."

They ended the call.

He stared at Stacey, raven hair cascading around her face. "Well, Sleeping Beauty," he murmured, "the boss says I'm to leave you. So, uh…"

Make her more comfortable? Leave her be?

She was still wearing shoes, though. Maybe she'd wake up if he slipped them off. He gingerly slid each low-heeled bootie off her feet. He also gently unclipped her gun holster and removed it from her hip, setting the weapon nearby.

He went and acquired both a pillow and blanket, setting her head on the cushion, covering her with the blanket.

And still, she slept on.

"Well, at least you aren't hitting me anymore," he whispered.

The parlor in his apartment was big. He had an entertainment center that faced the sofa and heavy, upholstered armchairs that flanked it. He went over to his desk across the room.

Jackson said to let you sleep. If you wake up first, help yourself to anything you like. Push button for coffee—I always set it up for the next morning.

He read the note over: it should suffice.

With that done, he headed past the kitchen to the bedroom. He was dead-tired, but not so tired that he could go to bed without a shower.

He'd spent hours at the morgue and then on the streets. He had a feeling that Stacey was not going to be happy with herself. She would have wanted a shower, too.

He studiously scrubbed his hair—glad he kept it cropped short—and then his body. He was standing under a spray of deliciously hot water when he heard the first scream.

Screams meant trouble.

He figured it was Stacey, dreaming again or waking up from a dream. But still, he raced out, just managing to grab a towel to wrap around himself.

He had an alarm system and high-impact windows, and he kept the alarm system set and the windows locked. There was no back door.

It had to be Stacey, but he had learned through the years to be prepared at all times. Stacey was sitting up. Her eyes were open, and she was screaming.

"Stacey!"

His shout had no effect.

He realized she was still sleeping. He sat behind her, drawing her against him as he tried his best to wake her gently.

Her scream faded; she went stiff as a board.

Then she went limp, lying in his lap. Her eyes closed and opened, and then snapped into focus on his.

She gasped, a pained sound.

Though he was seldom tongue-tied or at a loss for words, he found himself speaking too quickly. "You fell asleep in the car—dreaming. I couldn't wake you. I brought you in here. Jackson said to let you sleep. I left you a note—there on the coffee table, right there… I'm sorry. I don't know how to handle a situation like yours. I'd left you…you started screaming again."

She winced again, closing her eyes.

When she opened them again, she seemed to realize her position. Lying on the lap of a man still damp from the shower and wearing nothing but a towel.

"Oh, I… I am so sorry!" She struggled slightly to rise, compromising the knot on his towel, apologizing all over again awkwardly as she started to stand, lost her balance and fell on him again, blushing furiously. "Oh, Lord. I am so…sorry!"

"It's okay."

"I guess I was so overtired."

"It's okay!"

"No, no, you didn't want an idiot rookie who dreams things."

She was so distressed—and luckily, not with him. He found himself smiling and trying to assure her again.

"Stacey, you're fine. Really." He offered her a dry grin. "Trust me, much worse things have happened to me and probably will again. It's okay—you're okay."

She accepted his words, looking at him with a downcast sigh. She then blinked and looked away, taking a seat a foot away, but still on the sofa.

"Are you all right?" he asked.

"Oh, yes, fine, thank you. And again, I'm so sorry."

"Please, quit apologizing. I just wish… I just wish that I'd been able to do something—to stop you from going through such…distress."

She shook her head. "I need to go through it. It's…how I see."

"And you saw something?" he asked. He shifted slightly. He was losing the damned towel again.

She wasn't paying attention to him, though. "I'm trying to remember now," she said. "It was…disjointed. And I saw only just a little bit. It will come again, and again."

He stood, getting a firm grip on his towel. "Excuse me. I'll get dressed. I'd say that I was going to take you home, but I'm not sure you should be on your own."

She blinked and looked at him. "I wouldn't mind going home. I'd love to have a shower. You're—clean. That must be heaven." She smiled.

"I have a shower. I mean, not just in my bathroom. The guest room has an en suite." He hesitated. "Again, I feel like I wasn't that helpful during your nightmare. But I'm not sure you should be alone."

"I've dealt with this for years," she said softly. "Anyway, I don't have any clean clothes."

"I have clothes—and I believe they'll fit you fine."

"Your clothes?" she asked, another half smile curling her lips with skepticism.

"No. Women's clothing."

"Oh!" she said, flushing. "Oh, now I'm very sorry. Someone else lives here with you! Or, uh, spends time here with you. I don't want to interfere—"

"It's nothing like that. I have some of my mother's things here. And she's about your size."

She stared at him blankly.

"Yes, even I have a mother," he told her. "I'm one of five kids, and we're all over the country now. She keeps a few things here, though she spends most of her time with my sister in Chicago—who also has five kids."

She was just staring at him.

"Hey, quit it. I may be a hard-ass sometimes, but I have a family. And I'm a good uncle, really."

"I, uh…yeah. Thanks. I can stand myself if I can shower. But your mom's things—"

"My mom is very attractive and stylish," he assured her.

"Oh, I don't doubt that," she said, then she grinned.

"What?"

"It's really cute. I mean, that your mom keeps things here."

"Right. It's just adorable," he said impatiently.

"I'm sorry. I just imagined that…that you'd have…um…a busy personal life."

"You mean sex life?"

"Uh, yeah."

She seemed so miserably uncomfortable. He laughed.

"Don't worry, my life is fine. But I'm sure you know, we're not the kind of people who easily make real relationships. Just this line of work—and then pausing to chat with the dead now and then—can cause a bit of unease in others. With your dreams, it must be worse for you."

"Yeah…um, frankly, dating sucks," she admitted softly.

He nodded. "But I do love my family. And I'm happy to see them whenever possible."

"I, uh…then, thank you. I'm sorry. I didn't mean to be personal like that. If you wouldn't mind letting me have something that your mom wouldn't mind being borrowed… I'll shower." She was quiet a moment. "And then, yes, I'd like to stay. In the guest bedroom. I have a feeling that this might continue. And it might be important."

"Let me get dressed, and I'll get you a towel and some things."

He quickly turned, clutching the towel, and hurried to his room. He pulled on pajama pants and a robe, and then, before she could change her mind, he found one of his mother's night-gowns and robes and looked blankly at the closet for a moment. He saw a pair of tailored black pants and a shirt to match and even a cardigan and laid it all out. He remembered a clean towel and washcloth.

He walked back to the living room. She remained seated on the sofa, deep in consternation.

"Go take your shower. Then you can tell me about it," he said.

She nodded, rising. "Thanks." She started down the hall and then turned back. "Seriously, thank you."

"Sure. It's just a shower."

"No, I mean…for understanding. For believing."

"Well, I've yet to hear what went on in your dream."

She paused, studying him. She seemed very still. Regal, somehow. Her face with her beautifully crafted features was stoic and determined, her head high.

"I saw…the beginning."

"The beginning."

"I saw it," she whispered. "Bits…pieces…"

"Bits and pieces?"

"But I knew I was there. I was where it's going to happen. But…it was just the beginning. The moments leading to the next murder."

CHAPTER SIX

It was bizarre. Of course, she might be considered bizarre herself, just as the Krewe might be considered bizarre. And maybe it took the bizarre to step in when a case seemed to be just as unusual.

But the strangest thing at the moment, Stacey thought, was the fact that she was sitting on a sofa with Keenan Wallace, and he was in pajama pants and a terry robe. And she was in a T-shirt gown and a robe that belonged to his mother.

And she wasn't blind. He was an amazing presence. Height did that, and surely, that had to be most of it. But while his height made him appear lean, he had broad shoulders, tight abs and, she was certain, rocks and wire for muscles. Then, there was his face. A good face: his eyes were so intense and a deep blue. Broad forehead, strong jaw. Solid, high cheekbones.

She'd thought he was a total jerk. He'd made little effort to hide his initial distaste with her as a partner. But he was growing on her.

He was studying her—she was supposed to be speaking. She had stopped and was just looking at him. And he was waiting patiently.

"I…um. Anyway, this is the way that it has always worked. My dreams, or nightmares, in the past. I see something, a place usually, and know that something is happening that shouldn't be happening. Then the dream comes again, and I see a little more, and then each time the dream comes, it moves further into what is happening…or what is going to happen, or what might happen."

"You weren't even out of high school that first time, when I was on that case. I saw you then, but you were younger, and it was so briefly. Adam didn't want you involved with any of it."

She nodded. "But that wasn't the first time. My father was a private investigator. When I was about ten there was a double murder made to appear as if they'd been accidents—a doctor and his colleague. The wife of the one victim had been afraid for her husband. I believe he'd been getting threats—threats he thought nothing of but she took seriously. So, on her behalf, my dad started to investigate, following a man named McCarron. He was ostensibly a businessman, in pharmaceuticals, but his businesses were all rather dicey. But it seemed nothing could ever be pinned on him; he was very rich, you see, and had friends who were very rich, politicians, movers and shakers among them. My dad had video of McCarron going into the building where the doctor and the other man died—one supposedly from a fall and the other of a heart attack when he tried to help the first. I was young, and I didn't know much about the case, and I didn't see or dream any of that happening. But I did dream about a man coming after my father, breaking into our home office, and nearly killing him and my mother and, who knows, possibly me. The dreams were so bad, so terrifying to me, that my mother insisted on a psychiatrist. The psychiatrist was friends with Adam Harrison. Adam came in and listened to me. Then he, my dad, and the cops set up a sting. It was amazing. McCarron and a lot of people wound up with prison terms."

"What you have really is a gift," he told her. "I mean, it can't feel like that all the time, since your screams are pretty darned blood-curdling. I don't imagine it feels much like a gift."

She smiled. "Sometimes, no. But you know what it's like, in a way. You may not have bizarre dreams about violence that might happen, but you do have friends among the dead. You know what it's like to be very careful about your behavior in front of others. I've heard a few stories from other Krewe members regarding slips they've made and people who think they're out and out crazy."

"That part of it was okay for me." He paused a long moment. "I come from a family where it seems to be almost genetic." He stopped speaking again for a minute and shrugged. "When my father passed away, he came to his own funeral."

"I'm sorry...um, I guess... Do you still get to see him?"

He shook his head. "He moved on, but he was there for a minute. At the funeral, by his coffin. He was standing by it like any other mourner, looked down at himself as with approval, and turned and took my mother into his arms, telling her not to cry. He said he'd had a beautiful life and he wanted her to be happy. And then he was gone. Seemed like there was a glow of light, and he just disappeared into it. Maybe it was a shift of moonlight on the stained-glass windows of the church."

"I like to think that there is a light," she said.

"I guess we all do. I have friends who have said good-bye to others by seeing light as well, so maybe it was light. He was a good guy."

"He was an agent, too, like your great-great-grandfather Bram?"

He smiled and shook his head. "My dad was a cop. But actually, we do need to see Bram somewhere along the line, see if he knows anything. First thing tomorrow, though, the congressman. Congressman Colin Smith."

"I like it. He's going to see us?"

"It's nice to have people who can pull strings."

"Good. But...suppose he did want to get rid of Billie Bingham. Would he really slaughter those other women just to get to Billie? And while I may not like his stand on several issues, he makes a very formidable public appearance. He can be quite charming."

"Charm can cover a hell of a lot," he said. "But I doubt that he's that crazy. If he's involved with this, he has an agenda." He paused and gently touched her shoulder. "We're off course. Can you describe the dream?"

"I saw a room. There was a bed in it, and one wall had a hearth."

"Was it the room that Nan, Candy and their friends share?"

"I don't know yet. It was hazy."

"Billie's room—a room at her mansion? Or even a room at Cindy Hardy's house?"

"I'm sorry...so far it's just a vague impression that I'm seeing. And I know that someone is there. I don't know, can you sense evil?"

"I believe you can, and that everyone has an inner intuition that might warn of danger—or evil, as you say."

"I know that someone is there who is evil and intends to hurt a woman. I know that the woman is there. She doesn't know. She's just moving about, and he's watching."

"And you think this is going to be the fifth victim?"

"I'm sure of it," she whispered.

"Then, while I hate to make you scream in terror, let's hope you do dream again," he told her.

He stood up. "Damn, it's late. And tomorrow is early. It is tomorrow. Don't forget, if you're up first—push the Brew button on the coffee." He started down the hall to his room and then turned back. "Sorry, sorry—there's a bed in the guest room, as you've seen," he added dryly. "Much more comfortable than the sofa. Unless you prefer the sofa. Anyway, let's both try to get some sleep."

He smiled and gave her a wave.

She smiled back. She heard him enter his room, heard the door close.

He wasn't so bad, after all.

No, not bad at all.

She watched after him, appalled by the way her thoughts were roving. The door would open, he'd rush back out, he'd whisper that she was amazing, forgive him, he shouldn't be saying such things, he just wanted…

No, no, no, no, she told herself. *This is your first case! He's a work colleague. A respected agent!*

She stood and headed down the hall for the guest room, having an absurd idea that she would stop and, with an over-whelming impulse, open the door to his room and run in and tell him…

That he was compelling, and she had been alone far too much, and that she just wanted him to touch her. Hold her.

He had suddenly awakened so much more in her.

It was like being one of those people who was afraid of heights. They were so afraid that they would suddenly walk to the edge of a precipice and just keep going…

No, no, no.

She did have control of herself. She passed his door and hur-ried the few feet to the next. She opened and closed the door, leaning against it and gasping as if she had just escaped a great danger.

The danger had been herself!

Shaking slightly, she moved toward the bed, pulled down the covers and careened onto it. In minutes, sheer exhaustion took over.

And she was asleep.

She knew the dream was coming.

A protective and unconscious instinct tried to fight it. Somewhere in her sleep, whatever neurons played in her brain knew that the dream must come.

She wasn't sure where she was within the room, just that she was there. The walls were a blur, but she knew there was a hearth. She could hear that a fire was crackling, see that the flames were playing, blue and gold, and that smoke was rising.

She still couldn't see him; she didn't know how he had gotten in. Had he come through the front door?

He was in the shadows, as she was. There was a curious sound, as if something was being dragged, but she couldn't see what.

The woman in the room heard it, too. She started to turn.

But Stacey couldn't see her face.

She saw the flash of a knife, rising silvery and glittering, caught for a moment in the firelight.

The woman screamed.

"No!" Stacey whimpered, the sound loud enough to nudge her, wake her enough to know that she was dreaming.

But she didn't open her eyes; she wasn't out of the dream or the nightmare.

The killer had her. And while she couldn't see him clearly, she knew that he turned, and he looked straight at her—she could see a glitter as the firelight then reflected in his eyes.

How could he see her? He could not!

And yet it seemed he looked straight at her.

He lifted the knife in her direction. And he smiled.

Keenan walked to the far end of the kitchen, checking in the refrigerator for anything edible, then he turned to push the button on the coffee maker.

At that moment, Stacey came into the kitchen to start the coffee.

They slammed right into one another, then broke apart, laughing.

"Nice and early," he told her, stepping back a distance from her, his hands on her shoulders.

She smelled incredibly good.

He removed his hands from her shoulders and took another step back, still smiling. He had the thought that having her in his house, with no one else around, and remaining able to maintain their platonic partnership was not something that was likely to happen again.

He needed distance. They were professionals at very important jobs.

"You're up nice and early," he said. "We'll make sure we're at Colin Smith's office by eight, in time for our appointment. But it's barely six—"

"I'd like to go by my place. Please! I mean, it's great to borrow your mom's things, but I'd really love to get into my own."

"We have time," he assured her. He was still in his pajama pants and robe. "I'll just get dressed."

"I'll throw on my stuff from yesterday—and, I promise, I can get ready at my place in a matter of minutes."

They moved apart, retiring to the separate rooms. Fifteen minutes later, after each had downed a mug of coffee, they were in the car, heading to her place.

It was close, just a matter of blocks. And it was early when they reached her apartment, still just six thirty.

There was a woman at the entry to the apartment when they reached it. She looked to be in her midfifties, small and a bit stocky. She looked disapproving as Keenan stood by Stacey, who'd had her key out, ready, before the door had opened for them.

"I was worried!" the woman said to Stacey. She eyed Keenan. "Working all night?" she asked skeptically.

"You know I work all hours, Marty. This is my partner, Keenan Wallace. Keenan, Marty has the other ground-floor apartment here."

Marty offered him her hand. "All I have to say is this—when you work all night, work all night here, please! Two FBI agents in the building would make me happy."

"We just never know where work takes us," Keenan told her. Implication had been rich in the woman's voice. He didn't care. He smiled. Too bad it hadn't been what the woman had been thinking.

"We need to get moving," he said quietly.

"Hmph!" Marty said. "I have students, too." She eyed Keenan judgmentally. He wasn't sure where he came out in her mind.

He didn't really care. He didn't want to add complications for Stacey.

"Well, I'll be in the car," he said. "Marty, nice to meet you."

"And you! Nice, big guy. Seriously, please, *work* here."

He didn't respond; he lifted a hand and walked back to the car.

He slid into the driver's seat. While he waited, he'd go over his notes. Tedious as it might be, you never knew when you might see something that began to make more sense or pointed in a direction not yet taken.

He'd been there deep in concentration for maybe ten minutes, when a postal delivery truck pulled in just ahead of him. The young postman gave him a friendly wave and headed toward the house.

There were four simple mailboxes to one side of the porch; the postman had a bundle of mail, which he sorted for each box.

One of the items he carried was a small brown-paper-wrapped package that looked to be stained on one corner.

Keenan couldn't see the mailboxes from where he was, but something about the small package bothered him. He exited the car again, heading for the mailboxes.

"Sir, excuse me, who is that package for?" he asked as the young man opened the first mailbox.

The young postman jumped back, looking up to Keenan. The postman was only about five-nine, so he had to crane his neck. "Sir, the delivery of the mail is private. Interfering with a postal worker is against the law, as is opening or tampering with another person's private correspondence." He was stammering slightly, apparently trying to remember exactly what he should be saying.

Keenan produced his credentials, explaining, "I'm not trying to tamper with anything. I'm disturbed by a package that seemed to have leaked a substance and might be dangerous."

"Leaked?" the young man said with dismay, looking at the package—and then trying to determine if anything had leaked on him. He looked like a schoolkid who feared he might have cooties as he stood there.

Then he looked at Keenan, embarrassed. "I'm sorry. You may be FBI, but I can't let you see another person's mail—"

The door to the house opened, and Stacey stepped out, dressed in black pants and a beige leather jacket, hair brushed, minimal makeup in perfect, professional mode.

She frowned, looking from the mailman to Keenan.

"Is the package for Stacey Hanson?" he asked the postman.

"Yes, uh, yes, it is."

"Stacey, show the nice man your ID," Keenan said.

She did so, looking at Keenan with a curious frown.

"Then…here, miss," the postman said. He handed the package and a few letters to Stacey and quickly finished stuffing the other three mailboxes. He looked at them both, anxious to move on.

Keenan stepped in front of him, not wanting to physically waylay the man.

"I need your name, please."

The postman's eyes widened with unease. He stared at them both. "I didn't do anything; I'm a postal carrier. I do my job right—"

"No one is saying that you didn't. In fact, you're commendable at your job. But we may need to trace that package."

"Right. Please," Stacey muttered, glancing at Keenan with her frown of confusion deepening.

"Eric Bolton," the postman said. "My supervisor is Gene Estrella."

"Thank you," Keenan said, stepping aside to let him go on his way.

Eric Bolton hurried down the path to his vehicle but then stopped, turning back.

"What do you think is in that package?" he asked.

"Not sure. Thank you," Keenan said.

The postman hurried on again—his mail wagon jerking out to the road.

Stacey turned to Keenan. "What *do* you think is in that package?"

"No return address, Stacey," he said. "And suspiciously stained." He pulled out a pair of nitrile gloves from the small stash he kept in his jacket pocket and took the package from her. "I want to bring this to headquarters, get the lab on it."

"But...we don't know what it is."

"Do you know who sent this?"

"No, but—"

"Stacey, look at it."

She noticed the dark stain on the paper as well and looked at him again.

"This doesn't look like anything you might have purchased online."

"No," she admitted. "But...shouldn't we find out what it is?"

"Yes—in a controlled situation. I just have a hunch that whatever this might be, it isn't something good."

CHAPTER SEVEN

In the lab at headquarters, Rebecca Cabal, one of their best forensic investigators, first studied and photographed the package.

"Not that all the care we're taking may mean anything—this package was dropped off at one of the busiest mail drops in the city. It was handled by several people, at least. Who knows how many? But then again, there is the stamp, though I don't think that this envelope was stamped or sealed by anyone using their own saliva. There's a lot of info available on the methods used to catch crooks—most would-be crooks know enough not to leave saliva!"

Stacey had barely met half of the Krewe agents, much less those working in the extensive labs. So, she was happy to meet Rebecca. She liked her. Rebecca was tall with short red hair, not heavy but solid, quick to listen and pay attention and grasp a situation—and competent and knowledgeable about her own work. She had come into the technological age at the right time, Stacey thought, growing up with all the wonders that computers and science were bringing to the world.

"It could just be something hastily sent by an old friend—

didn't see that a cosmetic or some other such gift might crack and leak," Stacey said.

"Your friends don't use a return address?" Rebecca asked dubiously.

"People can be in a hurry. They forget."

She wondered why she was protesting. Rebecca was right. Keenan, standing by with his arms crossed over his chest, was right. This didn't look like a package that might be sent by a friend.

The package had been photographed, dusted and swabbed. With gloved hands, Rebecca opened it.

A stained note fell out. Along with a lumpy, red mass.

Both Keenan and Rebecca were silent. Stacey looked at Keenan, feeling a chill.

"That's not…"

"I believe it is," Keenan said quietly.

"Kidney. Human kidney. And I'm willing to bet that testing will prove it to be one of our Yankee Ripper's victims," Rebecca said. She looked from Stacey to Keenan. "There's a note with it. Pretty messed up, but…"

She used two sets of long tweezers to start painstakingly stretching out the note that had come with the lump of kidney.

She looked at Keenan. "You'll let me see what I can discover forensically? I'll send the photos to you. You'll have them before you even reach your offices. And the partial organ will go straight to testing."

He nodded grimly, glancing over at Stacey, expecting her agreement.

Of course, she nodded. But she was shaken.

She'd gone to autopsies. They were painful. She knew that those who worked and spoke for the dead—medical examiners and morgue workers and even morticians—had to learn to work with the body, the shell that was left behind. It was still difficult for her. Autopsies were bad, but the lump of human kidney on the examination table was beyond chilling.

She wanted to believe that they were wrong—that this wasn't a sticky lump that had once been a viable human organ. That a prankster had sent her a cow kidney.

But she knew that wasn't going to be the case.

It was bad enough that it was what it was.

Then she had to wonder why it had been sent to her. Yes, she was on the case; yes, she and Keenan were considered lead, but Fred Crandall was on the case, not to mention dozens of officers and agents in DC, Virginia, West Virginia and Maryland.

Why her?

And how did they have her home address?

They thanked Rebecca.

Stacey thought that she was moving normally as they left the lab for the elevator. But she felt a bit wobbly.

She heard the little ping on her phone, alerting her that Rebecca had been true to her word; the photographs she had taken of the note were coming through.

She wondered if the killer had known that the kidney might bleed through the packaging; perhaps Jack the Ripper had dried out his piece of human organ better before sending it to Mr. Lusk of the citizens' brigade.

It didn't matter; no matter how good Rebecca's camera might be, the note would be difficult to read. They probably already knew what it said, though. She guessed it would be the exact words that Jack the Ripper had penned years in the past.

But why?

A killer this brutal would usually be considered disorganized; to do what he was doing, this killer was organized.

Something bigger was going on here. She was convinced.

"Does he plan on stopping after his fifth murder?" she wondered as they stepped off the elevator.

"There's one thing every detective, scholar, et cetera agrees on—Jack the Ripper died, moved or wound up incarcerated. Because, in his kind of killing, no, they don't stop. They need the thrill, the adrenaline, the release, with greater and greater desperation. Unless…"

"Unless this is something else. A terrible and horrendous stage show for the police and law enforcement," Stacey said.

Keenan nodded.

He pushed open the door to his office. Sliding around to his desk chair, he woke his computer and logged in.

She drew the second chair around behind his desk as he was opening the pictures that Rebecca had sent.

"It's the 'From Hell' or the 'Lusk' letter," Stacey said. "But of course, we both knew it would be that."

"Yes," he said simply.

They both stared at it a second before Keenan brought up a facsimile of the letter that had come to the police in 1882.

They were exact matches.

"'From hell, Mr. Lusk, Sir. I sent you half the kidney'—spelled *k-i-d-n-e* on the original and here," Stacey said, "'from one woman prasarved it for you tother piece I fried and ate it was very nice. I may send you the bloody knife that took it out if you only wate a little longer.'"

"'Signed Catch me if you can Mishter Lusk,'" Keenan said.

"The killer imitated the handwriting, didn't he?" Stacey said.

"He made one mistake," Keenan said. "He didn't 'prasarve' it."

"I find it hard to believe that—given some attention to detail we've seen on this—he didn't realize that it was going to become…mush in the mail," Stacey said.

He was looking at her. "He must think of you as being a counterpart 'Mishter' Lusk," Keenan said.

"There, again, that doesn't make sense," Stacey said. "Mr. Lusk was head of the Whitechapel Vigilance Committee. Obviously he knows that I'm with the FBI investigating. But Lusk wasn't in law enforcement—he was with a citizens' group."

He nodded. He was still studying her. "Are you worried?" he asked.

She twisted her head at an angle, trying to understand the meaning behind his question.

She smiled. "I'm an agent. I excelled with firearms. I may not look like a large brick wall, but honestly, I'm competent. I mean, this is a job where danger is an inherent part of it, but we're also trained to deal with dangerous situations."

He nodded thoughtfully.

"Well?" she said.

"You're not afraid that he seems to have singled you out? He could have sent the kidney piece to one of Jess Marlborough's roommates or someone else involved. Or to me, or Fred Crandall or Jean Channing...or a dozen other people. He chose you."

"Oh, no, no, no, no," she said. "If you're even thinking of suggesting that I should be taken off the case—"

"Not in the least. You are the key in this case—you knew about Billie Bingham being discovered. And now, well, you're 'seeing' what *historically should be* the final murder."

"And maybe we can even stop it!" she said.

"That's the plan," he told her.

"Then, why were you asking me if I was afraid?"

"Because if you're not just a little afraid, then I'm worried about you, to be honest. We need to make sure that you're with other agents. At all times."

"That's not practical—"

"Practical or not, it's only sane. And not because you're a woman—though God knows, with this, he's very aware of you. Let's hope that he doesn't see you as his—"

"Mary Kelly?" Stacey broke in. She shook her head earnestly. "No, seriously, I'm not seeing that. Okay, many people may not like FBI agents or may be skeptical of them, but our work is a far cry from prostitution!"

"True. But I think you've been right all along. The whole Jack the Ripper thing is a ruse. Was it to kill Billie? Or was it, as we've theorized, to gain human organs? If so, you'd make a fine Mary Kelly. You're young and in excellent health and condition."

"So, what are you suggesting?" she asked.

"You can move in with me."

"What? No, that wouldn't be…"

"We're talking about life or death—not what's proper or not. Anyone targeted needs an extra pair of eyes watching their backs. You're my partner on this."

"You really think I'm targeted?"

"You received a human kidney in the mail. Yes. So, for now, we can check with the other agents, but since we're pretty much 24/7 on the case now, my place makes the most sense."

"All right—if you really don't think I should be alone."

"No man—or woman—is an island," he said dryly.

"Fine, then," she said. "I have an extra pullout sofa in my apartment, too. You can move in until we catch this monster."

"You should move in with me."

She grinned. "My dad doesn't leave clothes when he visits. He and my mom aren't all that far away. They don't sleep over often. You'll have to pack and bring your own things."

He leaned toward her. "He's obviously watched you—followed you. Knows where you live. He may know where I live, too, but… I think my place would be better."

They stared at each other and suddenly both smiled.

"It isn't a pissing contest, I swear," he told her, leaning back and grinning. "Nothing to do with the fact that I'm the senior agent. It's just a professional precaution."

"You have a point, but I think I do, too. First, Marty may well come and commit physical damage to you if you take what she sees as her safety net—me—out of that house. And here's another point. If he does know about me and has some diabolical plan, have you considered the possibility of baiting him at my place?"

"Okay."

"Okay?"

"Okay."

She looked at him warily. "You'll come to my place? That easily?"

He grinned. "I didn't really care where—I just wanted you to agree with not being alone. So, now, back to plan. We're on to see the congressman."

He stood and waited for her. For a moment, she didn't move. She just stared at him, and then she said.

"But we missed the appointment!"

He smiled. "The right people got it changed."

"Really? You're just telling me about it now? And what was all that about my apartment? You jerk!"

"Manipulation," he said. "Good to use in interrogation as well. Jackson went ahead and tried to get Colin Smith to come in to answer some questions. Smith put him off, saying that he knew nothing, and he wasn't coming into any law-enforcement agency—his constituents wouldn't like it. Jackson told him he understood, and that's why he had made an appointment that had to be adjusted. I believe Smith knows that if he didn't co-operate, Jackson would have gotten a judge to issue him a sub-poena to show up to answer questions in court. I'm sure Jackson was polite when they spoke—but that Smith knew he had to see us. We were a bit waylaid this morning—now it's time we go to him."

"Yes, it's time we see the congressman. But, still, wait! You just wanted—"

"You to agree to not being alone. It's fine with me if I move in with you for the time. We'll clear it with Jackson. But yes, it's me or another agent. You can take your pick. But—not being sexist—I don't think we should single out any other female agents. In fact…"

He paused, a curious look on his face.

"What?" Stacey demanded.

"He hasn't killed any males. Not in this manner, at any rate. But…the city is equally filled with healthy males."

"Maybe he has killed males, too?"

"We'll have Angela do a search of male murder victims in the area—DC, Maryland, Virginia and West Virginia."

"Not just those who have been murdered. We need those who have been reported missing as well," she added. "Though, if he is taking males…"

"He might have started with the homeless, the down-and-out men, just as he prayed on down-and-out women. Until Billie." He shook his head. "That's…off."

"Off," she agreed at nearly the same time. They were finishing one another's thoughts. That was, hopefully, a good thing.

And yet she was irritated at how easily she'd been manipulated. Maybe it wasn't such a bad thing to have someone watching her back—until the monster was caught.

Except that Keenan Wallace would be in her home. So close.

Nope. Don't think that way.

Surely, she could handle being in the same space as an extremely attractive male.

Aargh! She just couldn't think that way. At least he didn't find her as annoying as shoe-gunk anymore, but that didn't mean that he had come to think of her highly. Or *sexually* in any way.

She gave herself a mental shake. "All right, let's go. It's one horrific game," she said, "but…the game is afoot."

He nodded gravely. "We'll check in with Jackson and head on out." He started for the door and then paused and said, "He wasted a kidney. If he's selling organs…"

"I think we'll find that it was damaged or diseased in some way," Stacey finished grimly.

"We'll known soon enough," he said.

CHAPTER EIGHT

"I know you had an appointment, but it was supposed to be this morning. The congressman tried to fit you in—he wants to cooperate with and help the FBI, of course. But I'm afraid that Congressman Smith is busy now," the woman behind the reception desk at the DC offices of Colin Smith told them.

Keenan had expected that Colin Smith would balk when it came time for their interview with him.

Smith was a public figure. A married man with a bad reputation he insisted was unearned. Stories spread quickly, tossed about by opposing candidates and rival politicians, whispered about between staff members, but remained hard to prove. However, he had been accused often enough, on social media mainly, of being a womanizer and an adulterer.

In Keenan's mind, so much smoke surrounded Smith that, while many of his colleagues tried to cover for him, there just had to be fire.

"I believe he was informed that we were coming," Keenan said. "He was asked to come down to my unit's headquarters, and he refused. We understand. We're here. But we're not here to chat—or to complain about road construction. You can't have missed the fact that a known associate of his was brutally murdered. We're hoping he might know something that could help us catch a serial killer."

"He's—just busy. You should call his attorney," the receptionist said, offering Keenan a card.

Keenan tried not to show his annoyance.

All field agents were given customary lessons in the art of interrogation. Keenan knew that a successful interrogation didn't necessarily mean a confession, but a successful interrogation could provide some of the truth. Human behavior could give away so much.

Smith didn't want to talk at all. That could imply guilt—or that if he wasn't guilty, he did know something.

Keenan was already damned sure that Smith knew something.

The way someone waited in an interrogation room might mean something. The innocent often paced with confusion, wanting to know why they were there, and why they were brought in and then made to wait. The guilty sometimes became so anxious that they paced, twitched and knee-bounced until the adrenaline burned through them—and they fell asleep on the table.

Causing a suspect to wait and observing their behavior could give an agent or officer a direction to go with their questioning.

In Colin Smith's case, the man would probably consider himself smarter than any officer or agent.

Keenan smiled dryly. Smith would enjoy turning the tables. Refusing to see them, or keeping them waiting. He couldn't arrest or even detain the man—not for rumors or suspicion, no matter how rampant both might be, and not even on Tania Holt's word that Smith was the "Coffee Boy" from Billie Bingham's diary.

Keenan forced an easy smile, determining how to proceed, when Stacey slipped closer to the desk.

She gave the receptionist a sweet smile, leaning closer across the desk, her tone quiet and yet urgent. "Can you see if you have any sway with him? He really needs to speak with us." She appeared distressed as she added, "The press is going to go wild with all this. And if it's shown that the congressman has been nothing but completely happy to speak with the FBI, we'll be able to say that he's cooperating—which you just said he really wants to do. I mean, if it should be discovered that he was hostile and uncooperative—"

"He's not being hostile. He's busy," the secretary said. But she appeared to be growing uneasy.

Stacey remained pleasant and concerned, her tone worried. "I'm sure I've stressed to you how much it means that we just have a quick interview with him," Stacey told her.

The woman stood up, staring at Stacey. "I'll see what I can do. I just know...that he's busy."

She walked toward her boss's door, but it opened before she reached it. Congressman Colin Smith came out of the office with a young woman. She was about thirty, slim to the point of skinny, blonde and wearing a harried look. She clutched a tablet tightly to her chest.

Colin Smith, on the other hand, was on the portly side, with brownish hair—thinning, but he tried to hide it. He might have been reasonably attractive in his youth, but that youth was fading. He had become popular for a jocular charm, but even among his constituents—who hoped to ignore his behavior—the charm was fading as well.

He started to give an order to the blonde woman, but his mouth formed a silent O instead as he noticed Keenan and Stacey.

He looked at his secretary who looked helplessly back at him.

He turned his attention to the blonde, his voice booming as he said, "Thank you, Miss Bronsen. Now, if you'll go and get started right away on that project for the animal shelters, I will greatly appreciate it. And now...well, are these visitors from my beautiful district?" he asked his secretary, before turning his attention back to Keenan and Stacey. He seemed to force his charming smile.

"No, sir," his secretary answered with lightning speed. "I told them you were busy. They're from the FBI."

Smith tried hard not to change his expression. Despite his savvy, his smile did appear to be plastered in place.

"Well, goodness! A visit from our finest. I do have a terribly busy day and you were scheduled earlier, but, thankfully, some matters can be handled quickly. Please, agents, come on into my office. Let me see how I can help you today."

Stacey glanced at Keenan. They'd gotten lucky. The skinny blonde woman scurried away; the secretary went back to her desk.

Smith held open the door to his office as if he was welcoming them into his home.

They walked in. He followed them and indicated they should take the chairs in front of his desk.

Keenan caught Stacey's eye and she nodded subtly toward a credenza in the office. On it sat a very fancy espresso machine. Keenan raised his eyebrows in acknowledgment.

"To what do I owe this visit?" Smith asked. He didn't bother with the pretense of including *the pleasure of.* He sat behind his desk, left hand resting upon it, and leaned back in his chair. He looked at them guilelessly.

"We do hate to bother you, Congressman Smith," Stacey said easily.

"But your name has been linked with that of Billie Bingham," Keenan said.

"And you've heard about her horrific murder," Stacey put in.

"Of course, of course," Smith murmured. "Those poor, poor women. And Miss Bingham. Yes, I know the woman. We've met on occasion. She did receive invitations to the darnedest places! I wish I knew something. I do. This killer must be stopped. I'm going to assume that you and others are spending every waking hour determined to stop this scourge. Not that we don't have other matters of national and personal safety to be considered. Now, I do know others who would say good riddance to bad rubbish. But every man and woman born on this earth has a soul. So, if I can help you in any way whatsoever, I am certainly eager to do so."

"You did know Billie Bingham, correct, sir?" Stacey asked. "I've seen you with your arm around her in a picture, I believe, in a magazine."

Smith waved a hand in the air and managed a laugh. "Why, I don't even remember what event it was at—but yes, I did meet her. I thought she was one of my constituents, just wanting a picture with me!"

"Well, of course, sir, everyone would want their picture with you," Stacey said, leaning forward a bit. "I'm just curious, because the tabloids took off with it. Did you see her after, try to get her to…well, deny the allegations that there was anything going on?"

"No, no, no… You just can't help what people say. I'm a public figure. There are always opponents in the political field—people who want to egg things on, you know?" Smith said.

"We were hoping that you might know of someone who was with her or did know her well. If you could help us in any way that might help catch the killer," Keenan said.

He shook his head.

Keenan noted that Smith's fingers were moving, one, two, three, four. Not tapping audibly but moving nervously on his desk. And he could just see past the desk that Smith's leg was twitching.

"You're looking for some whacked-out madman!" Smith said. "I don't know any…insane people like that!"

"You've never been to Bingham's mansion?" Stacey asked.

Smith turned to her with wide eyes.

"We just ask because a car like yours was seen there," Keenan told him.

He didn't really know if Smith's car had been seen there or not—but it drew his desired reaction.

"You can ask my wife. I was home the night that woman was murdered. Can you really imagine me butchering someone in that manner?" Smith demanded.

Stacey quickly assured him. "Oh, no, sir! We were just hoping you could point us in a direction that you might know of someone who might know something. We have a witness who saw you at the house."

She was sure that his face paled, but he gave nothing away in his expression.

The man was the ultimate politician.

"I don't know what your witness thought she saw. But I've tried to help you. Now I'm done with this. If you want to speak with me anymore, I want my attorney present. And I suggest that you be very careful with your accusations."

He shook his head stubbornly.

Keenan rose, saying "As you wish," and thanking him for his time. Stacey rose along with him.

They left through the reception area; his secretary pretended to be working as they came out of the office, but she had been watching the door. She gave her attention to her work, as if she wasn't watching them leave and it didn't matter in the least to her whether they stayed or left.

When they were out into the hallway of the building, Keenan noted the other doors that were part of the congressman's DC suite of offices.

"He's lying," Stacey murmured. "I'd hoped to get something more."

"You did great in there," he told her.

She looked up at him, as if surprised by the compliment.

"We probably went through a lot of the same training—Adam

is big on his agents taking classes in every possible aspect of law enforcement. If you go in somewhere expecting a confession, you're going to be disappointed nine times out of ten. If you go in looking for grains of truth, you've gotten something. We got some bits of truth."

"And the truth?"

"Is that he's a liar, and he knows more than he's telling us." He hesitated, looking at the various doors in the hallway.

"You want to speak to the blonde woman, right?" Stacey asked.

"I do," he told her.

"We can open doors as if by mistake?"

"We can," he said, smiling. "First or second?"

She was already heading for the first door. Before she could touch it, the door opened.

The blonde woman was standing there. She froze, staring at Stacey in pure panic.

"It's all right," Stacey whispered.

The woman shook her head, then nervously licked her dry lips.

"You're afraid he'll find you talking to us," Stacey said. "That's okay. We'll go. You come on down. We'll wait for you at the coffee shop on the corner."

The woman nodded. She looked anxiously around the hall.

But Colin Smith wasn't coming out. He was probably busy making sure that his secretary warned him should the FBI be in his office again.

And his secretary was just busy being thankful they were gone.

"We'll be there," Keenan said. Not thinking, just in a hurry, he reached for Stacey's hand, drawing her quickly to the stairway.

She didn't protest; they hurried down the stairs together.

They didn't speak again until they were headed down the street. He awkwardly released her hand, apologizing quickly.

"Not to worry," she told him.

They walked on quickly to Cathy's Coffee, a gourmet pastry shop on the corner.

"Let's get some food while we're here," he said, surprised to realize that they hadn't eaten and that she was probably as hungry as he was.

"Anything with meat and cheese and bread," she told him. "There's a table in the back, kind of concealed by a post. I'm going to grab it. Coffee—no, ice tea, please—and anything that looks good and not too weird."

She headed to the table in back; he ordered.

As he waited, Keenan's phone rang. It was Fred Crandall.

"I've been going over the video from that pawnshop," Fred told him. "You can see the street, a car—and a man. I'm going to meet you at the station. Jackson Crow called me in to your offices along with Jean. Both departments are good with us teaming up for this—it is a task force, after all. He doesn't want the info on the kidney Stacey received getting out—even among anyone who is immediately involved. We're not giving this Jack the attention he craved from that. If it was attention he was after. It won't make it to the media. I'm heading to your offices; we'll get your tech to see what they can do with the footage from the pawnshop." He took a breath and hurried on. "Your technical unit is better funded than ours, even if we are one of the most…well, prominent police departments in the country. Where are you?"

"We just saw Congressman Smith; we were approached by one of his staff. We're going to talk to her, then we'll be right in," Keenan said. "You've seen the video from the surveillance camera, right? Can you see the victim?"

"Yes, the victim. But you'll see. You can't get a license plate—it's covered with dirt. And you never see the man's face. But if they can tighten it and clean it up some… I don't know. We'll be at headquarters when you get there."

"Thanks," Keenan said. "I'll call the medical examiner's office on my way in. For details on the victim from the basement."

"Fingerprints and dental impressions will have been taken by now. Even DNA, though I don't know how long that might take, and unless she's in the system—"

"I know. There will probably be nothing. I still think we'll get an ID. This guy chose one of the most notorious madams in history—he wasn't trying to find victims with identities we'd never discover."

A woman was handing Keenan a tray with their order; he ended the call, telling Fred that they'd see him soon. As he took the tray, he looked to the door. He was hoping that the young blonde woman hadn't changed her mind.

Keenan went to the table, setting down the food and filling Stacey in on the phone conversation he'd had with Fred.

She didn't ask what sandwiches he'd chosen; she just took the one closest to her and ate while she listened.

Then she cleared her throat, indicating the door.

The nervous blonde was coming. She walked to the counter and Keenan rose to meet her, asking her in an easy tone what he could get her. She laughed and said, "Decaf. I'm already a wreck."

"Stacey is over there. You can join her. Do you want anything else? Food?"

She shook her head and glanced at the door, as if making sure that she hadn't been followed. Then she noticed Stacey behind the pillar at the little table. She smiled at him, appreciating the chosen site, and hurried over to join Stacey.

He went back to the counter for decaf.

When he reached the table, she was already talking earnestly with Stacey. The blonde had evidently introduced herself, and Stacey seemed to have already eased her somewhat into conversation.

"The thing is—I don't think that he... Congressman Smith

killed Billie Bingham. But he's lying when he says he doesn't know her or didn't see her. I know because I was coming into his office one day when he didn't know I was there and he kept talking. He was telling someone that Billie was a...a bitch and that something had to be done about her."

Stacey looked over at Keenan. "Keenan, this is Peggy Bronsen. She's an assistant with Congressman Smith's office."

"Peggy, thank you for speaking with us," Keenan said. "I know that you're nervous. Do you have any idea who he might have been speaking with?"

She shook her head, biting her lip before she spoke again. "I backed out of the room. I didn't think that... Well, of course, it was before she was found...even before the body in Lafayette had been found. But I didn't want him to know that I was there because... I don't know. There was something in the way he was speaking. I mean, he's the kind of politician who *wants* to be known for being forthright and upright and honest and all. But those of us who are on his staff... I wanted to quit." She hesitated again. "He's a narcissist. Yes, he wants to be liked, and he wants to project the image that he's sweet and charming and firm but thoughtful, but...he barks at everyone. And the way he is with women is unnerving. Some girls just fall for him, and if things go wrong, he calls them liars. He's always touching people as if he's sampling them. Creepy! Every day, I've been afraid that he might see something in me. And now, the way all those women have been killed..."

"We understand," Stacey said. "If you're worried about your safety, can you send in your resignation?"

"He could find me!" Peggy said tearfully. "I'm not rich. I'm just an assistant. I was a graphic-design major, and I can come up with ads and slogans and create art for his different campaigns. I don't have a savings account to fall back on. I have to survive, and with what's been going on..."

"Okay. We'll figure something out," Keenan assured her.

"There is witness protection. And if this thing can be solved, it might only be temporary."

"Would I have to go to court?"

"At this moment, we still haven't proven anything," Stacey said. "But..." she added, looking at Keenan, hoping he would finish her statement.

He smiled at her. "We can get you protected. We need to find out who he was talking to."

"I know he's seen her before, too," Peggy said, "and I know his wife knows that he saw Billie, too. But it wasn't his wife he was talking to about Billie that day."

Keenan pulled out his phone, looking at her. "Do you have to go back to the office for any of your personal belongings?"

"I...uh," she said and then paused, looking at him a bit in wonder. "No. I have my personal laptop in my bag. There are works in progress, but...no. Nothing of mine is there. But you don't understand. They have my address. They can find me. I can't afford—"

"I'm calling my superior," Keenan explained. "We're going to put you in a safe house."

"Have I—have I given you enough to warrant that kind of protection?" Peggy asked. "I may be an idiot, I may not be in any kind of danger, but if he suspected that I heard—that I'm talking to you... Well, he said that Billie was a bitch and needed to be taken care of, and now she's dead. I'm really scared."

Keenan excused himself and left the table. He put a call through to Jackson and quickly explained the situation.

"I'm not sure how many times we can go this round. The police haven't the kind of funding to watch every frightened woman in the DC area. You feel that Colin Smith is somehow involved?" Jackson asked him.

"It seems likely."

"And yet you think that the killer is considering Stacey as his Mary Kelly, too?"

"She received the kidney. He obviously knows that she's on the case—and he knows where she lives. But, Jackson, this woman, Peggy Bronsen, is terrified."

"We're also watching Cindy Hardy, Tania Holt—Billie Bingham's assistant—and six terrified sex workers. Not to mention the two maids, but they're doing fine, loving protective custody. I guess Billie wasn't that great an employer. And despite the crime-scene investigators' best efforts, we have nothing from Billie's house… I suppose I shouldn't say that. We have hundreds of prints, enough to keep CSIs working for days to come. And fluids. In fact, we're awash in evidence that needs to be sorted through and may mean nothing at all. But so far nothing at all in the basement that would lead to the murderer. We're doing our best to stay low-profile with the media, of course, since whoever is doing this wants to generate the hysteria of a madman imitating Jack the Ripper." He paused and his sigh could be heard over the phone. "Thank God for Adam Harrison that we're well funded, because overtime on this case is going to be killer. Ahem. Bad choice of words."

"Jackson, if this is a case of organs being stolen, then a doctor has to be in on this. Doing the killing? Possibly. Although, as in the old case, it must be someone with a knowledge of anatomy. Surgeon?"

"Angela has been searching for local doctors who are involved in organ transplants."

"What about databases on people who need organs? If someone has suddenly come off a list, they might have been the recipient of an illegally acquired organ."

"True, and yes, we've started a search. If they're getting these organs out of the country, though, it's not going to be so easy. Anyway, as to now. Can you bring Peggy Bronsen to headquarters with you now? Detectives Crandall and Channing are here. Maybe it's time to look at the case from Jean's side, review everything that they have on the first murder."

"Right. Have you seen the video yet?"

"They just got here, and we're getting set up. Fred and Jean have gone over it. But we have better equipment. Bring Ms. Bronsen, and come on in."

"Will do," Keenan promised, and hung up.

He watched Stacey talking at the table with Peggy.

Stacey had a talent that many a seasoned agent still lacked: an ability with people. She honestly liked others and cared about them. It came through, and they responded to her.

"I was wrong, Jackson," he murmured aloud. And he smiled, thinking of his partner's appeal and the way she had stumbled over his words when the questions she had asked had become personal. "I was wrong about her!" That time, he just thought the words.

He knew that Jackson had partnered him with the best possible person on this case, with or without her extraordinary ability to dream the future.

He walked over to the table and took a seat, smiling. "Ms. Bronsen," he said, "would you mind coming with us right now? We're going to see to it that you're kept safe."

"Y-you want me to go back to the office and resign?" she asked, her hands shaking as she picked up her cup.

"No, no. We'll have you call in to work, just say that you're leaving immediately because of a family emergency and you'll send in any pertinent work. Don't get involved with explanations. Make it short and sweet."

"Now?" Peggy asked nervously. "You think that I should call now?"

"We can wait until we get in the car," Stacey said. She indicated the room and people around them, suggesting it might be better if all else was said in private.

But he asked her, "Do you think that there's someone else from the office in here now? Or anyone from the building who might mention they saw you here?"

She looked around and shook her head. "But they could pop in at any second. Especially that sourpuss of his!"

"Sourpuss? I'm guessing you mean his secretary?" Stacey asked.

"Agnes Merkle. She could have been a drill instructor. She comes here. I wouldn't want her to see me."

He leaned across the table, making unflinching eye contact.

"She's not going to hurt you or do anything to you—ever again. You will walk out of here between two federal agents. You don't need to worry about her, now or ever."

She smiled, still shaking, but maybe a little less.

"Shall we go?" Stacey asked.

"We're ready, right?" he said to Peggy.

She looked at the two of them and gave a tremulous smile. "Ready!" she said.

They stood up and walked out.

And while Keenan halfway expected the sourpuss drill-sergeant Agnes Merkle to come after them waving a letter opener, they left without incident.

"Do you see anyone out here that you know?" Keenan asked her as he opened the back door of his car.

She looked around quickly, then ducked into the car.

"No, I don't think so," she told him.

He didn't know everyone in her office, but he'd recognize Agnes Merkle if he saw her.

No. She was not on the street.

But he did want to see her again, at another time.

Eventually, he wanted to get some hooks into the woman and find out just what secrets she might be hiding as well.

CHAPTER NINE

The night had been dark when Jess Marlborough had last been seen alive.

But Brian, a whiz from Tech with an amazing ability to clean up and sharpen any video, film or still photo was incredibly adept. He was a lean fellow with wild red hair and a great deal of enthusiasm, and probably a year or two younger than Stacey's age—young but talented. He managed to brighten up the image of the street.

"Let's run the whole video right now," Jean Channing suggested. She looked over at Stacey and Keenan and explained, "Your call, but I haven't seen it all yet, either."

"Let's run it," Keenan agreed.

He was point man on the case, though Stacey knew that Jackson had intended on being in here while they viewed the surveillance video. But he and Angela had taken Peggy into Jackson's office. They were working with her, trying to go through her memory, hoping for anything else she might be able to give them.

Brian ran the video.

A large black vehicle drove up and parked outside the apartment building. It sat, nothing happening, for a few minutes. Waiting? Then, a man got out of the car.

Next to Keenan, Stacey let out a little gasp.

The shadows allowed them to see nothing of his face.

He seemed irritable as he met up with Jess Marlborough, just outside the windows to the little apartment the women shared. His movements were sharp, tense. He all but grabbed her arm to lead her to the car.

She had probably been late. A minute or two late. And that had kept this man waiting in an area where he didn't want to be seen.

But the irritation seemed to ease—was it forced? His hold released. He opened the passenger door for Jess.

She had been a pretty young woman. A little worn and jaded by what she had learned from life, but still brightened by a little ray of hope.

The man kept his head down the entire time. He was wearing a suit and a brimmed hat, looking like any banker or businessman might on his way from work.

"I can give you his approximate height and weight," Brian told them.

"That will be terrific," Keenan said. "I think I can tell you right now. You're going to find out that he's about five-ten in height and stocky. He was slim and athletic once, but he's quit his rounds of exercise and giving way to excess."

"You think it's Smith, right?" Stacey asked him.

"I do," Keenan said.

"But you couldn't prove it in a court of law," Stacey said. She gave him a grim smile. "We might know that it's him, but from this video—unless Brian miraculously comes up with something a little more—this only proves that a dark-haired man of approximately Smith's height was in that car on that street with Jess."

He smiled at her. "We know that. But Smith will have no idea just exactly what we got off the video. I think that, when we finish here, we'll pay him a visit at his DC home. We might have enough to bring him in, but I don't want to have him weaseling out on any technicalities or lack of evidence until we do have more."

They watched the video several more times.

"When the car drives in," Fred Crandall said, pointing at the screen, "you see the front of the vehicle, but I can't tell what kind. Looks like there is mud over everything. On purpose, I imagine."

"Give me a little time. I'll name the make and model," Brian told them. "There are all kinds of comparisons we can make with manufacturers' models online. Won't take me too, too long. But I should be able to make a match."

"When you do match it, we'll still be legally taking a shot in the dark," Fred muttered, shaking his head. "Think of all the black SUVs in Washington, Virginia and Maryland. Hey, there are plenty in the FBI and among detectives throughout the surrounding counties. High-quality SUVs from every manufacturer out there—all black."

"That's true," Keenan agreed. "And Smith—or whoever Jess's client was that night—made sure that he kept his face down the whole time."

"As if he knew there just might be a camera somewhere," Jean said.

"He was angry that he had to get out of the car. I don't think he had planned to get out," Stacey theorized, echoing Keenan's own thoughts. "She was late; he was growing apprehensive. He stepped out but remembered he didn't want his face to be seen. He yelled at her—Candy heard him—probably because he was just as angry at himself for having stepped out. Then he must have remembered he was playing the part of a gentleman, and he opened the car door for her."

"I think that sounds about right," Keenan agreed. "So, we've got possible links for Congressman Colin Smith to two of the murders. Can we connect him to the victim in Alexandria in any way?" He looked at Detective Channing.

"On our Alexandria victim, we still have just about nothing," Jean said. "I've walked the neighborhood in jeans and a T-shirt, tried to engage the street girls in the area. One girl took a look at the picture I was showing of the victim and went racing down the street so fast I couldn't catch her." Jean made a face. "And I run marathons! And other than that... I couldn't get close to anyone. No one was talking. I've gone over the medical examiner's notes, and all I know is that her organs were removed—completely—and that she was killed elsewhere and dumped where she lay. We've asked police at her last-known address to find out anything they could about her. We've been through government records. Her parents are deceased. She was an only child. We're just nowhere."

"A forgotten person," Keenan said. "As the others might have been. Except for Billie Bingham."

"It's sad but true," Fred put in. "We all know that cases can grow cold. We've got a big caseload. And sometimes, we're spurred into action because of a persistent loved one. And that usually means people not afraid of the police. Sex workers, even frightened ones, have a tendency to run from police and law enforcement, not to them."

"What if Billie was a wild card?" Stacey asked. They all looked at her. "An unintentional wild card, or someone who didn't quite fit the bill, but worked? The plan was to kill street people. Make it look like a deranged Jack the Ripper wannabe was on the prowl. Finish it up and slide into history and mystery like the real Ripper. But maybe Billie got in the way. Or maybe she was involved and became so irritating she had to be stopped. Despite her occupation and slightly older age, she was in excellent shape. From what I understand, she was pure business, in control all the time. She didn't abuse alcohol or drugs that might be dangerous to vital organs. That would make her a viable victim if they are taking the organs."

"I think you might be right," Keenan said. He filled the others in on their experience at Smith's office—and how Peggy Bronsen had come to them and what she had said.

"I always thought he was dirty," Jean said. She lifted her hands defensively. "That being important only because it has to do with our case."

Keenan liked Jean. He'd learned she'd started with the police straight out of college and earned her way up. She was dedicated. Nearing fifty now, she had never married but kept a lively-enough social life, continually taking martial-arts classes and ballroom dance. Her first devotion was, however, always to her work. She had short dark blond hair and bright hazel eyes, and was wiry and athletic and deceptively small.

This was often to her advantage. Tough guys thought that they could escape her in an arrest situation. They were sadly mistaken.

Jean continued. "So, our guy kills two street girls, and then, someone—still unknown—in Billie's basement, and then Billie. But you said that Peggy Bronsen doesn't believe that Congressman Smith did the actual killing, and I'm inclined to agree. If this is about black-market human organs, more than one person is involved. If we get Smith, will he give up whoever else is doing this?"

"I think he'd sell out his own mother if it would help him," Fred said dryly.

"If they are taking organs, there's big money involved. I think Jackson already has our forensic accounting department seeing what they can dig up on Smith," Keenan told him.

Jean looked down at her notes. "His wife is Sandra Smith, forty-seven. They have two grown children, one son living in Los Angeles, another working in London." She sighed. "Doesn't look like they're depending on him for survival. The LA son is working in movie production with a big studio, and the second son is on contract with a major pharmaceutical company—he'll be in the UK for another six months."

"Their colleges?" Stacey asked.

"Princeton and Yale. But the youngest graduated two years ago. So, no obvious major expenses or debts. I don't know why Smith would be so greedy. And if they are taking organs, where are they going? I can't believe that we have any of our transplant hospitals in on this."

"No known hospitals. If that is what's happening, there's an underground operation going on somewhere, or they're being shipped out of the country," Stacey said.

"Organs are only viable so long," Fred reminded them. "But they're being cleanly taken, according to our MEs."

"Then there's the kidney piece that was sent to Stacey," Keenan said. "We need forensics on that." He paused for a moment. "We're also checking into disappearances or any like murders of men. This whole Jack the Ripper thing may be to throw off law enforcement. Hopefully, we'll learn more on that soon as well. At this time, we do know that if we don't catch him, this man—or his accomplice or accomplices—will strike again. They'll need a Mary Kelly victim. We have the six women who lived with Jess Marlborough. We have Tania Holt, Billie's assistant. And we have Peggy Bronsen, the congressman's staff member, who is terrified of him. Any of those women might make a fitting victim, or the killer may strike somewhere we're not even thinking about."

"We're watching the home and surroundings of Jess Marlborough's friends," Fred assured him.

"And we have Peggy Bronsen and Tania Holt in protective custody. I believe we also need eyes on Cindy Hardy. She was vocal and furious," Stacey said.

"And you," Keenan added.

"Hey, I have you—the best of the best," Stacey said, smiling.

But all eyes were on her. Jean reached out and touched her arm. "Don't take this lightly—receiving a kidney from this killer, be he a madman or a businessman."

"We're not taking it lightly," Stacey assured her. "We're staying together, 24/7."

"That's a relief," Fred put in. "I'm still having your place heavily patrolled—your place, or are you two hiding out elsewhere?"

"My place. There's no need to stretch resources further," Stacey said. "We have way too many women to protect as it is, and I'm the only one who is both armed and trained."

"No one can watch his or her own back," Jean said softly.

"That's why we're taking every precaution," Stacey assured her.

The door to the conference room opened, and Jackson Crow joined them.

"We got a report from the gated community where Cindy Hardy is living," he told them. "She lied. Video showed her leaving the night Billie Bingham was killed."

"Possible victim—or possible murderer?" Stacey wondered.

"Should Jean and I take a run on her this time? We can ask if she wants protection," Fred suggested.

"Mixing it up might be a good thing," Keenan said, addressing Jackson. "Stacey and I plan on a meeting with the good congressman again—at his home."

"You might want to hurry," Jackson told him. "According to some congressional sources friendly to law enforcement, Smith is planning a trip back home. Due to leave tomorrow morning. You'll need to catch him this evening."

"We'll report to our forces, state and local, to keep up the vigilance," Jean said. "And we'll be back here eight sharp tomorrow, unless we hear otherwise."

"Great. See you at the task-force meeting tomorrow morning," Jackson said. "For now, go. Get on it."

He stopped Keenan and Stacey as they started to follow Fred and Jean out.

"Stacey, I know you don't want to be coddled. But that piece of kidney did come to you. Not only are you yourself at risk, but our chance to solve this could be in jeopardy if we're not careful."

"We're good," Stacey said. She grinned at him. "We have a plan, and Keenan is spending the night at my place."

Jackson arched a brow to Keenan. He didn't seem to be skeptically questioning them, but rather, he appeared amused and pleased.

"She's dreaming it—dreaming the final scene," Keenan said. "The last murder, the next in whatever is happening here."

Jackson looked at Stacey with a worried frown.

"Just—the beginning?" Jackson asked her.

Stacey knew that Adam had fully briefed Jackson on her background. "Just the beginning," she said.

He looked at Keenan again. "You can handle this?"

"He's great at—handling me. My dreams, nightmares, I mean. He didn't jerk me up or out, but he was there, ready to help. I…wasn't expecting to fall asleep when I did, and Keenan was able to deal with me, step by step. I wasn't taken out of it—and yet I didn't go through the terror of being alone. I don't really know how to explain. But it worked."

Jackson was smiling. "Glad to hear it. This could be the real key. Keep dreaming, Stacey, and keep our dreamer safe, Keenan, as she dreams."

"Will do," he promised. He looked at Stacey. She was smiling at him.

He looked back at Jackson, nodding in an acknowledgment.

"Jackson, you couldn't have given me a better partner," he said quietly. "Stacey, shall we?"

They made it out at last.

In the car, she turned to him, and said, "Thank you!"

"For?"

"The acknowledgment."

He didn't glance her way. He just nodded.

She laughed. "You must really have bitched about me at the beginning!"

He shrugged. "Maybe. You're still a rookie."

"But a rookie with great nightmares."

"A rookie with great nightmares," he agreed. He glanced her way. "In fact, I just can't wait until bedtime."

He half expected her to hop on his teasing. She didn't. She looked straight ahead. "I know. I'm just hoping, praying…"

"Yes?"

She turned to look at him again as he drove. "That I can see more. Get an idea of where the room is—where he's planning to do it."

She fell silent, appearing worried and deep in thought.

Eventually she said, "I don't know how it works. When my dad was in danger, there were nights when there was nothing. Then, the dream would come again. And later, it was the same. I don't think… I just don't think that we're going to have much time."

He reached out and squeezed her hand, surprising himself.

"I think you'll see it," he said.

"I must see it."

"Before it can happen," he said.

She allowed the touch to continue, almost as if it was reassuring. Good.

"Before it can happen," she agreed.

They drove in silence.

There were times when Stacey felt the reality that she was a rookie—and that it was good to be with an experienced agent.

"What do we do if he won't let us in?" she asked as they neared the congressman's house.

"Well, if we're lucky, their housekeeper will open the door. When they do, we gently but persistently make our way in. Then, we're in before they can get Colin Smith and he can throw us out," Keenan told her.

"He might yell 'Who is it?' and warn them not to let us in."

"He might."

"Where do we go from there?"

"We warn him that we'll be happy to go to a judge and get a subpoena. He's not going to want that—that will be too close for comfort."

"Will his wife be there?"

He looked over at her, grinning. "Hey, I talk to the dead. I'm not a mind reader. I'm assuming his wife will be here, but I have no idea. If they're leaving tomorrow, she may be packing."

"If she's going with him."

"It's all *if* until we get there!" He added, "Call Angela. Let's see if she can find us anything helpful about his address."

"Just—call Angela?" Stacey asked him, aware her tone was a bit on the skeptical side.

"Yep."

"She doesn't mind?"

"She's incredible. What she can't get to, she has someone else working on almost instantly. But this is the driving pursuit in our offices right now."

He was right: Angela answered when Stacey dialed. She quickly identified herself, though she knew her ID would have popped up on Angela's phone. Stacey told her that she and Keenan were nearly at Congressman Smith's home and asked if she could give them any info on the house and anyone else who was living there.

Angela informed them Colin Smith and his wife were in a row of historic townhomes that were now condos, with a large unit on the ground floor. The room above was owned by a diplomat who was assigned to the Middle East for the next several months.

"So, they're alone at the house," Keenan said thoughtfully.

"What does that mean?" Stacey asked.

"Probably nothing. But it's good to know going in," he said and then spoke loudly for the phone. "Angie, do they have live-in help?"

"They do. Anika Hans, from the Netherlands. She's in the States on a student visa," Angela told them.

"Here's hoping she's not at school," Keenan said.

He parked, grateful to have found parking on the street. The building that housed the congressman's DC dwelling was a colonial structure with grand columns. So close to the White House and the Capitol Building, it had received tender care throughout the years. It—and the other houses in the row—had most probably been built in the 1830s, after the War of 1812 and the burning of the area.

"Wonder if Dolly Madison ever came here for tea," he said, surveying the building as he stepped out of the car.

"Well, we can wander back to Lafayette Square and ask our spectral friends if they know," Stacey said dryly. "We should do that, anyway—see if your ancestor Bram noted anything the night that Jess Marlborough was killed."

"Not a bad idea."

They headed up a tile path to the front door. Signs on the little picket fence in front and on the lawn warned them that the house was protected by video surveillance.

The same signs sat in front of every house on the block.

There could be video surveillance of the congressman's comings and goings, thought Stacey.

Keenan rang the bell. The door opened, and they saw a young blonde woman.

"Anika?" Keenan asked.

She immediately looked confused.

"You have the food?" she asked. There was a slight accent in her words. "Two of you—to deliver Chinese?"

She had to be the student/maid, Anika.

"No, no, I'm sorry," Keenan said, producing his badge as he moved forward to step in.

The young woman instinctively stepped back; it was natural to give a man as large as Keenan space. Stacey seized the opportunity and followed him in.

"We're FBI agents. We need to speak with Congressman Smith," he said.

Stacey smiled at the girl.

"Oh! Oh!" Anika said, dismayed, stepping back farther.

They were in the house; they'd made it this far.

"Could you inform the congressman that we're here?" Stacey asked politely.

"I… Oh, he doesn't like me letting people in. I…um… Why are you here? Shouldn't you have made an appointment or something?" Anika asked.

They didn't have to answer. A woman of forty-five or fifty, slim and fit, with platinum hair coiffed in a soft bouffant around her features, came hurrying in from a doorway to the left.

"Anika, dear, is that the food?"

She stopped short. Stacey figured she had to be the long-suffering but stand-by-your-man—especially if he's a congressman—Sandra Smith. She seemed to be in casual mode, dressed in gray sweats that still fit her attractively, and thus the call out for Chinese delivery.

She stood dead-still, staring at them, her eyes narrowing. "And who might you be?" she asked.

"We're FBI, Mrs. Smith," Keenan said. "We spoke with your husband earlier; I'm afraid we just have a few more questions to clear up some discrepancies."

"Discrepancies?"

"Yes, ma'am," Keenan said politely.

"This is our home. How dare you come here! My husband is overworked, and that silly woman wanted a picture...and... She has caused enough trouble in this town. I'd like you to leave my house. Immediately," Sandra said indignantly.

Stacey believed that Sandra Smith had hated Billie Bingham and might even be glad that she was dead. She wasn't sure that Sandra believed that her husband was all innocence when it came to the woman.

"We are sorry to bother you—" said Keenan.

He didn't finish.

The congressman, now in jeans and a T-shirt, came out of the same doorway, obviously concerned about the ruckus going on in his foyer.

He, too, stopped in his tracks seeing the two of them there.

Then he grew angry. "What the hell are you two doing in my home?" he demanded. "Anika!"

"I thought they were Chinese food!" the young woman cried.

"I'm so sorry, Congressman Smith," Keenan said. "We've had a report that puts some of the information you gave us into a bit of confusion. We'd like just a few more questions with you, just to clear things up."

As Keenan spoke, Stacey saw that Smith's line of vision left Keenan's face; he glanced quickly—and worriedly—at his wife.

"Colin, this is just—" Sandra began.

He rallied quickly. "Sandra, that woman was a thorn in my side from the second she asked for a picture," Smith said. He hurried across the room, clearly with the intention of confronting Keenan, but then backed away a step. The congressman seemed uncomfortable with having to crane his neck to look into Keenan's face.

There was something inherently intimidating about Keenan's height, Stacey thought.

But Smith had to keep up a gruff front.

"You have more questions?" he demanded. "You really want

to clear this up? Then, fine—I want done with it. Really done with it. Let's go in to your headquarters. I'll answer questions all night if it will bring an end to it all!" He turned quickly back to his wife. "Sandra, I'm sorry. I'm getting this solved as quickly as possible. This is bull! Yeah, I know. Run for office, you become a public figure—a public target is more like it! But fine. I'm sorry, honey. You and Anika enjoy your dinner. I'll be back when I get back."

"Darling, we were going to head out tomorrow," Sandra reminded him.

"Well, now we're not leaving in the morning—I damned well won't look as if I'm running away," Smith said. "I am sorry," he repeated. Then he looked at Keenan and then Stacey. "Let's go. Let's get to one of your interrogation rooms where you can really give me the third degree. Am I being charged? Can you arrest me? I think not. So let's talk. And then you will stay the hell away from me!"

He might have been intimidated by Keenan, but he pushed his way past him. Stacey noted that he didn't push her—he'd risk Keenan before pushing a woman. She wasn't sure if that meant anything or not.

But then, she didn't think that he'd gotten his hands dirty, physically doing the killing himself.

He walked to the sidewalk and waited for them to show them which car was theirs, then crossed his arms and waited for Keenan to open the rear door for him.

Keenan arched a brow to Stacey; she nodded and slid into the passenger's seat in the front.

"I intend to report you. I am a powerful man, you know."

Stacey kept silent. Keenan cast a smile at the man through the rearview mirror. "Maybe," he said. "I mean, well, you are now, but…"

That angered Smith. He lunged up against the seat, as if he would do Keenan harm. Stacey spun around in her seat to face the back, her hand up flat and firmly blocking Smith on his shoulder.

"I don't care who you are," she told him. "Threatening a federal officer is a federal offense."

He sank back into his seat.

"You will pay," he promised her. "I'm going to have your badge."

Keenan glanced at her; his look said *Don't reply.*

She was wary as they drove to their headquarters; she didn't feel like dying because the man freaked out again and attacked Keenan as he was driving.

They reached their building and parked in the garage. "You people just think that Adam Harrison has more pull around here than I do. Well, come what may—he's just got himself a fancy title because he's rich and could get his own special unit going with his own special little plane to get you all around wherever. Ghostbusters! Yeah, I know that's what they call you. Even your own agency makes fun of you."

Stacey gritted her teeth. She was not going to engage. She knew that Adam Harrison's unit had one of the highest resolve records in law enforcement—which was one of the reasons they'd been brought in on this case.

Keenan exited the car; she did the same quickly herself, opening the rear door for Congressman Smith.

Glaring at her, he emerged. "Is Adam Harrison here?" he asked. "I'll bet not. He just buys himself people, right?"

"Jackson Crow is the acting field director here, sir," Keenan told him.

"And he's on the premises?"

"I'm sure he is—along with many agents. And our crime-scene investigators. They've found some disparaging discrepancies."

"Whatever it is, I've been framed!" the man proclaimed.

"Well, we'll do our best to see how that's been done," Stacey said.

He glared at her. "A woman agent. Right...yeah, you're going to help me. So, Mr. Special Agent Man, they stuck you with a woman."

Keenan stopped and turned to stare at him, smiling.

"Well, you did see just how fast she was able to block you, Congressman Smith. I rather like the way she has my back."

"I'll just bet you do!" Smith said.

He walked ahead, but he was further irritated to be stopped at the door by security; Keenan said that Smith was with them, and they went to the elevators and the office level.

"I'll get Director Crow," Keenan said, "if you'll escort Congressman Smith into the conference room."

He didn't mean the conference room. She knew he meant one of the two interrogation rooms they had on the office level.

She brought Smith to the first, indicating that he should take a seat.

There were several wooden chairs and a small table that resembled a little TV dinner table.

Adam and Jackson were both big believers in watching for body language. Body language was important.

"What the hell is this?" Smith demanded.

"We'll be right with you, sir."

"This is an interrogation room."

"Have you been interrogated before, sir?" she asked.

He drew himself up with great dignity. "No! However, I do watch TV!"

She smiled. "We'll be back. I know that you wanted to speak with Director Crow. Agent Wallace is just seeing to his availability."

She stepped out of the room. As she had figured, Keenan and Jackson were around the corner in the little space where— as on TV—they could observe Smith through their side of the one-way mirror.

"How much time do we give him?" Keenan asked Jackson.

"Let's see what he does now," Jackson said and then asked, "He came in willingly?"

"Not really willingly—but he didn't want us talking in front of his wife," Keenan said.

The three of them watched in silence. First, Smith sat. Then, he rose and paced. He sat again, then paced. He paused in front of the mirror, but it wasn't as if he could see them behind it.

He studied himself. He checked his face and touched it, as if he could erase signs of aging.

He winced, gritting his teeth and shaking his head.

Then he started pacing again until he sat once more, as if exhausted.

Then he suddenly yelled out. "Yes, I knew her. I knew her. I slept with the bitch! But I swear I didn't kill her. I slept with her—but I didn't kill her. I didn't kill her! Oh, God, you have to believe me!"

CHAPTER TEN

That was faster than expected, Keenan thought. He looked at Jackson. "How do you want us to play it from here?"

"Time to go in," Jackson said. "Stacey, you first. Tell him that I'm out of the office, and you're trying to reach me. See what he says to you—it may work for us or against us that you're a woman. I'm not being a sexist—but that man is, I'm willing to bet."

"I think it's a safe bet," Stacey said. "We spoke to a staff member who was glad he didn't find her sexually attractive and just treated her like dirt. And with everything that has gone around... I don't believe in skewering anyone without proof, but there's so much chatter about him—if any of it is true, and if any of the behavior I've witnessed counts, yeah—he's a sexist."

"You okay with this?" Jackson asked her.

She nodded.

"We'll watch from here, and I'll send Keenan on in when it's time."

Keenan stood next to Jackson and watched as Stacey went on in. She smiled at Colin Smith, taking a chair across from him.

"I'm so sorry—Assistant Director Crow is out of the building. He's going to come back as soon as he can." Her smile deepened, and she said gently, "We were already aware that you used Billie's services, or Billie herself, I guess I should say. And others."

Smith glared at her. "You don't know the pressure I'm under. The state of the world!"

"And, perhaps, the state of your own home," she said softly. "I mean, trust me, I'm a woman. And I've seen a lot of women who…well, we call them ballbusters. They get their teeth into a man and then make life miserable for him. And sometimes, you know, a man just needs to feel that he's in control of himself. He just needs to have a break. Sex that is fun and that is available with no headaches or problems or recriminations."

"Yes, yes, exactly!" Colin Smith said. He eyed her skeptically. "Are you one of those?" he demanded. "Is that why you know the type so well?"

"No, no… I'm not even in a relationship, Congressman Smith. I've just seen it. My mother completely emasculated my father, and it broke my heart."

Keenan saw that Jackson was grinning.

"What?"

"She's a damned good liar. I know her family. Her parents are the best—still in love—and they love her."

"I didn't kill her—I didn't kill Billie!" Smith said, his voice passionate. "I cared about her!"

"You were overheard saying that she was a problem and that something needed to be done about her," Stacey said apologetically.

"Yes! I needed her to cool it—we'd been seen publicly."

"So, who did you tell that to?"

Smith hesitated. "My secretary, Agnes. She's been with me for ages." He hesitated again. "She's overpaid and gets all kinds of vacation days. She's a battle-ax herself, but she watches out for me, and I make it up to her."

"What did you want to happen?"

"Money!"

"Pardon?"

"I was going to figure out a way to pay her to be more discreet. Billie could never have enough money. She was amazing in bed. Sorry. But she could do things… Anyway, that's how she made her start. And she trained her, uh, *escorts* well. But that woman… Wow! She loved money. I never quite got it. Jewelry meant everything to her. Clothing! That mansion of hers—all were costly. Billie could be bought. Well, obviously. She was a whore who ran a whorehouse. A high-class whorehouse, but a whorehouse, nonetheless."

Keenan glanced at Jackson, who nodded.

It was time for him to go and join the conversation.

He entered and closed the door, finding another chair to drag over to the grouping. He straddled it backwards, leaning his arm on the back of the wooden folding chair.

"Congressman Smith, we appreciate your candor," he said. "We have another problem. We have your car on video—your car and you—on a video-surveillance tape. And you were with a young woman named Jess Marlborough. The second victim in what they're calling the Yankee Ripper Murders."

Smith couldn't stop the change that came over his face.

Alarm showed as he swallowed and turned white, and then red.

"I…uh…um, no, it can't—"

"Congressman Smith, the video is quite clear."

"My car… I mean, no, I mean, everyone in DC drives a car like mine!"

"Technology is amazing these days," Keenan said.

Not that amazing, but Smith didn't know that.

"It's your car, Congressman Smith, and…" he added, deepening the lie "…your face."

"I should call my lawyer," Smith muttered.

Stacey and Keenan looked at one another.

"All right. Then we're done here," Keenan said, rising. "Every man gets his rights."

Stacey whispered, "What will happen then? I mean, I think he'll wind up held and possibly charged, and the publicity—"

"Wait!" Smith said.

"Yes?" Stacey said sweetly.

"I...uh... Look, I'm a man who loves women. Yes, I've frequented whores. And I was sorry, so damned sorry about Jess. I really did mean to set her up...help her. She was a beautiful person, heart of gold. She could listen, oh, Lord, could she listen. It wasn't just wham-bam-thank-you-ma'am. Jess was...different. I wanted to help her. It was devastating to hear...but oh, God! I didn't do it. I didn't kill her. I picked her up that night. And I dropped her off. I swear—I dropped her off right at the end of the street. She was going to run into a convenience shop and buy some cigarettes. I tried to get her to quit smoking. I told her how bad it was for her health." He stopped to laugh dryly, hysteria rising in his voice. "Bad for her health! Oh, God."

Then the man burst into tears.

Keenan and Stacey looked at one another, realizing that they both believed what the man was saying.

Then again...

He was a politician. By nature of the beast, politicians could be great liars.

Stacey didn't touch him, but she leaned toward him. "Mr. Smith, can we get you something?"

He shook his head.

"Jess is dead. Billie is dead."

"I'll get you some water," Stacey said. She stood and hurried out.

"Where was this convenience store, Congressman?" Keenan asked quietly. "As you've surmised, we've pulled a lot of video surveillance."

"In the middle of the block just north of her apartment," he

said. "Jess was so happy. She loved her friends—fellow hookers, if you will. She wanted to help them. They have a horrible
pimp—guy takes just about everything from them."

Jackson Crow came in.

"Congressman Smith," he said, "I'm Jackson Crow. And we're
going to need your help. We're going to need to know what
you know about others who might have been involved with the
murdered women."

Smith looked up at him dully.

"Jess…she approached me at a gas station. There was something about her smile. She was soliciting, yes. But there was just
that something about her… Anyway, I bought her a soda and a
packaged bagel from the station. She was so grateful. We agreed
to meet. Back at the gas station. I don't know how many times
I saw her. Enough so that we talked. And the night I last picked
her up, I'd found a way to give her a job in my building. I was
going to bring her in to meet the super—he was a con once
himself and tried to help people, even if they did have records."

Keenan looked at Jackson while excusing himself. "I'll see
where Stacey has gone for that water," he said.

They both knew that he was going to call Fred and that they'd
check out the convenience store where Tess might have gone
for her cigarettes.

He had his phone out immediately, pulling up the map fea-
ture, and hoping that the area around Jess Marlborough's apartment was up-to-date and accurate.

It was. He found it.

"Kevin and Kal's Kwikie Mart. Open twenty-four hours a
day.

Stacey was returning with a bottle of water for Smith.

He stopped her. "I know it's late, but I'm calling a friend. We
need more video surveillance—from a place not covered yet.
We've got to get on it—as far as the killing goes, it may give
us something."

"I'll just deliver this," she said, and went in.

By then he had Fred on the phone. "Sorry," he told the detective. "The day's not over. We don't have time to get a warrant. It's your stomping ground."

"No problem at all," Fred told him. "And my day wasn't anywhere near over. Jean is with me. We're reviewing files."

"And?"

"Well, that's it. We've been looking into doctors—anyone involved with transplants, anyone fired lately... If these organs are being taken, it wouldn't be worth much if there wasn't someone who knew what to do with them."

"I know that Jackson has staff here doing the same thing. We'll put results together for anything that pops out. It's a long, hard process—and the doctor performing the surgeries may be in another state or across the country. Frustrating," Keenan said. "We can compare notes later. We'll meet you at the store."

They hung up, and Stacey and Jackson came out of the interrogation room together.

"You're going to see if the convenience store has surveillance?" Jackson said.

Keenan nodded. "With any luck, we'll be able to go back a few days. Some places recycle them daily. But maybe we can prove if Smith did drop Jess off whether she was still living after she left him. How long do you think you'll be able to keep him here?"

"I'll have Angela step in and talk to him—she can keep him happy for a while. We'll feed him. I'll stick with him. Call me as soon as you know anything," Jackson said.

"We're on our way," Keenan said. "Fred Crandall will meet us; a local sometimes does a hell of a lot better than a Fed. And if not, I'll step in." Jackson headed back into the interrogation room.

"Let's go," Stacey said. They headed back to the elevator and from there to the garage. They were soon back out on the road.

Keenan looked over at Stacey. "You were good in there," he told her.

"Thanks," she said, turning slightly toward him. "Careful, I'm almost going to think that you approve of me, that you even like me."

He was silent a minute. Then he said quietly, "I like you just fine."

"Hmm. Well, I didn't want to like you—I mean, you were pretty rough on me at first," she said. "But I like you just fine, too."

"And so here we are, working together just fine," he said.

"Right—on our way to prove that our prime suspect might be innocent!" she said.

"Yep," he agreed, glancing her way. She looked intent, lost in thought.

"What is it?" he asked.

"Well, I was thinking about the dead girls...and then Billie Bingham."

"And?"

She shook her head, frowning. "It's there. Right there. I felt that I'd seen Billie before. Several times. But a long time ago. It's driving me crazy."

"Let it go, and the answers will come. Right now, it's time to hope to hell that we can get some video surveillance from the convenience store. And the thing is..." Keenan trailed off, focused on the traffic.

But Stacey knew what he was getting at. "Even if Smith is innocent, he may have the key to point us to the guilty party—whether he knows it or not."

Despite the insanity of their hours—and the strange dreams that had plagued her the previous night—Stacey felt a sense of ease as they met up with Fred and Jean Channing.

She really liked both detectives very much. Fred was thorough, an investigator who didn't mind any help, who didn't seem to care about making an arrest himself but was just going to do what it took to get a job done. Jean didn't have a chip on her shoulder, she just saw herself as an equal and an investigator; as a top detective, she was comfortable with her position, and her attitude was much the same as Fred's—all hands on deck, and it didn't matter who did what if they could catch the bad guy.

They met at the run-down little convenience store. The sign read Kevin and Kal's Kwikie Mart. Stacey eyed the old camera above the doors skeptically—it was dented and out of shape.

But just as they had seen in Congressman Smith's elegant neighborhood, the dilapidated shop in the poor section of town warned would-be thieves with a plaque in front that they were under video surveillance.

"I'll go first," Fred told them. "Actually, we may be in luck. I think we saved this guy from a robbery once. He might like cops."

Fred went in. They waited. Keenan, Jean and Stacey looked around the street. Stacey had noted that Keenan had something of a photographic memory. When he'd been somewhere, he seemed to remember everything about it.

They weren't on the sidewalk long. Fred was soon back out, a smile on his face.

"'Kal' is really Mohammed Abdul and a super guy—I remembered him, he remembered me. They were being robbed at gunpoint one night when I was close-by—we snuck in, got the perp, no shots fired. Come on in. He's got his computer up in the back, and we're welcome to go through the file. We're in luck—he's all digital and has footage going way back. Jean is great with a computer. She can probably find it fastest!"

"I wouldn't say I'm great, but I am fairly competent," Jean said dryly.

"That will work," Stacey and Keenan said at almost exactly the same time.

"Lord, you'd think these two had been working together for years," Jean said. "Let's go."

They all trailed into the store.

The exterior was deceptive. Inside, Mohammed Abdul kept a spotless and logically arranged store. Little shelf cards advertised rows of pharmaceuticals, household cleaners and different foods. The refrigerated section was even labeled—dairy, beer, soft drinks. There was a special row for diapers and baby needs.

Mohammed was a man of medium height, dark-haired, of an indeterminate age—he was polite and friendly but aware that they were on business. He introduced his wife, who was working at the cash register, and led them through a door to an office in back. There, he had his desk, computer, a fax machine and a printer, separated just a foot from row upon row of paper towels, dishes and toilet paper.

Jean sat at the computer; Stacey, Keenan and Fred hovered behind her.

"I knew her," Mohammed said, watching them. "I knew Jess, and she was a sweet, kind woman. She opened doors when she saw someone struggling. She reached for things off the shelves for the elderly. Anything I can give you, anything that will help catch her killer… I will do."

"Did she come in the night before her body was discovered in the alley?" Stacey asked him.

He nodded gravely.

"What time?" Keenan asked.

"Before midnight, I believe," Mohammed said.

"Precisely!" Jean exclaimed. She turned to look at them all. "Sir, your video shows not just Jess Marlborough coming into the store, it shows Congressman Smith's car—and even his face as he drives away."

"So, what Smith said was true," Stacey said.

"It doesn't mean that he didn't double back and find her in that alley," Fred said.

"No, but it does leave more questions," Keenan reminded them.

"Such as?" Jean asked.

Keenan shook his head. "When she was killed, it wasn't in the alley. There wasn't enough blood. Jean, you know that the victims were killed elsewhere. They were killed in one place, their organs were taken somewhere else, and then their bodies were dumped."

"Smith could have had an accomplice, someone ready to grab Jess once she'd been dropped off," Stacey said.

Keenan lifted his hands. "We can't hold Smith much longer; Jackson and Angela have been keeping him company. What we need now is for him to implicate someone else."

"Well, there's nothing more we can do tonight," Jean said. "And I don't know about you guys, but I've got to go to bed, or I'll be useless tomorrow."

They were all still for a minute.

"Look, every agent and officer in the surrounding counties are on this; we have nothing else to go on now. We've got to give it a rest."

"A rest," Keenan said, looking at Stacey.

Maybe she would dream. Maybe she wouldn't. But they did need sleep. And before they could get any, they had to return to Krewe headquarters and speak with Jackson again, and possibly Colin Smith.

"Right," Keenan said. He looked over at Mohammed. "Can you get copies of this to us—to the police and my office?"

Mohammed nodded. "I will be happy to! If there is anything, anything at all that can be done, just ask."

Keenan was quiet as they drove back to headquarters.

"Well, I imagine we'll be letting Congressman Smith go, but he'll know that he's being watched. And since that's happening, it should mean that possible victims are safe, at least," Stacey said.

"It should. Let's get in—and then leave this to others for the night."

Stacey leaned back in her seat.

She had to admit, at least to herself, she was glad she wasn't going to be alone tonight.

Keenan wasn't sure why he hadn't immediately realized just how incredibly appealing his new partner was. Maybe he'd just been too irritated and worried to take note of what he had seen and felt.

She was a beautiful woman; that had been obvious. It was the life within her, however, that created the depth of her appeal. Her energy seemed to emit sparks: she was determined and confident to take on anyone during any confrontation, including him.

When they returned to her home at last—having been back to headquarters and then to Keenan's place to pick up some of his things—it was late, and they were both hungry and tired. But even that didn't quell that spark within, though she did yawn several times while heating up a few little chicken pies— her own invention, chunks of white chicken meat, mushroom soup, carrots, peas, and a topping of potatoes with a dusting of bread crumbs for added flavor.

She made them, or similar things, on the weekend, she told him, and froze or refrigerated them for meals during the week, knowing she might be too tired for anything else if it had been a late day. As the food heated, they were both in thought, and Keenan set the table and poured glasses of ice tea, watching her as she busied herself with a salad. Locks of her dark hair fell over her forehead, and she occasionally gnawed on her lower lip, deep in thought. When she glanced at him, she flushed, and her eyes were bright crystals against the soft ivory of her face.

"Do you think that any of the men on the list Colin Smith gave Jackson will pan out?" she asked. "I wonder if he's being honest with us, or if he's been deceiving us this whole time. I know that my dad was on a case once with a complete psychopath—had no remorse at all for anything he'd done. Even at trial…"

Her voice trailed.

"Even at trial?" he prompted.

"Strange. I guess it's this case. I was just thinking about the McCarron trial, years back."

"The McCarron trial? What, you had to be about twelve or thirteen when that went on," Keenan said.

She nodded, pulling the finished pies out of the oven. "Twelve." She hesitated, glancing at him. "That was when I met Adam Harrison, and he convinced my parents that there really might be something about to happen. That my family could be in danger, based on the dreams I was having. It turned out McCarron was a bitter man—he'd lost a loved one when a transplant hadn't become available in time. Maybe that's why I'm thinking of the trial. No one stole anyone else's body organs at the time, but according to McCarron, that started his obsession."

"Yeah, I remember that trial—and the aftermath. McCarron came off like the handsome boy next door, appalled about the murders, and denying that he could ever do anything like that. Then, I remember the news in the months after the trial, he admitted to several other murders, including those of a few other people that happened to be for his own convenience and nothing about heartbreak. If I recall, he finally admitted to killing one man just because he'd taken his parking space."

"True. He admitted many things after he was convicted. His trial was in Virginia, and he was given the death penalty, so he started talking to bargain his way out. He was executed just a few years ago. There was a big uproar all over again," Stacey said as she set a steaming pie in front of Keenan and one at her own place. "But he was executed."

"So, we know he had nothing to do with these murders. I've yet to find a ghost capable of killing—unless they just scared someone to death. Possible, but those I've met aren't out to do harm. They want to protect someone or…protect a place, like your friends at Lafayette Square," he reminded her with a smile.

"I just keep remembering that trial. I don't know why."

"Well, it was a major event, and you were involved."

They sat and ate, both in silence for several minutes.

"I wish I could put my finger on it."

"You will. Thoughts just out of reach finally get closer. And then there are dreams."

She nodded dully, then suddenly stood. "Well, just leave this. I'm exhausted. I'm going to shower and hop in bed. Please, don't worry about picking up—I can get it all in two minutes in the morning."

She disappeared to her room before he could protest. She seemed distracted, probably worried about dreaming. She must be hoping that she would—and also that she wouldn't.

He heard the door to the bathroom close.

There wasn't much of a mess: two little single-serving pans and a salad bowl. He tidied up quickly, as there was no reason not to.

In his head, he went over every minute of their conversation with Colin Smith.

Yes, the man could be a liar.

Keenan hadn't been involved with the McCarron trial in the same way that Stacey had been involved, but he remembered it. On the stand, McCarron had come off as if he was Mr. Nice Guy, horrified that anyone could imagine him guilty of terrible things. Even when there was solid evidence against him.

Later, Keenan had heard that McCarron's prison interviews had been chilling. He'd killed people as casually as another man might swat flies.

Finished with the dishes, he went to grab his bag, glad that he'd stopped for his things. A shower seemed like a good idea. Hot water was relaxing.

He paused outside Stacey's door, wanting to make sure that

she was all right. He couldn't hear any movement in her room. Maybe she'd already fallen asleep.

He then went to check that the outer door to the building was locked, and he secured the door to her apartment on his way back in, and, finally, the windows.

Reassured, he went for his shower, pausing by her door but wondering why, and not wanting to examine the answer too closely.

He was just stepping out of the shower when he heard her first scream.

It was as if she'd stepped back in time, and yet she knew she hadn't.

It was the smoke in the room that seemed to blind her. There was a hearth and a fire burned within it. The smoke rose and swirled, combining with a gray mist in the air that might have swept in from the foggiest street.

Stacey was there, but she didn't know exactly where; it was as if she was all-seeing, omniscient.

And at first, there was nothing but the room and the knowledge that the killer was also within it. Close…knowing what was to come.

There was a surgical bag set down on the floor against the wall near the hearth. And she knew what it contained. Scalpels and saws. There was also a curious container near the bag, and she knew what that was intended to contain.

Pieces of life itself—the organs that belonged to the intended victim.

This time, the killer would not attack elsewhere and dump the body in an alley or a basement. Or for all to see in Lafayette Square.

No, the murder would take place here.

Someone moved about, humming softly.

The killer waited. His intended victim was blissfully unaware.

The killer watched and waited, anticipating, all but salivating...

Soon, there would be a bloodbath. Because this time, when he was done with the evisceration, he would relish the horror he would leave behind. He would slash her to ribbons, cut off her lips, her breasts, flesh from her thighs...

The woman turned; Stacey couldn't see her face.

She didn't know who it was...

She didn't even know if it might be herself, seeing with her eyes at last what she had seen through fragments in her mind.

Then the scream...

She didn't know that it was coming from her. She didn't know at all, until she was drawn back to the waking world, held firmly but gently in strong arms.

Stacey's terror had been real; her scream, bloodcurdling.

But when she woke and looked at him, she quickly rallied. She sat up and grimaced.

"You're okay?" he asked her. His arms were still around her.

She laughed dryly. "I don't know! Am I okay? Most people would probably say not. That's why it was so important to me when...when I met Adam. He made it so that I felt that I was okay, normal. Not normal but gifted rather than insane."

"Adam has that skill," he said.

He could let her go; she was strong once she was out of the dream.

He continued to hold her. Her dark hair was tousled and smelled sweetly and somewhat exotically of her shampoo. The skin of her bare arms was soft...

Let her go. The voice of reason whispered inside him.

But he didn't. He could argue that they really hadn't gotten through the nightmare yet.

"Can you remember anything more?" he asked her.

"No. I'm so frustrated. I'm there, and the killer is there... He knows I'm there, and he knows I know he's there...but I can't see a face, I can't see a size, nothing but a shadow, and the shadow is like this massive echo of the darkest evil. The victim sees the killer…"

She turned to him suddenly, moving in his arms. She didn't seem to want him to let go, to move away from her. She seemed to want to be exactly where she was. Her eyes were still glistening, her lips were soft and parted and damp.

"What does the victim see?" he said, to keep himself focused.

"The shadow, the evil, the intent. What I'm getting from the dream is this… It might be that the organs are being stolen. But there's more to this killer. He can't wait to cut up the victim. He's dreaming of bathing in blood. I mean, I think it's a man. I can't even see that, but I believe this kind of killer is usually male."

He nodded.

"I saw a box of some kind. A medical bag, and a box."

"So, the box was probably some kind of ice chest for the organs. And the medical bag carried the instruments to take them."

"But I can't see the killer!"

"You've brought us closer than anyone else," he assured her. "You'll see more. Think back. From what you've told me about your dreams, you'll get a little further and a little further. If by some chance you don't, you'll still have done more than anyone else," he said, touching her cheek, lifting her face to his.

She looked at him for a long moment.

To his surprise, she suddenly put her hand to his face and drew him to her, kissing him. Not a peck that meant thank you.

A wet kiss, filled with tongue and lips warm, generous, moving.

He'd be less than human if he didn't respond.

And he was definitely human. He leaned them both back on the bed and returned the kiss, deeply, passionately, feeling the warmth—and more—burst within him.

She seemed to realize, suddenly, that once again, he was wearing only a towel. At that point, she couldn't help but notice.

He grinned, thinking he needed to explain.

But she smiled when the kiss broke, looking up at him with her dazzling eyes. "I seem to have a tendency to interrupt your showers."

"That's okay. I was clean enough."

A worried look touched her features.

"I'm sorry, I shouldn't have... I mean, we're working. Jackson—"

"Jackson already thinks that we're sleeping together."

"Oh?"

"I think that Jackson made the best decision for his leads on this case because of the nature of the case and our abilities, but I also believe that he thought we just might work out."

"And...we've worked out?"

"I'd say so," he told her.

But she still looked worried.

"I don't want... I mean, I know you're feeling bad for me, I don't want... I hate to even say it, but I don't want...pity sex."

"You don't pity me?" he asked softly, amazed at the combination of tenderness, longing, hunger and urgency sweeping through him.

She smiled, looking a bit sheepish. "I've just never had..."

"Sex?"

"No, no. Just not...often. I mean casual. I just... How do you let a relationship go anywhere when you're constantly afraid you'll wake up screaming?" she asked bleakly.

"You can scream for me anytime—awake or asleep," he said softly.

"I'm going to be screaming now?" she asked.

"Well, moaning and all. At least, I hope," he said.

Then she smiled again, and her smile was beautiful, and he

wondered if she wasn't more gifted than she knew, that she was a gift herself, to him.

Because he knew the feeling; he'd cared for others.

He'd lost once. Because with all that he knew…he hadn't been fast enough.

Young, yes, but…

And nothing had ever really worked again. The past had haunted him with a greater clarity than any ghost had ever managed.

Forget the past, let her forget her past…

Live for the present.

He smiled down at her, straddling her, and laced his fingers with hers.

"You are the best thing to come into my life ever," he told her, "and if we're talking about pity or mercy…have pity on me."

She looked up at him, eyes wide, disbelieving at first and then crystallizing with understanding. He leaned down, and they enjoyed another incredibly wet and heated kiss, then his lips slid onto her throat and collarbone and down to her breasts. Their fingers broke free; he felt her touching him, felt her fingers moving down his back and her body shifting beneath his, arching and writhing.

Then the tension of their lives and the reminders of the past seemed to evaporate, and the need for her that was rising in him felt insatiable.

It was torture to wait, yet he had to know her body, feel the tension in her abdomen as his kisses fell there…on her thighs, upward…teasing, demanding. And the feel of her touching him, the incredible sensation of her lips and tongue and wet kisses over the length of him.

Then their bodies moved together. The night rocked. They slipped and shifted, came close to climax, drew back to savor the moment, moved onward again…

The release was fantastic.

"Told you. You definitely screamed," Keenan said into Stacey's hair as they lay, still tangled together.

"The screaming was you!" she said.

He laughed and said, "Maybe." He wrapped her in his arms, just holding her tight as his lungs gulped in air, and he heard the thunder of his pulse, pounding in his ears, slowly fading.

She curled against him, comfortable there.

"So, Jackson thinks we're sleeping together already," she said. "Maybe we should assure him that he was right on."

"Nah. Let's let him wonder!"

She shifted against him. For a minute, he felt a lump in his throat. He rolled to look at her and spoke earnestly.

"We've all had our pasts. For me...it was Allison. We were in high school. She was sweet, giving, popular, and she made those around her better people. She wouldn't allow bullying. Senior year, right near graduation, she was abducted. I already knew that I could see the dead. A ghost came to me. The ghost of a girl this deranged man had already taken and killed. She tried to get me to Allison, and she did, but...it was too late. She'd been left by the side of the road. Bleeding into the ground. I guess I've never really forgiven myself. I've always thought that I didn't form relationships because of my work, because others didn't understand. I envied Kat and Will, Jackson and Angela, and Vickie and Griffin and the other couples who work together, but of course, there was my work to keep me busy. So, yeah, I've had more casual sex than I'd like, but...you. You will never know, whatever the future brings, what you've meant to me tonight."

"What?"

She sounded indignant.

He was surprised. He was not a man who showed his emotions easily, if at all. He had just poured his heart out.

But she smiled and set her palm upon his face, causing him to look at her. "This better not be just tonight!" she said. "Please, don't let this not be just tonight!"

They made love again.

The morning was coming. And with it, the tension and heat of the case—and their desperation to find a killer before he killed again.

They didn't get much sleep.

And, still, when he woke, he noticed that he hadn't felt that damned good in…forever.

CHAPTER ELEVEN

"If the organs are being stolen for black-market transplants, I believe they're going out of the area," Jackson said. "We've pulled the name of every doctor capable of such operations. Police and our Krewe agents have been pulling info on time sheets, bank accounts and more for every transplant doctor in all states that you could get to from here in time to do a viable transplant. It's a wide net. So far, we can't find the least suggestion of illegal activity among them."

Jackson leaned forward in his office chair, pinning Stacey with his gaze. "That doesn't discount the theory. Makes no sense to me that a killer would rip up women and take all the major organs and not use them. Not when there's a premium on organs like that, and there are wealthy people not concerned with where they came from when they know they're not high on a donor list."

"South America?" Keenan wondered aloud.

"I think it would have to be Central or South America or one of the islands close enough to the United States—the operation would have to be pretty fast. Chilled and preserved properly, a kidney can be viable for not quite thirty hours, and that's the longest. It's less than six hours for a heart or lungs."

"A private jet could move quickly, if it knew when to go," Keenan said.

"Then someone with money is pulling all this off," Stacey said. "Or the clients are footing a hefty bill."

"Someone has probably been making a lot of money off this," Jackson pointed out grimly. "What price do you put on a human life? Those who will die without transplants and have the capability of paying just about anything are probably willing to look the other way when it comes to help."

"Right. But an organ doesn't just match anyone," Keenan said. "I admit, I don't know much about it, but there would have to be screening. Blood type, that kind of thing."

"And yet, if you have a nice list of people willing to buy a new organ," Stacey said thoughtfully, "well, anyone on that list would have been tested, and they would know what they're looking for."

"I wonder…" Keenan said.

"What?" Jackson and Stacey asked simultaneously.

"That's what we need!" Keenan said, a frown set deep in his forehead.

"What?" Jackson and Stacey repeated together.

"Sorry, sorry. We can't find a doctor. He—or she—is not going to be at a legitimate hospital. Whatever is going on is happening underground. There's a secret clinic somewhere—either near here, or on an island or in a different country somewhere close. When you're not working in the mainstream, you can't be found in the mainstream. We need to find patients. We need to find out who has come off the regular lists lately—who has been waiting for a transplant and suddenly removed their requests."

"Angela can manage to get that, right?" Stacey asked Jackson.

"I'm sure she can," Jackson said. "There have to be connectors somewhere and, in an enterprise this big, someone willing to talk. While the actual operation may be offshore, I doubt if rich clients are willing to give up their lives here. I'll get Angela on it. For now, I have a list of names—prominent citizens, men and women—who have used the services of Billie Bingham's escort service, if you want to get started on that. We're working on preliminaries, checking out who may or may not have been in the area at the time. We can eliminate suspects—two are men who have passed away. There isn't time to run in circles."

Stacey was quiet for a minute and then said, "And there's Cindy Hardy."

"You think she's involved?" Jackson asked.

"She lied to us. She did leave her home again the night that Billie Bingham and our victim in the basement were killed," Keenan mused.

Stacey looked at Keenan. "She had so much hatred for Billie Bingham."

"True. But what about our other victims?" Keenan asked.

"Something puts them all together," Jackson said. "If we're assuming right, and the victims were all sex workers," Stacey said, "it doesn't matter whether they were seen as high-class call girls or street prostitutes. They were all practicing the oldest trade."

"Then we're still watching Colin Smith," Jackson said. "The man put on a good show, but we all know how well people can lie. Based on my gut, I believe him. But that doesn't clear him."

"Or his wife," Keenan said.

"Do we have any reason to suspect her?" Jackson asked.

"No, but we're looking at Cindy Hardy. Hatred can run deep," Keenan said.

Jackson excused himself as his phone rang. He took the call quickly, giving guttural replies, and then saying a quick, "Thank you."

He looked at Stacey and Keenan again. "That was Dr. Beau Simpson. That piece of kidney that was sent to Stacey had signs of the early stages of kidney disease. So, one of our victims didn't turn out to be a good donor. But of course, heart, kidney, lungs and livers were also taken."

"I really think we're right on this. There's an illegal transplant operation going on somewhere," Keenan said. He looked at Stacey. "You nailed it early," he said.

He nodded at Jackson. "We'll get started, reinterviewing Cindy Hardy, and then we'll pay a visit to Sandra Smith. When those lists come in—"

As if on cue, there was a knock at the door, and Angela opened it and stepped in. "You're going to love this. You asked about the murders and disappearances of men in the area. Five men missing—the info has been sent to your email addresses. None of them were from this area. Three on vacation and two who had just moved here."

"So, they might just have wanted to disappear, or they moved on, or they might just be victims, and these killers are disposing of their bodies," Jackson said.

"They were all between the ages of twenty-five and thirty-five. Fit. In good health," Angela said.

"May be part of it all, maybe not," Jackson muttered. "If so, that means there's a lot more victims, and this thing is really monstrous."

"Well, there's more. You also asked about strange murders," Angela said.

"Yes?" Keenan said.

"Check your email. A human head was found floating in Chesapeake Bay. Mostly consumed. Maryland State Police had a reconstruction sketch artist working on it and a forensic anthropologist. Male, Caucasian, about thirty years of age."

"This has to be stopped," Keenan said. "All right, Stacey, let's visit some women."

"Do you really think either of these women would have the strength or know-how to kill like that?" Stacey asked Keenan as they headed to the garage, stopping just before they reached the car.

"You don't have to commit the murder to conspire to murder," Keenan reminded her.

She stood still, drawing in a deep breath. "I know this is a long shot, but something has been bugging me. Well, a couple of things... But... Keenan, I know there has to be footage of the McCarron trial somewhere. Do you think that we could find it and watch it?"

He frowned. "The McCarron trial? The counts against him were numerous. But he killed a transplant doctor and a man working his hardest to solicit people to sign donor cards."

"Right. Donor cards. People who will leave their organs to others *after* they die. Keenan, really, I'm sorry. But there's just something—"

"McCarron is dead," he reminded her softly.

"I know. And this isn't something I'm harboring because he ordered the murder of my family. I just need to see the trial again. Then I can set aside this nagging thought."

"All right," he said. He pulled out his phone. They were still in the parking garage, but he called Angela. Stacey listened to him ask her if she would do what she could to find all the video that had been taken at the trial. The judge had, thankfully, allowed cameras in the courtroom; he had wanted everything on record.

When he hung up, he said to Stacey, "If I know Angela, we'll have hours and hours of trial footage to review soon enough. Before that, let's go talk to some angry wives."

Cindy Hardy didn't want anything to do with them. She was upset that they were bothering her again about the woman who had, in her mind, ruined her life.

A woman who had made the world a better place by leaving it.

Stacey glanced at Keenan, wondering how he was going to bully their way in—and certain that he would manage it.

Cindy argued with Keenan when he called her from the gate. Only his warning that they had just a few more questions but could arrange for a search warrant if she didn't want to cooperate finally led her to opening the gate so that they could drive up to her house.

She stood at the door when they arrived, hands on her hips. She might have been small, but she could shoot out an aura of indignation and fury as if she were the Hulk.

"You people!" she exclaimed angrily. "Don't you have anything better to do than harass someone who has already been through hell! There's a killer out there—oh, yeah, let me think. Every one of those women could have kicked my ass in two seconds, so—"

"Mrs. Hardy, you lied to us. The residents' gate cards can be traced. You said that you didn't leave your home the night that Billie was murdered. Your key card showed you going out of here around ten o'clock, and not returning until the wee hours of the morning," Keenan told her pleasantly.

She stiffened.

"Oh…come in. Come in. You don't need to shout at me on the street!"

Keenan glanced at Stacey. He had a small grin on his face. He hadn't shouted at all.

Cindy Hardy had just about been screaming.

She went in and left them to follow. She walked quickly to the parlor and said, "Oh, how nice of you to visit. Sit. You've come to pry into my personal life because of some high-class whore who thought she had some kind of golden box? Lovely!"

"Are your children here, Mrs. Hardy?" Stacey asked politely.

Cindy glared at her.

"My children and nanny are at a ball game, Special Agent

Whoever!" she said angrily. "So, what is it? What the hell is it that you want to know?"

"Where you went that night. You lied to us. You said that you didn't go out."

Cindy sighed.

"Of course I lied to you! You were trying to pin the murder of that bimbo on me! Hey, if she'd sat on me, she'd have squashed me."

"Where did you go?" Stacey asked her.

"Out!"

"Out where?" Keenan persisted.

"You know, a nice policeman was out here recently to tell me that they'd be doubling patrols, that there is concern that I might be in danger with a madman out there running around. I'm not so sure I should be afraid of this madman. In my mind, he's done us all a public service. But the police were worried about me, which I found to be nice, proper and touching. And here you are suggesting that I've somehow been cruising the city, picking up whores and chopping them up."

"You still haven't answered the question," Keenan reminded her politely.

She let out a long sigh. "Out! I met a man, all right! An affair ruined my marriage and my life. But I'm not asexual. I'm trying to raise my children to be good and responsible human beings, and…well, I'm not bringing anyone here unless it's someone who will turn out to be something stable—if not permanent—in their lives. You have a problem with that?"

"Who is the man?"

"I haven't the least intention of telling you!" Cindy stated.

Keenan shrugged. "I can get a warrant."

"Really? That easily, to pry into my life? You're really going to think a judge is going to believe that I'm a sick murderer?" Cindy demanded.

"Okay," Keenan said. "Fine. We'll get going, then. But may I make use of your facilities?"

"What?" Cindy asked.

"Your bathroom. May I borrow your bathroom?" Keenan said. "I just never understood that way of asking, really. I'm not taking it anywhere. I'd just like to use it."

Stacey's lips curled slightly, and she looked downward. She had a feeling that Cindy might have refused, but Keenan's explanation made her wave a hand impatiently in the air.

"Down the hall, third door."

He walked down the hall, slipping into the designated door.

When he was gone, Cindy glared at Stacey.

"Shouldn't it be you who had to go? Your big, bad partner couldn't handle his bladder?"

"Men and women, Mrs. Hardy. Sometimes we all have to go."

"Well, and aren't you lucky, with that partner." Cindy shook her head. "So, you're an agent. A real agent. Do they let you out because you are with such a big, bad partner?"

"They let me out because I went through the academy and became an agent," Stacey told her, trying to control her temper. Really. The woman was obnoxious. Whether it had been with Billie Bingham or someone else, it was possible to see why her husband might have needed an escape.

"So," Stacey said, "the man you were meeting. He's married? Is that why you don't want to say?"

She kept her tone sweet.

She thought that Cindy was going to explode. She rose. She didn't come over to the sofa to stand over Stacey—if Stacey were to stand, she'd have her by a few inches—but she glared, her hands on her hips again.

"Oh, don't you just wish! Don't you wish you could cause more trouble for me! Well, you should watch out, missy. You never know when your big, bad partner won't be with you. You don't know this town. It can be one hell of a dangerous town.

A married man! How dare you. Get your subpoena! Get your damned subpoena. And mark my words, bitches like you can run into trouble!"

Stacey suddenly felt Keenan behind her. He had quietly left the restroom and returned.

"Mrs. Hardy, are you threatening my partner?" he asked gravely.

"Oh, never! Never would little old me threaten our federal finest," Cindy said. "I was warning her. This town will eat you alive if you're not careful. So, no, I didn't strangle and cut up a bunch of women who could beat my ass. I won't tell you who I was seeing. I have a right to my private life. Is that it? Will you please go."

"Oh, yes, definitely," Stacey said. "We've really taken up enough of your precious time and generous hospitality."

"Thank you," Keenan said lightly, glancing Stacey's way and nodding toward the door.

She nodded back and turned to head out.

For some reason, making that move, she noted the hearth.

The house was new but had been designed to recreate the look of a grand old colonial mansion.

The hearth was huge with a gray marble mantel. It stretched almost the length of the room.

A hearth. Like the one in her dream?

Frustration filled her. She never saw enough in her dreams. That strange fog shrouded the room.

There was a hearth in the hovel where Jess Marlborough's suitemates lived.

Hell, there was hearth in her own living room.

And yet, she paused. She took in every detail of the hearth. She wanted to remember it when the dream came again.

"There's something up with that woman," Stacey said.

Keenan looked at her, unable to restrain a certain amount of amusement. "Aw, and she likes you so much!"

They were back, seated in his office. He had his computer open. "Angela has sent all the video she's managed to get on the McCarron trial." He looked at her. "Time to figure out what it is that's bugging you." He got up, coming around to the side chair where she sat. "Take my seat, Special Agent Hanson. And go for it."

She stood, looking at him for a minute.

"I know you must think this is a wild-goose chase, looking for something from years ago."

"Hey, there's very little we discount here in the Krewe."

She offered him a grimace.

"There's just something I'm missing."

He frowned. "Maybe something important that just needs to be jarred. Whoever this is did send the kidney to you."

She hit the Start key on his computer. He took her chair, but she looked at him nervously. She smiled. "You don't have to sit there and watch me. Maybe you could go and get something done?"

He didn't bother reminding her that, often enough, just sitting and watching was part of the game.

"Maybe I'll check on another wronged wife," he said. "She wasn't exactly warm and cuddly, either."

"I doubt the Smiths' housekeeper is going to just open a door for you again."

"I'll think of something."

He left her and headed to Jackson's office. Jackson was in. He waved a hand to indicate that Keenan should take a chair.

"I'm going over and over everything. I'm trying to make sure that the press hasn't leaked out the details of the murders."

"I'm not sure we can help that," Keenan told him. "And I'm curious. Is this killer pleased or angered by the fact that we didn't let his letter—with a piece of kidney—get to the media?"

"I don't know. But I believe, if there is something else, it will go to the media this time." Jackson leaned back. "So, what are your thoughts?"

"Jill the Ripper," Keenan said.

"Cindy Hardy?" Jackson asked, surprised. "Physically, I don't think that the woman could have pulled it off."

"Maybe not. But maybe she knows more than she's sharing. She lied to us about being home the night Billie Bingham was killed. We went back and questioned her. She said she was with a man, but she wouldn't tell us who. She told me to get a subpoena. Can we force her to talk?"

Jackson looked at him, arching a brow. "Ever hear of pleading the Fifth?"

"Yeah. Well, I tried to look intimidating, anyway. But right now, I'd like to have a conversation with a different Smith—Sandra Smith."

"Think she'll tell you anything?"

"If nothing else, I might learn how she feels about her husband—and how much she knows about his outside activities." He shrugged. "She might be protective and loyal to the core—no matter what he's doing. But we can find out about her feelings, if nothing else. Jackson, Colin Smith is the only connector we have anywhere—he was seeing not just Billie Bingham but Jess Marlborough, too. We need to see if we can connect him to Andrea Simon."

"Go for it. We're watching Smith, you know." He picked up his phone and hit a few keys. "A friend of yours is tailing her, Axel Tiger. Will Chan is on Colin Smith right now, and Axel has been watching Sandra. We've attached our apps, and I know exactly where they are. Well, I know where my agents are." He looked up at Keenan. "Sandra Smith is at a boutique in a mall in Arlington. Give Axel a call; let him know what you're up to."

"Will do," Keenan said. He stood and headed out, determining just what he was going to say when he found her. They didn't want her to know she was being followed. And if he knew

Axel, she had no clue. He'd have to have something to explain why he was at the same mall. Well, everyone had a mother, and maybe his mom deserved a present from a cool boutique—for putting up with him and his siblings and the grandkids, too. He just hoped that if it was a place Sandra Smith was shopping, he could even pretend that he could afford to buy something there.

It was different, watching the trial now, as an adult, from what it had been back when she'd been a kid.

Then, Stacey had been worried sick about her father testifying. Though her mother had never said it, she, too, had been concerned.

What if the man hadn't been convicted?

He could snap his fingers, so it seemed, and make people wind up dead.

But McCarron had been convicted. He'd tried to wrangle his way out of the death penalty. He'd talked and talked after—not about others, though. Just about his own deeds. He kept trying to bargain for his life with the promise he could bring the police to more bodies.

Eventually, his time had come.

Now, watching the trial tapes, Stacey tried to find what it was that was bothering her so much. Something that had sparked in her mind, reminding her of the trial.

When she saw it at last, she didn't believe it.

She had to run it over and over again.

Watch every inflection made by the woman who had drawn her attention. Because, of course, she had changed. So much!

Was she sure?

She ran it all yet again. Because it made no sense. No sense whatsoever.

Parked and heading toward the chic boutique where Sandra Smith was known to be shopping, Keenan saw Special Agent

Axel Tiger leaning against a tall-top table outside a café. He appeared to be absorbed in reading on a small tablet.

Keenan knew better. Seeing Axel, he wondered why he hadn't thought to talk to his friend sooner. Axel had very recently and suddenly married.

A most unusual woman. Like Stacey, she more than saw the dead. Sometimes, she could touch an object or person and receive a strange intuition. Axel had told him that in trying on a dress, his new wife had helped catch a murderer.

She and Stacey needed to meet.

"Hey," Axel said.

"Hey," Keenan replied. "She's still in there?"

"Oh, yeah, trying on everything in the shop."

"Sorry about this. I didn't know they had you on surveillance duty."

"I'm on something back down in my neck of the woods tomorrow," Axel told him. "I volunteered. I knew you had this case. Thought I'd pitch in while I was still around."

For blending into a crowd, Axel wasn't really the man to pick. Tall and dark with striking light eyes, he was memorable. His ancestry included both the Seminole and Miccosukee tribes of Florida, along with whatever European his mom's family might have been.

Keenan knew he didn't blend in easily himself—six-five wasn't gigantic, but it was unusual enough.

But Axel could be so smooth, he was able to make it look like he just happened to be going the same way.

"You're leaving tomorrow?" he asked Axel.

Axel nodded. "Bodies on the beach," he said.

"And the local cops don't want it?"

Axel shrugged. "They're missing their heads and hands."

"Oh, I see. Well. What time?"

"Noon," Axel said, frowning.

"What about your lovely new wife?"

"She's not sure yet—she's working up here. She trains dogs."

"I know. She's got something going with the police—and us, right?"

Axel nodded.

"Think my new partner and I could meet you both in the morning?"

Axel looked at him with curiosity. "The dream thing, huh?"

"Right. How did you know?"

"Jackson talked to me this morning. I haven't even met our newest member yet."

"Would morning work?"

Axel laughed softly. "You mean me and my lovely new wife?"

"I do."

"Sure. Eight o'clock, the office?"

"The morgue."

Axel nodded gravely and said, "If that's what you need."

"All right, thanks. I'm going to get on in. I mean, they'll run out of clothing for the woman to try on at some point."

"Yep. Better get in there!"

Keenan didn't see Sandra at first; she was apparently in a dressing room.

He pretended to give his attention to a swing stand of purses, studying them intently—and with awe that a woman's purse could cost so much.

"Pure Italian leather!" a saleswoman told him cheerfully.

They might have been pure gold, for the prices being charged.

The saleswoman looked at him expectantly. Luckily, at that moment, Sandra Smith came out of the dressing room instructing someone unseen as to which pile of clothing she was purchasing and which pile needed to be put back.

Keenan pretended surprise to see her. "Mrs. Smith!"

She was surprised to see him—and not pleased.

"Are you taking me in, Special Agent Wallace?" Her voice

was low. She wanted to challenge him, but she didn't want to be heard.

"Should I be taking you in?" he asked. "I'm sorry. I mean... us asking your husband about his knowledge of prostitutes has to be extremely uncomfortable for you."

"You are monsters, all of you," she said.

"Mrs. Smith, we're doing our jobs, that's all," he assured her.

"Men are all such...idiots," she told him.

"So, oh, dear...then, you do know about..."

"I'm the wife of a congressman, Special Agent Wallace."

"Congressional terms don't go forever," he reminded her.

"Oh, is that it! You want to make sure that he's voted out?" she asked, her eyes narrowing.

"We haven't publicized anything about him. No one knows that he came to our offices to help us. His knowledge of the women who were killed is something that can help us."

The saleslady called out, "Mrs. Smith? You did want these, right?"

"Yes, thank you," she said, still staring at Keenan, tall and perfectly fit and regal. "Do you mind, Special Agent Wallace? I need to pay for my purchases—and I don't want to waylay you from your shopping. Though, frankly, I don't see you wearing anything in here."

"My mother's birthday is coming up," he said, then he added pleasantly, "Trust me. We're completely tight-lipped on this case. If the gossip rags are casting aspersions on your husband, I swear to you, we have had nothing to do with it. Quieter is better for us."

She pushed back a lock of her perfectly coiffed hair. "Run my husband through the mud however you like. I will not be thrown, and we will be back on the campaign trail, making all of you look like petulant children who couldn't solve a murder committed right in front of them. Excuse me."

She headed to the counter with a credit card and paid quickly, asking that her things be sent to her house.

"Oh, you don't even want to take this cute little top?" the friendly saleswoman asked.

"You heard me!" Sandra Smith snapped. "Sent to my house!" She spun and left the shop without so much as a glance back. The saleswoman sighed with relief and muttered, "Cow!"

Then she realized that Keenan was looking at her and that he'd heard her. Her cheeks flushed crimson.

He grinned.

"I, uh... Did you need some help, sir?" she asked.

"No, thanks. Sorry, I can't afford a thing in here!"

The girl grinned at him and said softly, "Neither can I!"

He waved and strode out.

Axel was gone—subtly still on the trail of Sandra Smith.

As Keenan headed for his car, his phone rang. "You've got something," he said to Stacey without preamble.

"Something. Something that doesn't make sense in the least!"

"What's that?"

"Come on in. You're going to have to see it to believe it."

CHAPTER TWELVE

"Do you see what I'm talking about?" Stacey asked Keenan.

She was sure that he was going to have to study the video several times, as she had.

But he spotted it far more quickly.

"Yes," Keenan said, leaning back in his chair after freezing the screen. "It's Billie Bingham," he said.

"I've watched nearly all the footage. She didn't testify, but she was in the courtroom every day. I didn't get it at first, but it explains the familiarity I felt when I saw..."

"Her corpse," Keenan finished for her. "Well, yes, she changed her hairstyle, and back then she looked like such a serious and prim young woman. But that is definitely her. And I guess she became the reigning queen of escort services here about six to eight years ago... I don't know. I didn't pay that much attention to tabloids, but she was certainly becoming notorious at least five years ago. After this, though... So, Billie Bingham was at McCarron's trial."

"And now she's dead!"

"Yes, a victim of this killer," Keenan said thoughtfully, still looking at the screen.

"Keenan, I've watched this so many times; she looks at Mc-Carron. And he looks at her. As though they know each other. But she wasn't one of the delusional women testifying for him, saying he was a good man."

"Tell me everything that you remember about your dad's part in all this, the investigation, and the murders."

Stacey waved a hand in the air. "In the end, as you know, McCarron admitted to a number of murders—not just the murders of Anderson and Vargas. But that's what he was on trial for. There were other charges having to do with the murders. Charges that had to do with his attempts to bribe doctors for friends, that kind of thing." She hesitated. "My dad was a private investigator; he was working for Anderson's wife, and he had pictures of McCarron going into the building and coming out of it. There were no eyewitnesses to the murders, but they had proof that McCarron hired the man who was supposed to kill my father." She paused, trying to remember what might be relevant. She looked at Keenan, frowning. "This may not have anything to do with anything, but why was Billie at that trial, looking as fresh and pure as a baby doll? Was that a planned costume for court, or did she make the change into what she was after the trial? And—" she added, frustrated "—what can it have to do with this case? Except that Billie was there, and now Billie has been murdered?"

"One of the men murdered was a surgeon who specialized in transplants. Heart transplants, to be exact. But he headed the department. And Anderson was a philanthropist, right? And an outspoken advocate for organ donation?"

"Yes," she said thoughtfully. "In fact, their bodies were discovered by another transplant doctor, Dr. Henry Lawrence." She gasped suddenly. "Is his name on the lists of doctors? I know he was up-and-coming. He was a protégé of Dr. Vargas's. I remember that he cried at the trial. You should have seen the way that McCarron looked at him. McCarron just kept staring at him, as if he hated him so much. Well, of course, you can see it. It's all in the video. Or, I should say, videos. There are hours of viewing pleasure to be found there," she added dryly.

"Anything else from the video?" Keenan asked her.

"I guess that was it," she said, worried that all she had done was recognize someone who couldn't be the killer—since she was already dead.

Keenan pulled up the list of names of transplant doctors they were currently investigating. "I can't find Dr. Henry Lawrence here," he told Stacey. "I'll have Angela search for him. He may have been so traumatized by what happened that he left the field and the area completely. But you're right—if Billie Bingham was at that trial, who knows what else might connect."

"But Billie is dead."

He smiled at her. "That doesn't mean that Billie wasn't somehow involved." He pushed back and told her, "There is an agent you haven't met yet, Axel Tiger. He's a friend of mine. He worked a really strange case in Florida—his home—recently."

She smiled. "I know that I'm far from knowing the whole Krewe—I am, as you've often liked to remind me, a rookie."

"I think I mentioned others with very different talents."

"Axel has a different talent?"

"Axel is extremely talented, but no, he's not the one with the unusual talent. His wife tried on a dress—and that led her to a murder victim. You see things in your dreams; she sees them when she touches things. Axel was down in Florida for a time, and came back to headquarters after a very sudden wedding. But a good one! Beside the point. They're going to meet us tomorrow morning at the morgue."

"At the morgue?"

"I'm going to ask her to touch a body." He hesitated, looking at her. "And you."

Stacey didn't protest. "Okay. So, where do we go from here, until tomorrow morning?"

He couldn't help the smile that curled into his lips. "Well, there's the concept of working like normal people and going home for the night."

"I love that concept. But I'm coming to know you. You have another idea."

"Lafayette Square. I'd like to see my great-grandfather, if we can find him. He's always investigating something. He'll go after a dog owner who doesn't pick up after his pooch if there's nothing else going on. But if I know him, this case will have caught his attention, and he'll be watching from vantage points we could never achieve."

"Let's do it. We'll stop by Angela's office first and ask her to search for Dr. Henry Lawrence?"

"Yes." He glanced back at his computer. He hadn't gone through all the video of the McCarron trial as Stacey had, but he'd seen something of it.

"I thought of someone else," he said.

"Who?"

"Dr. Vargas's widow. She might be able to tell us more of what was going on at the time."

"You think it could relate to now?"

"Who knows? We must try any possibility." He pulled out his phone. "I'm going to check in with Fred and Jean, and we'll let Jackson and Angela know our thoughts and what we're doing."

He made his call to Fred, filling him in on his conversation with Sandra Smith and what they had discovered about Billie Bingham through the old tapes.

"Jean and I paid a visit to Congressman Smith's office—not to speak with Smith, who is supposedly a cooperative witness, but to his secretary. Agnes Merkle. She is something!"

"And what did you get from that experience? Anything?" Keenan asked him.

"A great deal of appreciation that I'm not related to that woman nor have ever had to work for anyone like her."

"Great. Anything else?" he asked. He glanced at Stacey. She shrugged.

"Well, she admitted that she talked with Billie for him, and they discussed a monetary value on Billie's silence over her relationship with Colin Smith. She also said it was none of our business—no matter what his sexual appetites, he was a good man. It wasn't his fault if his home life was less than perfect."

"So Agnes doesn't like Smith's wife."

"Doesn't seem to like her much. We're going in some circles, checking on Peggy, seeing if she remembers anything else that happened in the office that might help. We've started on the missing men and found it to be a similar situation. The skull belonged to an Ethan Jones, and his disappearance was reported after he'd been missing for days—and it didn't much upset the police. His disappearance was reported by a fellow who shared a cardboard-box home in the center of Baltimore. He said that Ethan really liked to sleep on Poe's grave in the churchyard cemetery, but people just kept kicking him out. No family to be found. We're working on the other disappearance in the area. We'll have more later. I hope. This case can't go cold—or get worse before it gets better."

They agreed to catch up the next day; Jackson would be calling another task-force meeting the following afternoon.

They finished the call.

He looked at Stacey. "Let's go and pay a visit to the ghosts of Lafayette Square."

"Took you a hell of a long time to get back here," the ghost of Bram Wallace told Keenan. He studied Stacey as he spoke. "And this is your new partner, eh? A pleasure to meet you, miss."

Keenan was already slightly aggravated by his great-grandfather's manner. It didn't seem to bother Stacey at all, though. Bram certainly knew that she worked for the FBI.

But Stacey was simply curious to hear if Bram did have anything for them. The ghost of Philip Barton Key II stood next to Bram, casually watching movement in Lafayette Square.

"Sorry. There are leads we've been following," he told his grandfather.

He didn't remember Bram in life; the man had died when Keenan had been a toddler.

But he was easily able to see the family resemblance that had passed from Bram to Keenan's grandfather and father and on to Keenan.

Bram was tall. Not quite six-five, but almost. And, Keenan thought with some amusement, the ghost of his ancestor liked to stand very straight near him, chin in the air, because no matter how old Keenan might become, Bram would see him as a youngster who needed to be schooled.

"We've been vigilant here," Philip assured them. "But...well, I don't think this fellow—or these fellows—will operate in the same area twice."

"Did you see or hear anything?" Keenan asked Bram.

Bram nodded gravely.

"I saw a car. Black—the same car that Philip saw," he said.

"Oh," Keenan said, hoping he didn't show the depth of his disappointment. He had hoped for something a little more.

"I saw the car," Bram said. "I didn't see the body—not until later, much later, after the dawn broke, after you and all the others came. I was out and about, you know."

"Of course you were," Stacey said.

"Right," Keenan agreed. "Understandable. You couldn't have expected someone to have left a mutilated body in Lafayette Square. I wanted to see you; Stacey wanted to meet you. We really weren't expecting you to have anything."

"I didn't say I didn't have anything," Bram told him, frowning. He turned to the ghost of Philip Barton Key II. "Young people today! No patience."

"We are on the trail of a really vicious killer," Keenan reminded him.

"On the trail," Bram growled. "Get on that trail fast! I've seen the newspapers, and that's not the half of it, I'm sure."

"Sir, do you know something that might help?" Stacey asked.

Bram nodded gravely.

"I didn't see anything but the car moving away. Swiftly—but following traffic laws. It's not what I saw that might help. It's what I heard."

"And?" Keenan said.

"They must have just carried the body from the car and put it down," Bram said. "There were two of them—a man and a woman. I'm not completely sure what they were saying. She wanted something done right; he just wanted to be gone as soon as possible. I was already headed down the street. It was so late at night, so early in the morning, that there was nothing much going on. I wasn't even sure where they'd come from, but at the time, I thought they were just a couple out doing some late-night partying—tourists, even if they did have a Washington politico car. But after, of course, when I heard what had happened, when I talked to Philip and saw all the reports... Well, it had to have been the killer or killers. Whatever it was, they were in it together. Maybe they were a couple just having a tiff after a late night. But with us both seeing that car and a mutilated body being left, I may be behind the times, but to me that sure as hell points toward something."

"He's cute," Stacey said as they walked around the square.

Keenan eyed her as if she'd lost her mind. "Cute?" he queried.

"An older, grouchier you," she said.

"A very grouchy me," Keenan said. He stopped walking, and Stacey almost slammed into him. He was looking around.

"I doubt the murderer is coming back here for anything,"

she said. "The next murder, he intends—or maybe now *they* intend—for it to happen indoors," she finished quietly.

She'd seen the room shrouded in the mist. She'd seen the hearth.

"I love Lafayette Square," he said, looking around at the historic buildings. He shook his head. "I love DC. Politics can get ugly, but the ideal remains, and people, our people, fight for their ideas and beliefs, and I also like to believe that, even when we take steps backward, we'll take steps forward again."

"I love it, too," she said.

They were in public, but she took his hands. "And I'm a dreamer; I always believe that we'll make it better, too."

"Smith—whether he's in on the killings or not—is a scumbag."

"And, yes, sometimes, scumbags get into office. We have to believe they'll be voted out."

He nodded, gave himself a shake and apologized. "I'm sorry, I just… If Smith is in on this, he was making one of his statements, leaving the body here, in such an historic area."

She smiled. "Much of DC is historic, you know."

"Yes, of course. And…it's home," he said. "Shall we?"

Her smile broadened. Home, yes, and it meant more now than at any time since she'd moved in. He was referring to her apartment, and it was nice that he said it that way.

They'd only been together one night, she reminded herself.

And that didn't matter; he was coming home with her again.

He made a face. "Should we grab some kind of fast food on the way?"

"How about I call for sushi and we pick it up?"

"That will work."

He didn't pull his hand away. It was late; not many people were out. She had a feeling that it didn't matter. It wasn't taboo in the FBI for two agents to be together—though, usually they weren't in the same unit. With the Krewe, it was different, she knew.

Jackson Crow and Angela were married, for one. They were

most often in the office, managing the many agents out in the field. But not always. Sometimes they were drawn in on cases, separately or together.

It was all part of the extraordinary way the Krewe worked. She chuckled thinking that Jackson Crow had possibly set them up, knowing that even among the different she was different, and Keenan could not only handle it but encourage her.

Over their takeout sushi, eaten right in the car after they picked it up, they both admitted that they'd taken White House tours—hoping to meet Abraham Lincoln or one of the other presidents rumored to haunt the Executive Mansion.

Neither of them had met Lincoln.

Stacey was eager to get home. Long days had turned into long nights.

To her surprise, when she opened the front door, she found that Marty Givens was waiting anxiously, as if waiting for her.

"You're here!" she said.

"Uh, yes. Home after a very—"

"Very," Keenan added.

"—long day," Stacey said.

"Yes, of course, but… Special Agent Wallace, I am so, so glad that you're here, too!"

Her pleasure couldn't simply be the fact that it probably appeared that Stacey finally had a date.

"Yes. I'm here, too," Keenan said.

"There was someone out there tonight," Marty said. "Someone sneaking around!"

"There was?" Keenan asked.

Marty nodded gravely.

Stacey lowered her head, counting slowly. She lifted her head and smiled at Marty. "Marty, the alarm was set, right? On the main door. I heard it tick when I set my key in the lock."

They had a high-tech system; keys for the apartment were

specially crafted so that they armed and disarmed the main door
alarm by being the right key.

"And I know," Stacey continued, "that you have bolts on your
door, right? You're as safe as you can be. And I'm sure you know
if our friends are home in the other apartments?"

Marty nodded but still looked upset.

"Nothing like a good alarm system," Keenan said.

Stacey reminded herself that Marty lived alone and that she
was a good person.

"We're here now. Two FBI agents. We're watching out for
everything, I promise," Stacey said.

"But you haven't caught him yet, have you?" Marty asked.

"No," Stacey admitted.

"Marty, we'll be here all night," Keenan said, smiling and
speaking with gentle reassurance.

Marty smiled at last. "Thank heavens! Well, I think I can go
to bed at last."

Stacey forced a smile and a pleasant good-night. There was
no way out of it: Marty would always trust a man with a gun
more than a woman, trained agent or not.

Marty started up the stairs and then turned back, smiling
happily now.

"So, so, happy that you're here!" she told Keenan.

"Thanks, Marty!" he said.

Stacey had already turned to head into her own apartment.
He followed her in, leaning on the kitchen counter as she set
her bag down.

"I guess we have approval all the way round," he said, grinning. "Pseudomom seems to like me!"

"My mom will surely like you," Stacey said. She shook her
head. "She probably thinks only a man can keep someone safe,
too."

"Some stereotypes are hard to break." Before she could reply,
he added, "Safety is in numbers. I wonder if someone was prowl-

ing around. Don't take offense; we need to make sure that we're vigilant."

"Keenan, Marty tends to be paranoid. And I know she's alone, so, I swear, I try to be very nice."

"You are nice. But we'll stay on alert."

"I thought we were already on high alert."

"Higher alert."

She smiled. "Guns on the sink while we're in the shower?"

"I think one will do," he said, grinning.

There was no pretense after the night they'd already spent together.

But he was serious about the gun. She slid hers into the drawer of her nightstand; he brought his into the bathroom, setting it on top of her laundry hamper, within easy reach.

They showered together, for long moments just standing together beneath a spray that was hot enough to wash away some of the day, even though there was nothing that could really rinse away the intensity of their case.

But it was night. And they were working endless hours. This time was precious.

They were both determined to use it.

She wasn't afraid with Keenan. If she slept, if she dreamed, if she woke screaming like a maniac, it was all right.

That added a touch extra.

Not, she thought quickly, that he really needed an extra touch of anything. He was so right for her in so many ways. He seemed to know just how to touch her. They could laugh and tease, and grow passionate and urgent, and even then, laugh again.

As he carried her to the bedroom, she wondered at how she'd never imagined that something so beautiful could exist in her life, that she could be with someone, loving the taste and feel and scent of him and the way he felt against her, and also know that she dared lie with him through the night.

He kissed her sweetly, wetly, hot as he touched her lips, trav-

eled her body. The feel of being with him, so desperately wanting more and more…as if they could all but inhabit one another's
flesh.

Lying beside him…breathing. Just breathing.

"This is…amazing," he said.

She rested her face against his chest, wriggling her nose a bit
as she shifted, and his chest hair teased her.

"Yes."

"I mean the sweeping, mind-blowing, ripsnorting, sheer nir-
vana climax part is so damned great, but man, this is amazing,
too."

She laughed.

"*Ripsnorting?* My, my, Special Agent Wallace, you do have a
way with words."

"Well, you know what I mean. At least I think you know
what I mean."

"Exactly," she assured him, leaning up on his chest, lowering
to kiss his lips, slowly, and lingeringly.

She felt her need for him swell again, but by then, they were
mentally and physically exhausted.

Soon enough, she was asleep.

And thus, back in the room.

The room clouded with fog or haze, thick and dark, smell-
ing and feeling like evil.

She couldn't place where she was; she only knew that the
killer was there, and the killer knew that she was there as well.

And the victim.

She couldn't see the victim; she didn't know where she was.

She didn't even know if she herself was the intended victim.

But she did know something of the killer's mind. This time,
there would be no neat strangulation. Difficult as strangling another person could be, it required great strength in the hands when
done manually, without any type of garrote to aid in the deed.

This time, he wanted blood. A knife slashing in the air. No

hesitation, but slow enough. And the mutilation would go and on and on...

The organs would be preserved. That, after all, was what sanctioned the carnage. He was prepared. And he would do it as he knew to do it, keeping every needed organ as pristine as he knew how. Yes, yes, but then...

The slashing of the throat—hard enough so that the blood loss would render his victim powerless...but not enough to kill instantly. He wanted to see this victim squirm and squeal and, yes, even choke out a few screams. He wanted to see her eyes, as she knew that death was imminent.

Close, close...closer.

The victim knew that he was there—and that he had come for her...

Who is it, who is it? Something screamed inside her.

But the fog was so dense and gray, the miasma so great.

The knife, even against the blinding depth of the fog, was glistening, high in the air, ready for the first strike.

A scream of terror broke free...

Keenan held her, smoothing back her hair, whispering her name and shaking her just slightly, gently.

The scream faded; her eyes opened.

"Keenan..."

"You're okay. You're with me."

She stared at him wonderingly. "I'm so sorry; you're sleeping with a freak!"

"You're not a freak. You're amazing. I'm so sorry that you being so amazing has to be so painful for you as well."

"It helps that...that you're here with me."

He held her quietly and waited, and she sighed with frustration.

"I can't see his face; I can't even see his victim's face!"

"You will."

"But when?"

"In time," he assured her. And he waited again; he let her go through her own thoughts and put them into words without pressing her.

"Okay. I did learn something. It's one person who commits the murders. I still don't know if he's really medically trained, or if he's been shown exactly what to do. It was as if I could slip into his head. Keenan, he couldn't wait to rip her to shreds! He was thinking about the organs... He must have help. Because he was thinking that his indulgence in the terrible killing was sanctioned by someone—the someone who wanted the organs, I imagine. More than one person is involved, but...who I don't know."

"But we know what we're looking for," he told her.

"You think it really makes a difference?"

"A tremendous difference."

"I'm still sorry. I don't get enough sleep—and I make you not get enough sleep."

As if it had been paying attention, the alarm clock blared suddenly.

"See? We got plenty of sleep!" he told her. "Up and at 'em, as they say. We have a date with—"

He paused, wincing.

"With?"

"Some incredible people and...a medical examiner and a few corpses."

CHAPTER THIRTEEN

Stacey thought that she would have recognized Axel Tiger as a law-enforcement officer of one kind or another whether he had been introduced to her as one or not.

Though not as tall as Keenan, he had a similar build. Stacey had noted that many Krewe agents were not giants at all—it was in the way they moved. Their jobs required they kept fit. But Axel had crystal eyes against bronze skin, dead-straight hair and an incredibly intriguing profile.

Beyond a doubt, he was an interesting man.

His new wife, Raina, was taller than Stacey, with rich, dark auburn hair and eyes a lighter shade than her hair, an amber color. She had a great smile as she took Stacey's hand, greeting her warmly.

"And you're not an agent, right?" Stacey asked her.

"Nope. I'm an animal trainer—domestics, whatever they may be. My forte is dogs, but I've worked with just about everything else you might consider a pet. Or," she added, her smile deepening, "anything anyone else thinks of as a pet."

"She's working with a lot of police and agency bomb-and-cadaver dogs," Axel told Stacey.

It was a strangely cheerful conversation to be having in the reception area of the morgue while they awaited Dr. Beau Simpson.

"But I'm here because Keenan thinks I might be able to help. And if I can help you catch a murderer, I'm so happy to do so!"

Dr. Simpson came out for them, bringing them first to mask and gown up, then heading into a room that was quite cold and seemed to be filled with giant, silver-colored filing drawers.

Of course, Stacey knew, what was filed was bodies. Some awaited loving family members or friends to claim them and set them to rest with flowers and prayers.

Others would meet with a pauper's farewell, no fanfare whatsoever. Decent, but cold, lacking the greatest of human gifts—love.

She'd seen death before, but today seemed especially sad as she looked at the rows and rows of "filing" cabinets.

"Okay," Beau said. "You just want me to open the drawers on Jess Marlborough, Billie Bingham and Lindsey Green. Anything in particular you're looking for?"

"A last look," Keenan said.

"Right."

If Beau was surprised, confused or even perturbed by the request, he didn't show it. He didn't even ask why a dog trainer had come with them. He apparently knew Raina already; he had greeted her as a friend.

He opened the drawer that contained the mutilated remains of Jess Marlborough first. Keenan and Stacey stood on one side; Axel and Raina on the other.

Beau looked away.

One by one, they laid a hand on the cold body.

Jackson had told Stacey that every once in a rare while, those who did see the dead found something as they touched the deceased.

She felt nothing, just the chill of the preserved body. Life was gone.

She waited for the others. Raina let her touch linger, but then she glanced at her husband and shook her head slightly.

They went on to the body of Billie Bingham and repeated their motions.

Cold, so cold. All life gone, not even the memory to the soul once inside.

It was the same for the others, Stacey thought. Raina gave that almost imperceptible shake of her head.

At last they came to the body of Lindsey Green.

The insides were not ripped up, but she wore a red gash around her neck like a sick Halloween necklace.

This time, Raina held on a few moments longer; she didn't shake her head.

Beau turned to look at them all, one by one.

"Thank you," Keenan told him. "I know we're taking up your time."

"Don't forget, there's a victim in Virginia, too, if you need."

"We won't. Thank you." As the drawer closed, Keenan managed a smile. "I don't know that ME as well as I know you."

"You need anything with him, you let me know," Beau said.

"Will do," Keenan said gratefully.

They left the morgue, agreeing to meet up at the office directly.

On arriving, they took seats in the conference room. Jackson joined them, ready to listen to whatever Raina had to say.

"I don't really have anything," she began.

"But you did have a vision from the last victim," Axel reminded her.

"Right. I felt something from her, yes. She was asked to the house. I'm not sure who asked her. She was looking for...work. She had met Billie at a club. She was anxious and eager to find out if she was...worthy, I guess, of being one of Billie's escorts."

"What was she doing in the basement?" Keenan asked.

"She thought that Billie was down there. I don't know why. I had an impression of her going down…and then she was completely surprised. She was killed in a whirlwind attack." Raina was silent a minute. "Her killer came at her from behind. She never saw what happened." She paused again, hanging her head sadly. "She knew she was going to die. I felt her thoughts in those last minutes. Heartbreaking. But…it was like a replay in my mind. I don't think that she's lingered here, that she's still with us in spirit. It was a residual thing that I felt. I wish there was more. I know what she knew at that time, but… Doesn't really help, does it?"

"Now we know she was lured, then attacked," Keenan told her.

"Oh! One thing. I picked up…a scent. A scent of perfume."

"Perfume, or aftershave?" Stacey asked.

Raina was thoughtful and then said, "I really think perfume. I think that she was killed…by a woman."

And yet, in her dreams, Stacey was fairly certain it seemed that the killer was a man.

"Well, the thought does seem to be that there's more than one killer involved in this," Jackson said.

"Billie?" Stacey said. She looked around at the others. "Lindsey was attacked before Billie. Did Billie kill her—before she was killed herself?"

No one answered as they considered the possibility.

"And does that mean that there's just one killer left, or that more than two people were involved?" Keenan wondered aloud.

"We're trying to keep our eyes on all the key players," Jackson said. "Jess Marlborough's roommates. Tania Holt. Peggy Bronsen. Colin and Sandra Smith. Cindy Hardy. Protecting anyone who might have been a witness—and who might be seen as a last victim in the Ripper round of this. But we have checked into missing persons and found those who vanished, along with the skull of one man. This might just be one stage of a truly wide-range operation."

Jackson studied Stacey for a long moment. "Anything more?" he asked.

"The person physically committing the murders is male," she said. "That's the clearest part of my dreams."

"All right, then, keep up whatever pressure you can on Colin Smith," Jackson said. "He's still a primary suspect."

"We're going to show up there as soon as we're finished with the task-force meeting," Keenan told him. Then he asked, "The info that a piece of kidney was sent to Stacey hasn't gotten out, has it?"

"No, but the kidney was sent to her, so we can't let up on watching Stacey's back, either," Jackson said.

"We've got to get to the airport," Axel said. "I have a few things to get from my office, then we'll head out." He nodded to them all and stepped out of the room.

"I'm going to drive him," Raina said.

"Good, then," Jackson said. "I'll check in with Angela, see what our searches have turned up."

He left the room.

"I'll be right back," Keenan said, following him out.

Stacey was left alone with Raina. She smiled weakly.

"Do you have the dreams often?" Raina asked her.

"In general, no. When they do come, it's like watching a scene unraveling, bit by bit. I saw the body in Lafayette Square, and that was it for that part of the dream. But now I'm seeing a room where the killer is with the victim. He's functional, but seriously deranged. He can't wait to rip up his last victim."

"But you can't see his victim. Or exactly where it is?"

"No."

"Well, from what Jackson has told me, you will," Raina assured her. "I heard this isn't the first case you've helped with.

And," she added brightly, her tone filled with admiration, "you're an agent."

"I always wanted to be."

"I've always loved animals," Raina said. "And I think my more natural talents lie in helping with both police and agency dogs—and pets! I'm happy to come in, though, anytime you think I might help. Or even if you just want to talk." She hesitated a minute. "Have you met Jon Dickson and Kylie Connolly, yet?"

"No."

"Oh, no, you wouldn't have—they're in Scotland, vacationing and investigating for a friend who apparently has a haunted castle," she said. "Aren't all castles supposed to be haunted?" she said with a smile. "But Kylie has had...strange events in her life to go along with this. She had a past-life regression and wound up finding herself as a murder victim. I'm just telling you all this because...well, the Krewe exists because Adam knew there needed to be an honest place for those of us with these strange talents. I just didn't want you to feel like...the Lone Ranger."

"Thank you. That is reassuring!" she told Raina.

Raina was quiet for a minute and then asked her, "You've experienced dreams that tell you things a long time, right?"

Stacey nodded. "When I was young, my father was involved in a major case. The man going to trial was responsible for all kinds of criminal activity, including murder. Some people he killed himself. He also hired killers to do his killing. He wanted my father dead, and he hired a man to kill him. That was when I first starting dreaming. And thankfully, my mom hired a psychiatrist, and the psychiatrist called in Adam. Adam and some agents were there—the assassin was caught, and he talked. He went down for conspiracy to commit murder, but he did it with a plea deal because he told the prosecution everything he knew about McCarron. And it was a lot." She shrugged. "Then, later, I dreamed about a friend who was getting into trouble with drugs. Again, Adam helped out, and Keenan was even in on that, but when we started working together, it took me a bit to realize just where and when I'd seen him before. I barely saw the agents—everyone wanted to keep me out of it. I hadn't yet graduated high school at the time." She shrugged. "I've had other dreams—prophetic dreams, I guess. But they're often just about…walking into a store. Losing something and finding it. Things that are mundane, and yet… Well, they made me a loner."

Raina was listening to her intently. "So, you came into this knowing about your talent—that you could see the dead?"

"A Revolutionary War heroine helped me in the last case, so, yes," Stacey told her.

"Believe it or not, you're lucky. I didn't know a thing until I tried on a dress and looked in a mirror and saw a murder. I was freaked out, to say the least! But after that, well, I had to get involved. I know how much this case means to you. I don't think any of us really knows our capabilities, until something happens. Once you accept there might be more, intuition kicks in to a greater degree. This may sound strange, but it might help if you let yourself go. Don't doubt yourself. If there's an instinct that takes hold or even teases at your mind, let it go. Follow anything. I think most Krewe members get to that point. And if something bothers me now, I tell Axel right away. I'm not even sure what I'm saying. Trust yourself, I guess. Explore any thoughts, feelings or sensations you may have. I know that in a court of law, we need proof. And that's the way it should be. But even cops who don't see the dead have intuition. Lots of them hone it. With you… I'm imagining that your intuition is right on. Don't hesitate; go with it."

Stacey smiled. "Thank you. Thanks so very much."

"Kylie and I had decided that we would silently call ourselves the Twisted Two," Raina told her, a very wry smile on her lips.

"Now, I guess, we're an ever-so-slightly twisted threesome. I guess the name still works!"

"I'm now part of the Twisted Trio!" Stacey said. "I love it."

Raina gave her a grim smile. "I just wish that it worked better, that I could give you more."

"You've given us something," Stacey assured her. "Thank you!"

"Keep dreaming," Raina said softly.

Stacey laughed. "No choice!" she said.

"At least you won't be alone—and please, don't be alone," Raina warned.

"Trust me, I won't!"

The conference-room door opened, and Angela came in, greeting them both and getting right to it. "Stacey, I've got a number and address for you. Dr. Henry Lawrence, working at a hospital just outside Richmond. It took so long because he's no longer doing transplants. He's working in general surgery. I verified that he's there—day shift, doesn't work weekends—but he is there, and I have a home address as well, not far from the hospital. I didn't speak with him; I wasn't sure what you were hoping to get from him, so I'm leaving it to you and Keenan."

"Thank you!" Stacey said. "I'm not sure what I'm hoping to get from him, either. Maybe, just maybe, he knows something about someone who was on the outs with the transplant world." She was thoughtful. "He was the one who found Dr. Vargas. He worshipped the man—Vargas was his mentor. Maybe that's why he left transplant surgery. He just couldn't cope."

"Maybe," Angela said. "Events like that... Well, we all know. Some deal with them. Some don't. But apparently, he's still a good surgeon. He just turned his talents in a different direction. Well, see what you can find out."

She gave them a wave and left the room. Axel poked his head in, saying goodbye to Stacey and telling Raina that he needed to get to the airport.

Alone, Stacey looked at the landline in the conference room. It wasn't going to be easy, trying to reach a surgeon on his own line. She might as well get started.

Angela had given her several numbers: Henry Lawrence's work extension at the hospital, at his office, at his home and a number for his cell phone.

She hurried to the phone, not expecting to reach him, but at least hoping to leave a message.

To her surprise, he answered his phone.

"Dr. Lawrence, I'm sure you won't remember me—"

"Are you an old patient? I have a great memory. How can I help you? Have you called the office for an appointment?"

"No, Dr. Lawrence. I'm not a patient. My name is Stacey Hanson."

"Hanson!"

"Yes, sir. Special Agent Stacey Hanson, now. We never met in person, but—"

"Your father was the one who helped put McCarron away."

"Yes, that was my dad."

"Amazing man."

"Yes, thank you. I think so. I'm sure you must—"

"I'm sorry. I'd be delighted to help you in any way. I have a very complicated hernia to take off in just minutes. Can we talk later?"

"Yes, of course. I'd like to get out to see you—"

"About the old McCarron case?"

"I'm afraid so. I know it's painful for you, but you must have heard about the scourge of murders taking place in the DC area—"

"Of course, but I do have to prep for this surgery—"

"Doctor, my partner and I will come to you. We'll find you at the hospital. Thank you, sir. Goodbye!" she said.

She hung up before he could protest. She didn't blame him; he wouldn't want an old wound reopened. But if he could say

anything at all that might jar her memory or lead them somewhere—anywhere—closer...

Keenan came in.

Jackson was about to start his task-force meeting, a brief one,
but they'd all go over—and over again—every little scrap of
information that they did have.

"We'll go see the battle-ax secretary when we're done here,"
Keenan told her.

"Then we need to go to Richmond," she said.

"Richmond?"

Stacey nodded firmly. "Angela has found Dr. Henry Lawrence. Maybe he'll know if there was another bitter man out
there like McCarron. One who would kill to readjust a donor
list."

"Do you think the killer possibly *can* strike again?" Stacey
asked Keenan as they drove to Congressman Smith's DC office.
She was thinking about the task-force meeting. Fred Crandall's
team of police was there, as was Jean Channing's team, and of
course, all Krewe members who could make it. Dr. Beau Simpson also attended, along with Dr. Victor Bowen of the Alexandria morgue.

He had brought them a piece of new information, one that
they had expected. Beau Simpson had sent him the piece of kidney Stacey had received when it hadn't matched his victims, but
it had, indeed, matched up with Andrea Simon, the mutilated
victim found in the Alexandria alley.

"Diseased—the poor girl suffered as an alcoholic; her liver
was damaged to an extent that her other organs might have been
damaged as well," Bowen had said. He was an older man, slightly
hunched, precise and clear in his speech. At the end of the meeting, he'd assured Stacey and Keenan that they were welcome
to inspect the remains of Andrea Simon at any time. "I've been
at this for almost forty years," he told them. "I've seen a lot of

horrors. The only saving grace is that I do believe the girl was killed swiftly and then, that the organs were taken immediately. After she was strangled, well, she didn't feel anything. But if I'm right, the killer didn't get what he wanted. Not from her."

"We don't think that these outrageously staged murders are the only killing being done," Keenan had reminded him. "They serve a purpose, and they draw attention. Please, keep an eye open for anything out of the ordinary that reaches your morgue."

The ME had seemed a bit amused. "We rather do that anyway," he told Keenan, and the two men had smiled grimly. They'd exchanged a few words with Jean. She was still canvassing the streets near the alley where Andrea Simon had been found, asking for and viewing video surveillance, and helping Fred with the protection units that the police had taken on.

Everyone was working.

Everyone was frustrated. And afraid.

No one wanted another killing to take place.

It was the fact that so very many agents and officers were working the case that made her ask the question. They had so many of the people of interest under surveillance or protection. "The killer does seem very bold," Keenan said. "All we can do is keep looking and hope we're getting close enough that he's getting nervous."

Stacey really hoped that was the case.

"Is Smith in his office today? I take it we know, with agents watching Smith and his wife."

"Smith has not left his home yet," Keenan said. "Not since we got in the car, at any rate. Congress is on hiatus. That leaves him a clear schedule. He's probably calling all his buddies, one by one, warning them that they might have been on one of Billie's lists that could become public, or making sure that they know that his name came up because of a picture—and thus he was falsely maligned and worthy of their sympathy. Then there's his campaign ads. Next one could be a damned hard one for him."

"It's strange," Stacey murmured.

"What, in particular? Since all this is strange."

"Cindy Hardy and her husband wound up in a bitter divorce because of Billie Bingham. But no matter what Smith did—with Billie or another woman—Sandra Smith is not going to let go of her position. But what do you think she'll feel if he is forced to resign or if he's voted out of office?"

"People react to circumstances differently," Keenan said. "We can go at Battle-Ax Agnes Merkle and find out what she thinks on that count."

It was evident, when they reached the suite of offices and opened the door to Congressman Smith's office, that Agnes Merkle wasn't just surprised to see them: she was alarmed.

She stared at them as if they were twin demons brought up from hell, spewing fire and brimstone with each step they took.

But she folded her hands on the desk in front of her, glaring at them.

"He isn't here."

"Oh, we believe you," Stacey said pleasantly.

"We've come to speak with you," Keenan added.

"For what? What do you want? Haven't you done enough? Colin is a good man—a really good man. And you're dragging him right through the mud. Well, you might just discover that all your horrid questioning and harassing of that man will get you nowhere. He has very loyal constituents."

Stacey smiled. "We're here to help him."

"Yes, he's been very cooperative with us."

Agnes looked at them skeptically.

Stacey glanced at Keenan, her pleasant smile deepening. "He hasn't been back to the office since he came down to help the FBI, has he?"

"But he's contacted you, of course. Seriously, a wife is a man's love. But a secretary is truly the most important person in his life."

"I have my place," Agnes said primly.

"He's brokenhearted. Just brokenhearted. You see, he did care about both Billie and one of the younger women who was killed. He cared for her a great deal. And he wants to help us catch whoever is doing these terrible things."

She arched a brow, doubting them.

"We need to know if he was telling you the truth. He said that he'd talked to you about Billie. She was making some waves. And he said that she needed to be taken care of, and that he was talking to you when he said it."

"Oh, no! You think that he meant that I should do something to her?" the woman gasped in dismay.

"No, no, of course not," Keenan said. "We don't believe you capable of such a terrible thing."

"I should hope not!"

"But what did he mean?" Stacey asked.

"He told you that he called me to talk about Billie? You're not just making this up?" she asked warily.

"I can't believe he hasn't spoken to you since we had him at the office," Keenan said, shaking his head.

"Because it's true—you make his world go around," Stacey said earnestly.

Agnes looked down at her desk for a minute.

"We're trying to clear things up," Keenan said. "Congressman Smith is trying to help us, but he admitted to making use of Billie's services. We're not interested in who is sleeping with who. All we want to do is solve these murders—and stop others. We'd hate to see you become involved—"

"Your good name out there," Stacey put in.

"—when all you've done is be a good secretary," Keenan finished.

"Oh, good Lord!" Agnes Merkle said, her words explosive. "Money! Billie was a money-grubbing monster. I never saw what any of them... Well, men are fools. Sorry, Special Agent

Wallace, but men are fools," she snapped. "Yes, he talked to me about her. And if you just knew her... Money was her game. It was all she ever wanted. And I was going to make sure that she received her hush money. Are you happy? It wasn't coming out of campaign funds. He inherited a good business from his father, who had been a peanut farmer and had made out extremely well. He had a machine that helped shell the things, and it sold well, and Smith has his own money. Okay? Is there anything else?"

"Just one thing," Keenan said.

"What else?" Agnes demanded.

"Did you ever hear him talk about a young woman named Jess Marlborough?"

"I know that name," Agnes said.

"Yes?" Keenan asked her.

She made a face, glaring at them. "I heard it in the news—just like everyone else all over the country and beyond. She was a Yankee Ripper victim. That's how I've heard the name."

"He never asked you to get an apartment for her, finagle a way to pay a few bills?"

"He wouldn't ask me for the pennies needed to care for a two-bit whore," she said tightly.

"We know your financials, Agnes," Keenan said pleasantly. "You're very well-paid."

She straightened indignantly. "And you think that I...that I might be performing some special task that would warrant the amount I make? That I might be anything like Billie Bingham?"

Keenan managed to keep a straight face as he replied, "Oh, no, Agnes, I wasn't suggesting anything of the kind!"

"Indeed not!" she said.

"But you do handle problem people for him."

"I am an excellent secretary, and I minored in accounting. I am more than a secretary. I'm glad that wretched Miss Bronsen sent in her resignation. She was worthless! A young graphics major." She paused to snort. "She was paid too much without a shred of loyalty. I swear that young woman flirted with the congressman. She wanted more than she was getting. She's looking for greener pastures, I imagine. Thought a pretty face was all that was needed—and whatever other talents she might have offered. I can handle all problems, and that's why I'm paid well!"

"Of course!" Stacey said, and Keenan echoed her sentiment.

"Is that all?" Agnes demanded. "Despite your best efforts, this is a busy office!"

Keenan smiled. "Thank you. Thank you so much for your time, for speaking with us."

He turned. Stacey quickly followed.

"What do you think?" she asked as they left.

"I think we might have stirred a hornets' nest."

"Ah—telling her that Smith told us that he'd called her about Billie?" She grinned. "Or suggesting that her income might suggest sexual services as well?"

He nodded and smiled. "I was thinking about her being angry that Smith would have told us that he talked to her about Billie. The sex thing—she is so uptight, I just couldn't help it."

"Oh, you just feel that way because all men are fools."

He laughed softly. "I wish we had a tap on his phone."

"Don't we have enough to get one?"

"Even if we did...if he's doing anything illegal—or even immoral—he'll have a burner phone. Any calls from his house will make him sound like a Boy Scout. But it will be interesting to see how his future progresses." He shook his head. "I don't see it. His wife and secretary. Standing by—even if he goes down."

"Very well-paid secretary; a proud congressman's wife," Stacey reminded him.

"And yet Cindy Hardy went right for the throat. I can't help but wonder who knew who—and who knew what about who."

"Could Billie have been in on this, and when she became too troublesome, whoever else decided that she could both be out of the picture and part of the charade?"

"Anything is possible. Anyway, we've got a long drive. This Dr. Lawrence is expecting us, right?"

"I told him we were coming."

She might have told him that they were coming, but when they reached the hospital, he wasn't there. A nurse suggested that they try his office; it was near.

A receptionist at his office said that he didn't take appointments that day: it was one of his surgery days.

They thanked him and headed on out.

Stacey was grateful that Angela was thorough. They didn't need to ask for his home address because they already had it.

"Do you think he's hiding something—or he just doesn't want the past brought back up?" Keenan asked her as they returned to the car.

"He cried on the stand while McCarron denied having killed either Dr. Vargas or Mr. Anderson. He was a young doctor at the time, and he found his mentor murdered. Vargas's neck was broken when he went down the stairs. And I guess Lawrence thought he could save him. Maybe it's just something he really doesn't want to remember," Stacey said.

"If that's the case, I'm sorry. But we have his home address, and we've come this far. We're going to find him."

CHAPTER FOURTEEN

One of the continual trials of living and working in the DC area was traffic. Any major city offered that kind of daily challenge, but getting out of DC had been a nightmare, even using some of the shortcuts Keenan knew, and he knew the area as well as one possibly could.

Then they had to deal with Richmond traffic.

But Keenan was more determined than ever that they weren't heading back without talking to Dr. Henry Lawrence.

They got back into the car. Lawrence's home was just north and west of the city. As they drove, Stacey murmured, "Beautiful country."

"There are a lot of old Victorian plantation homes out here. Not the ultralavish kind. And despite the Civil War, many survived. Compared to the Blue Ridge, it's flat land out here, but flat land that rolls in gorgeous blues and greens." He grinned at her suddenly. "My parents almost bought out here once."

"Oh? What stopped them? Certainly not ghosts!"

"Nope. Ticks. They walked in the beautiful little patch of forest land around the house and discovered they were covered in ticks!"

"Ah," Stacey murmured. "We haven't had much of a problem in Georgetown."

"But this countryside is so beautiful. You have Richmond and the District of Columbia just ninety miles apart, big places, stone, concrete, woods, buildings. But here, it's nice, huh?"

"As long as you can get a tick population under control," she said. She straightened in the passenger's seat. "I think that's it ahead. Addresses aren't that easy out here, but according to the GPS, that should be his house up ahead."

At the end of a circular drive stood the house. It had a broad porch, soaring white columns and a white, two-person swing right on the porch.

"There's a car in the drive," he said. "Fancy!"

"Well, he is a surgeon, and a good one. And as beautiful as these houses are, it's far more reasonable to get a house out here than in the heart of the city."

Keenan pulled up behind a sleek sedan on the circular driveway. They got out of the car, looking at the house.

He shrugged to her, smiling.

"Ten to one, a housekeeper answers the door."

"Maybe," Stacey said, and then added, "Okay, probably."

"Is he married? Does he have a family?" Keenan asked.

"You know, not back when I was a kid, but that was a while ago now. And Angela didn't say. I should have tried to find out more. I mean, that would have been easy enough."

"He's not a suspect. We're just anxious for his help."

"But he was a transplant doctor," Stacey said. "Working with the best."

They walked up the steps to the porch, and he rang the bell.

It was answered by a housekeeper in uniform. She looked surprised; they probably didn't get that many visitors.

Keenan glanced at Stacey. They smiled at one another.

"Yes?" the housekeeper said.

She appeared to be fiftysomething, a bit squat, with iron-gray hair swept severely back. Her eyes, however, were bright blue and friendly.

"Hello, may I help you?" she asked, her manner pleasant and easy.

"Hi, I'm Stacey Hanson, Special Agent Hanson, and this is my partner, Special Agent Keenan Wallace. I called Dr. Lawrence earlier today and asked if we might speak with him. We thought he'd be at the hospital, but he wasn't, and we see his car—" she paused, sweeping an arm out to indicate the dark blue sedan in the driveway, though they really didn't know if it was his or not "—and we're just hoping for a few minutes with him. We drove down from DC. Not a terrible drive, but…"

"Come in, come in, yes, Dr. Lawrence is home. He's playing one of his video games, can you imagine? The man works so hard! I'm always trying to get him to relax a bit, and I was delighted when he made it home early today. Please, if you'll wait in the foyer for just a minute, I'll get him for you."

She opened the door wide and indicated that they should come in, and then hurried to whatever rooms lay to the left.

The house was nice: it wouldn't have been owned by the ultrawealthy back in the day but by someone who had worked hard and was doing all right. The ceilings were high. A hand-carved stairway led to the second floor. The foyer, where they waited, gave way to an expansive parlor with doors opening off to other parts of the house on either side.

They were there barely a minute before the housekeeper returned, frowning and appearing to be very perplexed.

"I'm so sorry. Dr. Lawrence says he can't see you right now. He's extremely busy with an urgent medical report," she said.

"I thought he was playing video games?" Keenan asked.

"I…uh… Well, I guess I was hoping he was," the woman said, stammering. It was evident that she wasn't at all fond of lying, even when told to do so by her employer.

She stood there awkwardly.

Then a door opened, and Dr. Lawrence came out.

"It's all right; I'll see these people," Lawrence told his house-keeper.

His housekeeper, evidently uncomfortable, quickly escaped.

"I just have to close out on my computer," Dr. Lawrence told them. "Give me a minute."

They stood alone in the foyer.

Stacey spoke softly. "Seeing him…he's changed. Everyone changes, but I remember him so clearly from the trial. He broke down several times. Every time McCarron was on the stand—denying his culpability—Henry Lawrence looked as if he would burst into tears again."

"Well, physically, he came out fine," Keenan said. "He's got a good height on him—he's about six-two—I could see that in the video footage. His hair was a sandy-blond back then, he's just gaining bits of gray. I'm estimating he was in his early thirties at the time of the trial, which makes him in midforties now." He lowered his voice still further. "He seemed to have an intense and quick manner about him then."

"And still, though we've barely seen him," Stacey murmured. "The way he moves, it's probably gained from years of learning his way around patients in an operating room."

"Let's hope that he's not too quick or jerky with a scalpel!" he muttered and fell silent.

The good doctor was back.

"Miss Hanson—or Special Agent Hanson, now," he said, studying her. "You grew up well," he told her.

"Thank you. I'm hoping you've been well."

"Well enough, thank you." He looked at Keenan.

"And you, sir?" Lawrence asked.

"Special Agent Keenan Wallace, Dr. Lawrence. And we're sorry to bring back painful memories, but you were on the road to being one of the foremost transplant doctors in the country—until McCarron murdered your mentor."

Lawrence shrugged. "There are other challenges. I performed a hernia surgery today that may well be the most complicated to ever hit the books. I've saved lives when people might have died of ruptured appendixes. There are different rewards." He looked at them both and then indicated an antique sofa and matching side chairs in the living room just past the foyer. "Please, have a seat. You've come this far."

They followed him and took seats. Lawrence studied Stacey intently.

"How is your dad?" he asked her.

"He and Mom are both fine, thank you. The two of them are retired, I'm out of the house, so they've bought a camper. They're off now in Yellowstone, I believe."

"Your father is a good man," he said. "Amazing that he made it to the trial."

"And now, Dr. Lawrence," Keenan said, "someone is killing vulnerable women—and others. We believe that there's more going on than a killer who enjoys killing. We believe that they're being murdered for their internal organs, and that all these organs are going out on the black market. You were a transplant surgeon. We're looking to find out if there was anyone you knew back then, someone who maybe dropped out of the field completely, who might be behind this."

Dr. Lawrence frowned thoughtfully. "That was the whole thing with McCarron. He was bitter over the lists. Said they weren't fair. I can't begin to tell you what goes into the lists, and how a person just might match if there is a chance for an organ to survive. Such an operation—killing people randomly for their organs—is crazy. You would—well, frankly, you'd waste so many."

Keenan shrugged. "This killer may not care about waste. Seriously, what is just one kidney worth on the black market? A half million or more, right?"

"What price do we put on human life?" Lawrence asked softly.

"For most of us, lists and playing by the rules are the lot that life has cast us. But ask yourself—if you were incredibly wealthy, and you knew you were going to die without a new heart in a few years, wouldn't you pay anything?" Lawrence asked.

"I honestly don't think that I could ask another person to die so that I might live," Keenan said.

"Oh, well, I agree!" Lawrence said. "I'm just explaining to you how there is a market for opportunities that are under the table and beyond the lists."

"Was there anyone back then who made you suspicious?"

"McCarron. He wanted to shape the entire way the hospitals handled things. He was bitter. His cousin fell down the list because he'd been drinking. McCarron pointed to all the movie stars during those years who drank like fish, some of whom mysteriously acquired new livers. McCarron was a monster of his own kind. I don't think he minded getting his hands dirty, but he thought he was above everyone else, or at least that other people were of lesser value." He paused and shrugged. "Someone killing street people and hookers? If McCarron was alive now, I'd say, right there, there's your killer. But McCarron is dead. I was there—right there—at his execution."

"McCarron is dead," Stacey said. "But I was hoping you might remember something from the trial that might point to someone else taking over his empire. Or, even forgetting the trial, you might know something about someone who was interested in transplants when you were working or since. Any hints of someone not entirely aboveboard."

He shook his head. "Medicine moves on. Everything is better now than it was just a few short years ago. Transplant is still a specialty, and a sad specialty. When you give a healthy heart to someone dying of heart disease, you know that someone else died. Often young people. Cut down in accidents. Dying far too young…" He shrugged. "It's not that I haven't lost patients since I moved in a different direction. Medicine is magic in a way, but not all-powerful magic, and sometimes there's just no way to cheat death. But I don't think about the fact that someone else died. Unless it was a donated kidney. That can be beautiful. Watching someone who received a kidney from the loved one who donated it… Wow! That's a feeling. And partial liver transplants—to imagine that a liver will regenerate, if not scarred—is amazing as well. There are no partial heart transplants, yet, not that I know about. Lungs…yes, left, right. But despite all that, most of the time, someone has died. Now, I just fight for life. For the lives of my patients." He looked at Stacey again. "I'm not meaning to be rude, but what made you think that anything from so long ago might be relevant?"

"Billie Bingham was at the McCarron trial," Stacey said. "She was the killer's last victim."

Lawrence frowned and then shrugged. "The courtroom was always filled. The judge wanted all the proceedings to be open. McCarron was guilty of so many crimes. Drug running, money laundering—and the murders that came along with it. I saw programs on his talks with FBI interviewers when he was trying to get a stay of execution. He killed, or ordered to be killed, so many people. It's not surprising that anyone was there in the courtroom, really."

"She was there. And she's now among the dead," Stacey told him. "Do you know of anyone else at the time who was following Dr. Vargas's work—or perhaps someone who was angry with Anderson, perhaps believing he pushed them into filling out donor cards—and then watched someone die who wasn't high enough on a list or didn't qualify for a transplant?"

"There's hundreds—probably thousands—of people out there who are angry because someone couldn't receive a transplant. Another reason that, with Dr. Vargas gone, I just wanted out," Dr. Lawrence said. "And I don't know anything about the donor lists. I don't want to know anything about the lists. Give me a ruptured appendix any day." He shrugged. "I can get you some names of other doctors who were interested in Dr. Vargas's work and expertise at the time. If that will help."

"Anyone back then who didn't get the transplant they needed?" Keenan asked. "A case that stood out?"

"They'd be dead now," Lawrence said dryly.

"Sorry," Keenan said. "I meant, could there be anyone who needed a transplant and wasn't high enough on a list—but is alive now."

He shrugged. "Not that I know about. Anyway, I will help you the best I can. McCarron was a monster. It's a good thing he's dead. He killed, though, because someone failed him or…"

His voice trailed. For a moment, he looked as if he felt he had spoken too much.

"Well, his brother needed a transplant. Didn't get it. That's what his motivation, according to the prosecution. And to think… Well, I was so desperate to save Dr. Vargas… Anderson, too, but I didn't touch Anderson where he lay at the foot of the stairs, just Vargas. I was a doctor; I knew that his neck was broken. I still… I wanted to save him."

"Understandable," Keenan said. "Well, we're very grateful for any help you can give us."

"Of course. I'll get you names. Do I email you?"

Keenan handed him a card. "That would be great. But this was a two-hour trip in traffic. Could you just scribble down anything you can think of? We'll be out in the car."

Lawrence looked aggravated for a moment, then shrugged. "Sure. I'll get you what I can think of now. You don't have to sit in the car."

"We'll be on the porch. Enjoy the beauty out here," Keenan said.

Henry Lawrence stood with a shrug. "Sure. I guess you don't get a lot of grass and trees back up there in the old District of Columbia."

"Some," Keenan said pleasantly. "We're in Georgetown—it's nice. But nothing like this."

Lawrence strode to the front door and opened it for them. I'll do my best," he said.

Keenan and Stacey walked out.

"Had to try the swing," he told her.

"It's very pretty. Of course we must try it."

They sat together on the swing, not quite touching.

"It is beautiful here," she said. She pointed across the road. There was a small cemetery there, filled with old and broken gravestones and funerary art, angels with chipped wings, obelisks at odd angles, and other pieces of memorial art. It was overgrown and fenced in; no longer active, Keenan thought, and somehow both historic and charming where it sat beneath the darkening sky.

The house was surrounded on both sides by trees; to one side, there was a little copse with pretty benches. Large pots with flowering plants were set next to the benches.

"Pretty, pretty place," Keenan murmured.

"Yes, Dr. Lawrence has created a very nice home for himself."

"So, what do you think?"

"I don't know what to think at all, really," she said. "Every step of a person's life has an influence on them. I guess Vargas was like a superhero to Dr. Lawrence. I know the whole situation back with the McCarron case had an influence on me."

"Right. You became an agent, ready to fight for truth and justice."

She cast him a grin.

"Stacey, you took it all and turned it into something good. I'm serious," he told her.

"Well, since I've just begun, I'm hoping! But Dr. Lawrence didn't turn his back on medicine—he's still a good doctor. He wouldn't be working at the hospital if he wasn't."

"But he did know all about transplants."

"Well, they can't be doing the transplants legally," Stacey said. "You don't think that a man who gave an oath to save human lives can be doing this?"

"Stacey, a medical doctor must be doing this. That's the only way for a transplant to work—and it's sketchy at that. An experienced doctor has to be doing this."

"I don't know—I don't know!" she said. "He was so bereft over Dr. Vargas! How could he have turned that into…killing people to maybe or maybe not save others?"

"The human condition is that sometimes sickness, evil or whatever sinks in. I'm not saying this man is guilty of anything. I'm just saying we can't rule him out yet."

"A lot of people came to that trial. I know it's still a stretch that it can be related."

"You weren't at the trial, but you watched every minute of it. Your father was a key in the prosecution's case against Mc-Carron. Yes, a stretch, but it does seem that it's all related. Mc-Carron's trial, Billie—and illegal transplants now."

She nodded. "I guess I'm playing devil's advocate. I do keep feeling that, somehow, it is connected. But it's hard to see Vargas as…as the madman in my dreams!"

"Let's see this list he's giving us," Keenan said.

"Right," she murmured. But she had stopped listening to him. She was frowning intensely.

"Stacey?"

She looked at him.

"Did you hear that?"

"Hear what?"

"I could swear…there was a whisper."

He sat still, listening. Dr. Lawrence inside, talking to his housekeeper? No, all he heard was the wind.

"What did you hear?" he asked her.

She shook her head, as if confused, and then stood, walking down the path toward the street just a few feet.

He followed her. Closed his eyes. Was it the power of suggestion? Or did he really hear it? First, it sounded like one voice.
Soft, pathetic.

"Please...don't go."

Stacey looked at him. "Yes?"

The sound got louder.

Now, it was almost a chorus. A chorus of the dead. And he
was sure he heard it.

"Help!"

"Please."

"For the love of God!"

"It's the cemetery," he said. "I've found the dead usually are
fonder of hanging around places they enjoyed in life. We can
go over there..."

"We have to wait for Dr. Lawrence to give us his list. And
there's a wall and a gate, and it looks like it's locked."

"Stay here. I'll just cross over to the front," Keenan told her.
Then he spun and gave her a serious look.

"What?"

"Do not go back into that house. Do not go back in there
without me!"

She nodded.

He strode quickly down the driveway, hurrying across the
street.

It was a true country road: there was no traffic.

The wall that surrounded the cemetery was about waist-
high; he could easily leap it. The gate advised with iron writ-
ing above the iron bars that he had come to Mount Hope. The
date beneath was 1777.

He had a feeling that many graves within would be those of
Revolutionary War soldiers—maybe Confederate troops and
their loved ones had been buried there as well.

But a plaque advised that the cemetery was owned and op-
erated by the Catholic Church, and that tours were allowed

through arrangements with the parish. A phone number was listed as well.

Keenan had no problem with the idea of jumping the wall—easy enough to say that he had heard someone in distress from within.

But he paused outside.

The voices were gone.

"Hello?" he said quietly. "I'd like to help."

Nothing.

Then he heard something like a snort of disgust. "Not there, genius!"

He turned, realizing that the cries they'd been hearing weren't coming from the cemetery.

They were coming from the charming little copse next to the house. The outdoor sitting area with benches and large ceramic pots with flowering plants.

He started back across the street, and looking over at Stacey, he saw that she had made the same realization.

She was starting in that direction.

The door to the house opened, and Dr. Lawrence appeared.

"I have my list," he told them, and he frowned, looking at the two of them.

"Thank you!" Stacey said, making a quick turn.

Dr. Lawrence handed her the list. "There it is—take it. And please! I will greatly appreciate it if you would be kind enough to get the hell off my property!"

CHAPTER FIFTEEN

To Stacey's surprise, Keenan smiled at the doctor who was spewing anger at them now. He wanted them gone; he wanted to be left alone.

Keenan just nodded and headed to the car.

Worried, Stacey went quickly after him.

"Get in. Let's go," he said.

"What? We can't! I didn't just hear something, I saw a man. He hasn't been dead for centuries or even decades—the T-shirt he was wearing was from a band that's only a few years old. Keenan, there are dead people—newly dead people—back there somewhere—"

"And Dr. Lawrence asked us to get off his property. Without a search warrant, anything we find will be thrown out of court. Don't worry, I'm not leaving. Well, we are leaving. We're driving down the street and out of his sight. I'll call Jackson, and he'll get a warrant."

"Can we get a warrant at night like this? Keenan, those cries... that man..."

"Yes, the one who called me a genius for trying the cemetery first."

"You did see him."

"Perfectly."

"You've been far more suspicious of Henry Lawrence than me," she said. "But, Keenan, could he have buried those missing men—if they were murdered for their organs—on his own property? How stupid would that be?"

"Incredibly stupid. But he is a respected surgeon. Stacey, I don't know. What I do know is that he wanted us gone. And that he did do transplants. He could have known Billie back during the trial. She was in the seats watching, day after day. And he was there, testifying."

"He...can't be such a monster," Stacey said. "But then, someone is. We need to get back there now. But what will you say that can call for a search warrant?"

"That I heard screams."

"They won't find anyone. The dead were screaming."

"Yes. But Raina didn't go with Axel. We're going to get her and one of her cadaver dogs down with us when we have the warrant. The dogs will hone right in on a human body. And we will find out what has gone on here."

He pulled off the side of the road to make his calls back to headquarters.

"We have to wait," Keenan told her when he was done. "Jackson promised that he'll have a warrant for us within a few hours. They'll notify the local police, and he'll be here himself with Raina and one of her pups. She has the one dog that has been her pet forever that she adores, but she'll bring the German shepherds she's been working with for the DC police force—she's working with two dogs she seems to think have something special."

"Like we have something special?" she asked him dryly.

He smiled. "Dogs already use their instincts better than we do. Anyway, not to worry. We'll hover close. And they will get here with a warrant—traffic will have died down. It really won't be long." He sighed. "Wish we had someone else to keep an eye on the house. We could eat. Sit down in a restaurant with plates, maybe a massive steak or…"

Stacey laughed. "Don't get started; we have to stay here."

"For two hours," he said wearily. "In the car. Well, it's not like I haven't done the waiting and watching thing often. I just wish…"

"What?"

"That there was one more of us. We could get that steak."

"There isn't one more of us," Stacey said. "So, we sit. My angle is somewhat blocked by that stand of pines. Can you see the front of the house?"

"I can. I'll know if he comes or goes. Through the front, at least."

Stacey leaned back in her seat, as he was doing. He looked relaxed.

She knew his attention was on watching the house.

"If Dr. Lawrence is the killer, it can't be just him. There was a woman involved, we know that now," Stacey said. "Well, we've known that this can't be a one-man enterprise, anyway. But…he's all the way out in the country here. Are any of the women who are connected capable of doing this? Battle-Ax Agnes Merkle, for one, and then, the two wronged wives, Cindy Hardy and Sandra Smith. We can also try talking to Peggy Bronsen again, but the vibe I got when Agnes was talking about her was that the secretary was really jealous of the younger woman. Peggy is very attractive. If Smith is a womanizer, he may well have found her appealing—and asked her into his office more than Agnes."

"Peggy never said that he assaulted her or ever acted inappropriately."

"And I doubt that he did. He probably just enjoyed her appearance and her company." She looked at him worriedly. "She's still being protected, right?"

"Yes."

"So…maybe one of these women is working in conjunction with whoever the killer is. Or another woman entirely. Maybe… maybe our instincts are all off! Maybe Tania is really evil, and Jess Marlborough's roommates are terrible people, posing as desperate girls on the street just trying to get by. Nan could be pretty feisty!"

He gazed over at her. "Please don't drive yourself crazy, second-guessing your instincts for the next two hours."

She made a face at him. "You mean I don't drive you crazy?" she asked.

He smiled. "I don't think our instincts are that off. Cindy Hardy has been a question mark from the beginning. We still don't know who she was seeing."

"Maybe her mystery date is Dr. Henry Lawrence," Stacey said.

"Maybe."

"But they can't have seen each other since the night that Billie Bingham and Lindsey Green were killed. Someone would have seen her come and go. She's being watched."

"Burner phones. They can connect, and we have nothing," Keenan told her. "So, who is your money on?"

"Cindy Hardy," she said.

"She isn't very nice," he agreed.

"I'll bet you're thinking that it may well be Sandra Smith."

Keenan grimaced. "She isn't very nice, either. And Agnes is a total witch. Thing is, it's not illegal to be not nice. It's not even illegal to be downright mean. And we always have to be careful. Some of history's most heinous murderers have been able to charm people."

"Oh, true!" Stacey said. She fell thoughtfully silent for a bit. "Keenan, do you think that we're missing the boat entirely? We know—because of Bram—that there was a female involved. Logic tells us that there is more than one person involved, but only members of the Krewe would understand why we're convinced at least one of the players is a woman. And we could be wrong because Bram could have been wrong. But say that it is a woman. We're looking at nasty people. Do you think we could be fooled by that? Maybe Peggy was trying to make Colin Smith look bad, or maybe one of Jess's roommates sold her out?"

"We don't know, but they have been watched." He was quiet a minute. "I believe that Adam—" he made air quotes "—anonymously made sure that their rent was paid and he sent groceries—keeping them off the streets. And their pimp is still in jail, no bail, so if they are innocent, at least they're safe."

"But nothing has happened yet. I'm sure the killer is gearing up for his next strike."

"We work with what we have. And maybe we have something here."

"Maybe," she murmured. She glanced at him and grimaced, and then closed her eyes.

Waiting.

Watching.

Waiting.

It was certainly a very unglamorous part of the job. At least she was waiting with Keenan.

Even if it wasn't exactly quality time, she was still glad that she was sitting in a car with him. She could say whatever came into her mind. She could close her eyes and rest.

They were running on empty.

Just sitting still...

She closed her eyes.

Night was almost fully upon them. She was so ridiculously tired...

She drifted, and she began to dream.

This time, the dream went a little differently. She was in the room again. The fog was as thick as ever, swarming, moving as if it was something that lived and reeked of both a warning and a promise of evil. The killer was there.

He knew that she was there. And he was angry.

"Catch me when you can, Stacey."

He knew her name. He spoke to her from the depth of the shadows, calling her by name.

"Catch me when you can!" he said, repeating the phrase from a Jack the Ripper letter, real or hoax, that answer never known.

"If you can, Stacey…"

Her name was a hiss. And something about the sound made her nerves leap to life and fear invade her.

"Stacey! Stacey!"

She heard her name again, this time spoken firmly and tenderly. She opened her eyes.

Keenan had leaned over to draw her against him.

She straightened up, not awkward about him holding her but embarrassed that she had fallen asleep in the car again.

"Wow. I'm sorry."

"Did you see something? About this place?" he asked her.

"No," she told him, letting out a long sigh. "I was in that damned room again—and I can't see. With the killer who I can't see, and the victim I can't see."

"I know you're frustrated," he told her. "And I know your dreams are disturbing. But there is a bright spot to your sleeping."

"There is?"

"Yep. They got the warrant. Adam knows every judge in DC, Virginia, West Virginia and Maryland. Jackson is coming with Angela and Raina—with the local police department on call, though the sergeant Jackson talked to was apparently dubious that they'd be needed. Dr. Lawrence is a fine surgeon, you know."

"And maybe he is," Stacey said.

"What did you see in the room this time? Anything new?"

"The killer saw me, talked to me—he was saying, 'Catch me when you can'."

"Pulled out of a letter sent to London police," Keenan said.

"And he addressed me," Stacey said. "By name."

He pulled her close to him, despite the bucket seats. "I know it's disturbing. But we know that he knows your name. He sent you the kidney."

She nodded. "He's so smug, Keenan. Are we completely on the wrong trail?"

"No. I don't believe that we are," he told her.

It had grown dark. A light was shining on Dr. Lawrence's front lawn. It barely reached into the trees and the benches at the side of the house.

"Has…anyone appeared? Said anything else?" she asked.

"The fellow who called me a genius?" he asked dryly.

She smiled. "Anyone?"

He shook his head. "They must think that we've driven away—I wanted to be out of sight, and I didn't want to be seen walking around. Once the warrant gets here, anything that we find will be legal."

"Do you think that the ghost in the T-shirt and jeans is one of the men on a missing-persons report?"

"I think it's likely," Keenan said. He smiled at her. "I know you've been through these dreams before. And you're an excellent partner, an amazing rookie. But might they get to be too much for you?"

She looked at him smiling and slowly shook her head. "No. I'm ready to dream more. And listen more, open up to all possibilities."

"Cool," he said, still evidently a bit confused.

"I talked to Raina today. She made me feel more grateful for being…weird, or gifted. Take your pick!"

"I say *gifted*," he told her.

"They're coming," she said.

"Jackson and team? I don't see lights—"

"No, the ghosts are coming, heading this way, out of the forest."

She smiled at him.

Open up.

She had done so, and she had *sensed* that they were being sought, and when she had turned, she had seen them.

Four men. One was in a polo shirt and khakis. Their leader was the man in the jeans and rock-band T-shirt. One was in a short-sleeved cotton shirt and cargo shorts, and the last was in jeans and a T-shirt that advertised a theme park. They were all in their twenties or early thirties.

Keenan and Stacey both got out of the car.

"See, they didn't run!" the young man in the cargo shorts said.

"And they see us!" the theme-park-T-wearing man said.

"We're FBI. Trying not to be seen waiting," Keenan informed them. "And we are assuming that something damned bad happened to you and that's why you're hanging around. You're buried on these grounds somewhere?"

"Hey, so, he is a genius!" rock-band man said.

"You are buried here," Stacey said. "D-did Dr. Lawrence kill you?"

"Don't know. Here's what's sad," rock-band man said, and he looked at Keenan as if he was a bit embarrassed by having behaved like a jerk. "Not one of us knows what happened to us. We were attacked. Jumped. Each of us! Then, a searing pain in the head. Blackness…falling, falling, falling…into a whirling pit of darkness. And then, here…and, miraculously, finding one another."

"It's horrible. Not a clue. We don't know what happened," the cargo-shorts man said. He had dark hair with a clipped, businesslike cut. He seemed to be the oldest in the group, but at that, not much past thirty if he had even reached the triple decade mark.

"We just woke up here," the fellow in the polo shirt said. He was fit; he might have been playing polo or some other sport before he was taken by surprise. "We don't even know just where the hell we are!"

"How we got here, and how on earth we are...what we are," rock-band man said.

"Just blackness," Cargo Shorts said.

"We're getting good," Rock Band told them. "We can get around—we've gotten to know one another. Kinda cool—if we're crossing the road and a car comes, it doesn't matter." He winced, shaking his head. "We are aware that we are deceased. I've tried to learn to open the mailbox, but I can't quite do it. So we don't have an address."

"You're in Virginia, just northwest of Richmond," Stacey said. "I'm Stacey Hanson, and this is Keenan Wallace."

"Oh! Sorry. Let me make introductions," Rock Band said quickly.

He was Tim Dougherty, Polo Shirt was George Seasons, Cargo Shorts was Ronnie Gleason and Theme Park was Harvey Ryan. They introduced themselves and started to offer their hands.

Keenan and Stacey shook them...in a way.

"So, you're out here, I take it," Tim Dougherty said, "because the doctor who lives in that house might be the one who murdered us?"

"Talk about a genius," George Seasons said, grinning, his smile taking the sting out of his words. "This is his property."

"And when have you ever seen him out in the yard?" Harvey Ryan asked.

"Do you know when you were buried?" Keenan asked. "Was it together, or one at a time? Do you know anything?"

"I know I was on vacation," George said. "I had a few too many at a bar near Lafayette Square. Then, like Tim said, sudden pain. Blackness...and then waking up or whatever to find

Tim staring at me. Then, pain again," he added softly. "Realizing I was dead."

"I'm so sorry," Stacey murmured.

"You think that maybe we're here," Ronnie Gleason said, "because…it was so sudden. So unfair. Then again, I like you guys, but man… I'm not sure I want to spend eternity hanging out with you in a little bit of forest."

"Hey, these guys see us. They must know something. Are we…stuck here?" George asked anxiously. "It could be worse. I mean, I don't mind being…well, something. But I don't particularly like it being here."

"If we tried to leave the area, would we go up in dust, disappear, cease to be?" Harvey asked.

"We don't really have all the answers," Keenan said.

"And maybe you are here to help us," Stacey said. "We would have driven away with nothing, but you called out to us."

"Yeah, forgive me for that 'genius' thing," Tim said to Keenan.

"Not a problem."

"Do you know what happened to us?" Ronnie asked.

"To be honest, since your bodies have never been found, I believe you're all still listed as missing persons. We don't know what happened to you. We are out here because of some vicious murders that have taken place in the DC area. A killer the media has dubbed the Yankee Ripper."

"Ripper…like Jack the Ripper?" Ronnie asked.

"Yeah. Like Jack the Ripper," she said.

"But none of us was a prostitute," Harvey said. "Not that men can't be, I mean. We couldn't have been killed by the same killer, right? This had to be something else."

"Great. Another serial killer. Does it really matter?" Tim asked, adding glumly, "Dead is dead…and we're dead."

Harvey looked at Keenan. "Jack the Ripper gutted people, right?"

Keenan and Stacey glanced at one another.

"Uh, yes," Stacey said.

"Were we...gutted?" George Seasons asked, looking glum.

"We don't know since we haven't found your bodies yet," Keenan said.

"Go find them! Maybe if we get real burials, we get to go to...well, heaven," George said. "I... Yeah, I believe in heaven. Something more. More than this!"

"We don't have that kind of answer," Stacey said softly.

"But you'll go get our bodies, right?" Tim said.

"Yes, but if we go before our warrant gets here... Well, it gets complicated in court. With a search warrant, everything we find is admissible—"

"If you found a body, it wouldn't be admissible?" Tim demanded.

They didn't have to answer. Keenan saw headlights coming down the road.

"Our team is here. They'll serve the warrant," Keenan said.

"Should we...go away? Hide?" Harvey asked nervously.

"We're ghosts. Why the hell would we hide?" Tim said wearily. "They can't see us anyway."

Keenan looked at Stacey; they both grinned.

"Actually, these people will see you just fine," Stacey assured them.

"You mean..." Ronnie began, "you have more people coming who will see us?"

"Exactly," Keenan said.

"Where have you been all our lives?" Ronnie asked.

"You mean, where have they been all our deaths?" Tim said, shaking his head.

A car pulled ahead of Keenan's. The doors opened. Jackson stepped out of the driver's side, Angela from the passenger's side, and Raina—with two huge, handsome German shepherds emerging with her as well.

"Dogs!" Harvey said with pleasure.

"Must be cadaver dogs," Tim told him. "But yes, please, bring them on!"

"Hey, guys," Angela said, waving. Raina was making sure that her dogs were behaved and under control, paying attention to her.

Jackson called out to them. "I'm heading straight to the house with the warrant."

"We'll get moving!" Keenan called to him. Angela and Raina were both staring at the ghosts. One of the dogs barked.

"Angela, Raina, please meet Tim, Ronnie, Harvey, and George. Guys, that's Jackson heading to the house. Now we can find your bodies," Keenan told them.

"Dogs!" Harvey said. "I have always loved dogs!"

"Brutus and Butch," Raina said, introducing the dogs. "We'll get off the road, and I'll let them loose. They're not quite done with training, but they'll find you!"

"They're beautiful!" Stacey said. "Is it okay to say hi?"

"Today? Yes. Usually, I'd say no, as they need to concentrate. But these are still learners, and it would be good for them to recognize you as a friend. Won't hurt to give him one of these treats," Raina said, handing her a handful of little nuggets. "They'll love you more."

Stacey hunkered down to talk to the dogs, thanking them for their help.

"That way, in the trees, I believe, just beyond the cozy little garden sitting spot…where no one ever sits," Tim told Raina.

"Fine. Let's see what these boys can find."

They moved in. She gave the dogs their freedom.

Brutus, nose sweeping the ground in front of him, headed right for the area that Tim had indicated.

Butch did not. He ran farther into the forest.

"I'm after him!" Stacey said, heading after the dog like a bolt of lightning, calling out, "It's good he likes me."

"No! Not alone, you're not!" Keenan yelled after her. "Even with the dog!"

But she was moving. She knew he would race after her and be glad that he had very long legs.

They didn't have to go far.

The dog was on to something.

A corpse, Stacey thought. Because Butch wasn't fully trained, but he did know what he was looking for.

Butch was already digging furiously in the ground.

Stacey watched him.

The dog was barking and barking. Stacey glanced back at Keenan and then at the dog. "Oh, we have to stop him! It's a—"

Crime scene.

"Butch!" she said firmly, walking forward to grab the dog's lead. "That's enough, boy. You've done your duty! Good dog!" She petted him and praised him and gave him some of the little dog treats that were his reward for a job well done.

The dog whined and obediently sat.

Keenan strode forward to the spot where the dog had been digging.

"I think that Tim knew where their bodies were," Stacey said. "But Butch hasn't graduated yet, so maybe—"

"Butch did just fine," Keenan told her.

"Well, I mean, of course he did. He's a dog, and—"

"Stacey, no," he told her, redirecting her attention. "There's more than one burial site here. Look."

And then she saw the forearm and hand sticking out of the dirt, bone glowing, patches of flesh having rotted away.

CHAPTER SIXTEEN

The night was alive with lights now, and people.

There were far more than four bodies to be discovered.

Keenan stood with Stacey, aware that the four ghosts stood just behind them, watching all that went on as well.

The bodies were in various stages of decomposition. Some were little more than bone fragments; others retained flesh. All had been covered in lye to help with the process—*dust to dust*.

The dogs found another spot in the woods, and then another.

Jackson had duly served the warrant—to the housekeeper, not Dr. Lawrence. His housekeeper had been completely flustered.

She couldn't find Dr. Lawrence. He had apparently suspected he was being watched, slipped out the back and made his way through the heavier woods behind his house.

A manhunt was on.

As the hours went on toward morning, the area was flooded with police officers and agents, then the medical examiners and, finally, forensic anthropologists.

Angela remained with the housekeeper; the woman appeared to be at a total loss. She swore she'd thought that Dr. Lawrence had been working in his study. She'd had no clue that he'd left.

He couldn't have gone far. He only kept the one automobile. It remained in the driveway.

Because of the scope of the investigation, Dr. Beau Simpson was called down, along with Dr. Bowen out of Alexandria. Detectives Fred Crandall and Jean Channing arrived.

Something big had broken.

"That's… I think they found me," George Seasons murmured. "I'm…bone. Bits of bone. I guess… I guess I've been here a long time."

"I'm still rotting," Tim Dougherty said. He sounded angry.

"But you've been found," Stacey said gently.

Dr. Beau Simpson had hunkered down by a grave in the woods closest to the house where it seemed that Ronnie and George and Tim had been buried.

Beau stood and looked at Keenan and Stacey grimly, brushing the dirt off his knees with gloved hands. "At this moment, we believe we're going to find over a dozen bodies, several male, but there are young women here, too. Bones and bone fragments…and, trust me, enough so that this county is more than happy to have federal intervention and help from anywhere." He hesitated, looking at them. "The bodies are so decomposed, it's hard to say…but on a few, yes…it appears that vital organs have been removed. Cause of death, from what I've ascertained so far, appears to be blunt trauma to the head. This is preliminary, of course, but the damage on some of the skulls is evident."

"Oh, Lord!" Tim whispered behind Keenan.

"So, it seems that this has been going on a long time—murder committed to steal organs, most probably for illegal transplants," Keenan said.

"Either that," Beau agreed, "or we have a tribe of cannibals who aren't interested in consuming anything other than human organs."

"That's sick!" George breathed behind Keenan.

Yes, sick. But so was killing one man to *possibly* let another one live.

"This is amazing, what you've discovered," Beau told Stacey. "Now, if they can just find Dr. Lawrence and bring him in…"

He turned away and headed back to the closest patch of graves.

"You have to catch that bastard!" Tim said, pain in the whisper of his voice. "Oh, God! All these people. Me!"

"He's out in the woods. So are dozens of police officers and agents. He will be caught," Keenan said. But he was restless. He knew that other law enforcement—good cops, good agents—were on the hunt. He and Stacey had done their part.

But he couldn't just wait any longer. No, he didn't know these woods or anything about the surrounding homes or estates—all of them on good stretches of property. But he couldn't stand still.

He turned to Stacey. "Listen, I'm going to—"

"Not without me," she said.

"Stacey…"

"I move damned fast, and you know it. Please, Keenan! I'll never have any peace. If we can get Henry Lawrence…just get him locked up…maybe the dream will stop because we have taken the steps to change what might have happened."

He looked at her skeptically.

"We'll take Butch," she suggested.

"Butch is busy—"

"No, they're trying to make sure that the dogs don't disrupt the scenes now. Brutus will stay with Raina and be here if they need him. Butch can come with us."

"All right, all right, wait!" Keenan said. He strode over toward the closer gravesite. Raina stood there with the dogs, behind the work being done by Beau, Dr. Bowen and the local ME.

"Bodies are fresh enough here—forensic anthropologists are deeper in the woods, places Stacey and the dog found," Beau said.

Keenan knew not to come too close while the MEs were still

working. "Right," he said, and then he called to Raina. "May I borrow Butch?"

"Sure," she said. "Butch, go on."

She released the dog's leash. Somewhat to Keenan's annoyance, the dog ran toward him, and then past him, making his way straight to Stacey.

"Which way?" Stacey asked him.

"Maybe we should ask Butch."

"Maybe. He's being trained as a cadaver dog, but he's also had general search training. Let's get something from the house, something with Henry Lawrence's scent on it."

He left her with the dog and strode quickly to the house. Angela opened the door.

"I need something of Lawrence's," he told her.

Angela quickly understood. There was a jacket hanging on a hook by the door. She called to the housekeeper. "This is the doctor's, right?"

"Yes, ma'am. Oh, yes, ma'am, oh... I just don't believe this! Dr. Lawrence. And I live in this house—with him. Oh! Maybe I should thank God for my age...or..."

She was going on. Angela handed the jacket to Keenan. "Mrs. Tremblay is going to need a sedative," she said. She smiled grimly. "Go."

He hurried back to Stacey, who had, thankfully, waited. The ghosts of the four men buried on the property stood behind her.

"We're going to get him," Keenan assured them. "Look at the officers running around—he can't escape this kind of a dragnet."

"Thank you," Tim said, and the others nodded.

"All right, Butch, which way?" Stacey asked, loosening the big shepherd's leash.

Butch sniffed the jacket and barked.

His nose toward the ground, he started off as if he was headed back to the known burial site.

Then, he turned so suddenly that he almost lifted Stacey off the ground.

"Hey, I can take the leash—" Keenan began.

But she was already running with the dog.

He followed.

Butch ran up and down along the road, sniffing at the many cars parked there now.

Then, he barked and tugged against his leash to cross the street.

It was close to 3:00 a.m. There were no cars on the street. Stacey let the dog lead her across the road to the old cemetery, Mount Hope. Butch went to the gate, barking.

"How the hell could Dr. Lawrence have gotten across the street without us seeing?" Keenan wondered aloud. "All this commotion, but…"

"But?" Stacey asked. Butch was trying to get through the iron grill of the gate; the bars were a little too close together.

"If he ran south, the road takes a little bend. He could have crossed there, and we don't know if the entire place is walled or gated, and even if it is, it's easy enough hop over."

"For you, maybe," Stacey said. "Probably for me. But… Butch?"

"Butch can jump it. Here, I'll give you a hike."

He was glad of his hours at the gym; Stacey wasn't heavy, but he was boosting her straight up to sit on top of the wall.

Butch had evidently decided that Stacey was his master. He jumped at the wall, once, twice, and then he backed up, eyeing it, then came back running and made a flying leap.

He cleared it.

Keenan jumped up after the dog.

The cemetery was shrouded in darkness with only the multitude of lights from the Lawrence estate stretching over it to provide any kind of visibility.

"Butch?" Keenan said.

Butch barked. Stacey and Keenan drew out their penlights together and started into the darkness of the cemetery.

"Be careful," he warned, almost tripping over a stone broken so that only an inch or two of it remained, hidden by the grass surrounding it.

He shone his light the best he could.

Butch and Stacey were moving, quickly.

He kept pace, reminding himself that Stacey had passed the academy; she had a gun, and she knew how to shoot.

But someone involved in this knew her and might well have it out for her. They passed tombs and stones and came to a site where a large cement flag played over a group of graves. Behind it was a holding house, a place for the dead to rest when the ground was frozen and graves couldn't be dug. Life-sized angels with chipped wings and noses stood guard.

Butch stopped there, barking.

Where a door to the holding house had once been, there was nothing. Not even a gate. Butch sniffed at the entry, whining.

"Watch the door—and my back," Keenan said, heading into the house.

He had barely crossed the threshold when he heard a thudding sound.

And then Stacey's voice. "Don't! Don't make a move. It will not break my heart if I have to shoot you, Dr. Lawrence."

Keenan stepped back out of the house.

Stacey had her weapon trained on Lawrence. He stared at her; he was dusty and dirty, and his eyes were bright, as if the very pale light there had captured the glow within them.

"No, no, no—you don't understand! I didn't do this—I swear to you, someone has been using my land. I'm innocent, I swear it!"

"There may be two dozen bodies—*on your land*—but you're innocent?" Keenan demanded.

He saw then what had caused the thump. An angel's head lay on the ground. He saw that Tim Dougherty's ghost was standing behind Dr. Lawrence, and Tim was looking very proud of himself.

"I didn't do this! I didn't kill anyone!" Lawrence cried again.

"On your knees, hands behind your back, please," Keenan said.

"I didn't do this!"

"Then, why did you run?" Stacey demanded.

"Because…because I panicked. I saw you people coming back, saw that the other guy had an envelope, and I just… I panicked."

Keenan cuffed him as he spoke and drew him back to his feet.

"I didn't do this!"

"Dr. Lawrence, your guilt or innocence isn't up to us," Stacey told him. "That will all be up to a jury of your peers. I'm assuming you have a good lawyer. Make sure it's a criminal lawyer. Let's go!"

Keenan led Lawrence, reading him his rights as they went.

Stacey hung back a step. He heard her whisper, "Thank you!"

She was speaking to the ghost of Tim Dougherty.

The ghost replied, "No. Thank you."

He went back across the street.

Jackson was talking with the local authorities; it was decided that it would be a federal case, and a federal arrest.

Dr. Lawrence would be held back in DC.

Keenan was glad to turn him over to Jackson.

"We can go home now," he told Stacey.

She nodded. "We can go home," she said.

In the car, she was silent a long time. He thought she might fall asleep again as he drove. But then she turned to him. "Keenan, it isn't over. Not unless Lawrence talks. You don't think he can be innocent, do you?"

"Let's see. He was a transplant doctor. Dozens of bodies found, and it's looking like they'll discover that the organs were taken.

Half of them were on his property—half in the forested area beyond. What do you think?"

"He didn't do it alone."

"We're going to have to hope to hell that he talks, and faced with the death penalty, he may choose to do just that. Stacey, it's after four in the morning. It will be close to six by the time we get back. We need to rest. To sleep."

"'Perchance to dream,'" she murmured.

"I hope that, at least tonight, you don't dream."

She smiled at him. "One night would be nice. And we do have Dr. Lawrence."

"We do," he agreed.

"But it isn't over," she said softly.

"No, but I do believe we've begun the ending," he said, and he cast her a smile. "I wonder if anyone is going to have hitch-hiking ghosts."

"Pardon?"

"Tim, Ronnie, George, Harvey—those guys aren't going to want to hang around where they were."

"Do you think they'll get to move on?" Stacey asked. "Now that Lawrence is in custody."

"I don't know, Stacey. I honestly don't know." He glanced her way with a frown. "What happened tonight? Lawrence didn't just walk right up to you, did he?"

She shook her head. "He was carrying something…a broken piece of funerary art."

"An angel's head."

"He might have meant…well, he might have meant to crown me with it, though it would have been stupid, since you were right there. Tim followed us. He may not be able to open a mailbox, but he managed to scuff some stones on the ground. I heard Lawrence coming and was spinning around. I don't think he would have gotten me, but I know that Tim believes he was helpful. And I'm happy for him to believe that he saved me, be-cause…he needs to believe that he mattered."

He squeezed her hand.

"You are the best rookie. Ever," he told her.

She smiled and leaned back. Her eyes closed. In a few min-utes, she appeared to be asleep.

At this time of night, the drive back wasn't as bad as the drive there, and he made it right before six.

Stacey seemed to have slept easily. Keenan nudged her gen-tly to wake her.

Her eyes opened. She stared at him for a minute. Then she smiled. "Keenan, I didn't dream!"

"No, you didn't dream. Let's get in for some real sleep. What do you say?"

She nodded and opened her door. They walked the path to her house, and she pulled out her keys.

The door swung open. Marty was there, looking at them anxiously. "Oh! I was so worried about you!"

"We're fine, Marty," Stacey said.

"There was someone out there again," Marty said. "Sneaking around the house. I was worried. I couldn't sleep."

"We're here now."

"I called the local police, and they did come. But they didn't find anything. They thought I was a crazy woman. They told me that it was legal for people to walk on the sidewalk. They said that our neighbors were probably out. But I could feel it, you know? Someone was sneaking around. Where have you been?"

Keenan reckoned that one thing about making a discovery out on a country road meant that the media hadn't had a chance to seize on it yet.

"Working, Marty," he said pleasantly. "We desperately need some sleep. It's day—hey, nothing happens by day, right?" he said.

That wasn't true.

But they had to escape Marty.

She nodded and swallowed. "Okay, the door is locked. The alarm is back on. I'm glad you're safe. Good night."

"Thank you, good night," Stacey said.

Marty headed up the stairs. They watched her go, and Stacey opened the door to her apartment, walking in with an exhausted sigh.

"I'm so tired!" she murmured.

"You go have the first shower."

"Not on your life," she told him. She swirled and smiled and kissed his lips.

They showered. They held close; they made love.

Seconds after, she was asleep.

He let himself drift off as well, ever aware of her, even while he slept.

No alarm rang; there was nothing they had to do early. They would have a go at Dr. Lawrence themselves, but they knew that others would be handling him as he sat in jail.

Jackson would talk to him early, and then maybe Angela.

The MEs and forensic anthropologists and dozens of CSIs would be busy.

But they could sleep late.

It was almost noon when he felt Stacey stirring and he opened his own eyes.

She kissed his lips quickly and gave him a brilliant smile.

"I slept, Keenan. I slept so well. I didn't dream. Do you think that means..."

"I'm so glad you had a good night's sleep," he told her softly. "I don't know what it means." He shrugged, not wanting to ruin her morning.

He knew that they were just beginning.

And she knew that, too. But for the moment, they could be pleased with the night that had passed.

"It means breakfast!" he said. "I'm starving."

"Me, too."

She leaped happily out of bed. She left the room just seconds before his phone rang.

It was Jackson.

And, as Keenan had expected, the end was just beginning.

Stacey wanted to make omelets; Keenan was happy to chop up tomatoes and peppers to go in them and grate cheese.

They enjoyed the meal, managing to talk about something other than the case for a bit.

But the case was an elephant in the room. And with breakfast enjoyed and over, they left for the office.

"So much will happen today—mediawise," Keenan told her as they locked up.

"Of course. People... Well, the media is important. When it isn't skewed."

"It's always skewed these days."

"I don't think that this is the kind of thing anyone needs to skew," she told him. "Wouldn't it be great if Dr. Lawrence did just start talking?"

"It would be great," Keenan agreed. "But unlikely to happen."

"He knows he could face the death penalty."

"He's still claiming innocence. I talked to Jackson; he was with him this morning. He sent Angela in. He still claims that he had no idea that people were planting bodies on his property. We've questioned the housekeeper. She was terrified and panicked and so was given some sedatives. She also swears that she knew nothing about the bodies. And she's lived on the property for about a year, though she goes on weekends to stay with her niece. The bodies were buried deep enough to keep them from being disturbed by animals. Most were covered with lye, but... I'm not an ME. Beau Simpson is the best, and he's seen enough to believe that the organs were definitely taken from them."

"So—we get a crack at Dr. Lawrence, too?" Stacey asked.

"Oh, yes. Separately, I think. Then maybe together. We'll see."

Jackson Crow was holding the press conference right when they arrived; news was seeping out about the many bodies that had been found on the property of the very respected Dr. Henry Lawrence.

Jackson could handle a press conference like no one else.

Yes, Dr. Lawrence was being held. He was being held, at the moment, but they needed to remember that while he would probably face many charges, he would have his day in court.

Reporters asked him dozens of questions; he fielded them all well. The discovery was so new and so much was still under investigation that he couldn't say that indeed, the Yankee Ripper had been caught or even that these were the bodies related to the murders that had taken place in DC and Northern Virginia. The case was, he repeated several times, still under investigation.

Stacey and Keenan arrived at their office in time to sneak around the growing crowd and watch the press conference from the television in the conference room.

When Jackson came back upstairs, he met with them there.

"From the preliminaries we have so far, it definitely appears that these murders were committed to acquire the organs from the victims. Here's where I'm curious. We found many men. But also young women. Why did this killer go from secretive attacks on these people—quick killing, quick removal of organs—to making such a display with his so-called Ripper victims?"

"Is it even the same killer?" Stacey mused. "I mean, one would hope that an operation like this is the only one in existence, but..."

"We know we're looking for more than one person," Keenan said. "Dr. Lawrence has to talk to us. Maybe once we have identified the bodies and hopefully placed him with at least one or two of them in the same place at the same time, he'll realize that he's really in trouble."

Stacey frowned and said, "Billie Bingham."

Keenan and Jackson both looked at her.

"Billie Bingham. She was at the trial. Maybe she met Lawrence then. But maybe, just maybe, they had a falling out. And he wanted to get rid of her, but Billie Bingham was a public figure. There would have been tons of media attention if she had just disappeared. Make it look like she was a victim of a crazed killer, and no one would look for the others, those without family to hound law enforcement to the ground over them being missing. Or those who were just down-and-out. I mean, it may be a bit out there, but she was at the trial."

Keenan looked at Jackson. "Right. It may be far out there, but so is everything that has to do with this case. Forensic accounting could go over her books again. I'm assuming she's been audited many times and that she had a way to keep her cash-flow documents, but there might be something there to indicate that she was financially gaining from all of this."

"I'll get people on her financials again," Jackson said.

"And Lindsey Green in her basement—Raina felt something from her at the morgue. She didn't know who had killed her. A surprise attack from behind," Keenan said. He inhaled and said, "Maybe Billie was the one to kill her. She'd be waiting for someone to get the body and expecting that another woman would be killed that night so that the supposed Ripper would have his Elizabeth Stride and Catherine Eddowes victims. Naturally, she'd never expect that her killer meant for her to be the ripped-up Catherine Eddowes victim."

"It's possible, certainly. Billie's assistant had no idea that anyone else was in the house," Jackson said.

"Right," Keenan said. "Well, we're going to go and take our cracks at Dr. Henry Lawrence."

"I'll get Forensics working," Jackson told them. "Good luck."

They walked down the hall to the interrogation room.

"It's a good theory. The more I think about it, the more the theory makes sense," Keenan said.

"That this whole elaborate scheme to kill prostitutes was a way to get rid of Billie Bingham?" Stacey asked him.

"Quite possibly. But still, say Billie was in on it. Billie was dead and set up in Lafayette Square when Bram thought that he heard a man and a woman arguing. If everything we've heard about Billie is true, she might have wanted a bigger share of the money," Keenan said.

"Maybe. Are you going to ask Dr. Lawrence about it?" she asked him. "Or am I?"

"Hmm. What do you think? Is he going to respond better to you because you were, in your way, involved with the Mc-Carron trial?"

"Doctors can have god complexes. Feeling superior. Maybe he'll respond better to a dude who is almost six and a half feet tall."

"I say we still go in separately, and we both bring up Billie's name."

"He already told us there were dozens of people there. And that's true."

"Doesn't matter. He's going to be tired. He's been stripped of his finery. Maybe he'll feel more like talking. We'll both come at him."

They turned in their weapons, signed in and were escorted to a holding cell. The guard bringing them in said that Fred Crandall was in the viewing room; he had been watching Henry Lawrence since he'd been brought to the interrogation room.

"You first—memory lane," Keenan decided. "I'll see if Fred has gleaned any more information since last night."

"As you wish," Stacey said.

Keenan slipped into the viewing room, nodding to Fred.

"A hell of a thing!" Fred told him. "I stayed until about five in the morning. I figured we were on to something complicated, but man...that was a damned body farm. How the hell did you get on to all those bodies?"

"The earth just looked…odd. I asked Jackson to arrange for dogs. And well, you know the story from there."

Fred was a good guy, but if Keenan had told him that the ghost of one of the victims had come after him, he might have reported Keenan as needing a psych evaluation.

"By the way, where's Jean? Thought your respective precincts decided you two needed to pair up for this."

"They did, and we did. Jean was out there with me. I'm still geared up—wanted to watch you questioning this guy and thought it was better you two than me. Always thought I could go in with Jean and I'd remind him he could face DC charges and she could remind him that he'd also face federal charges— and the Commonwealth of Virginia, if he was wavering. She'll be here in a bit; she thinks it might be nothing, but she went to see a woman who called her precinct this morning. In the task-force meetings, we were talking about those who'd fallen off transplant lists. Could be a fluke or a fake. You know how many calls we get."

"It could be important. When did this call come?" Keenan asked him. He looked through the viewing window. Stacey was just sitting down with Henry Lawrence.

The doctor was staring at her as if he'd like to slice and dice her. He was tired, aggravated, and looked as if he'd been forced to roll in the mud.

"Dr. Lawrence," Stacey said.

"I've been set up," he told her.

"But you're a transplant doctor."

"I was a transplant doctor."

"You know how to transplant human organs. Tough science. In fact, I don't know how you've been pulling it off. But then, you must think that you pick up throwaway people and their lives don't matter. Still, you must make sure that your wealthy clients live. I mean, if you're going to get paid, right?"

"Idiot woman!" he said. "I told you—I don't do transplants

anymore. Everything you're saying is untrue. You can't just grab anyone."

"But you can go for the young and healthy and hope for the best, right?" she asked.

"I keep telling you—"

"But you did know Billie Bingham."

He sighed. "Look, I don't even live in DC. And whether I was ugly as sin or not, I'm a surgeon. I'd never need an escort service. I'm a surgeon."

"Billie wasn't the famous Billie Bingham, back in the day of the McCarron trial."

He sighed again. "My lawyer is going to dice you people to pieces," he said.

"Dice. Interesting choice of word," Stacey said. She stood. "Well, enjoy your accommodations!"

"Wait! Wait. You should believe me. You, of all people. Your father was important in that trial. You know that I was devastated. That I tried to save Dr. Vargas... Hey! Don't you walk out on me!"

Stacey walked out.

She joined Keenan and Fred in the observation room.

"Your turn," she told Keenan.

"You got a rise out of him," Fred told her.

"But no confession, no names."

"I'll take a different tack, ask him who he thinks might be setting him up, who might be involved."

Keenan walked in to talk to Henry Lawrence.

"What is this? Musical cops? You know your boss was in this morning. You can ask me questions from here to eternity. I didn't do it."

"I just find it hard to believe that you didn't know that Billie Bingham was in the courtroom during the McCarron trial. She was beautiful—staid-looking at the time, but young and very beautiful. She had to have caught your attention," Keenan said.

"I'm a surgeon. Women flock to me," he said.

Beyond a doubt, the man was a narcissist.

"Then again, all those bodies. Right under your nose. It's difficult to believe all those people were buried and you had no clue."

"I have an office and long hours at the hospital. When I'm home, I'm holed up—sleeping, working or relaxing. I'm not staring at the woods."

Keenan felt his phone vibrate in his pocket. It was Stacey, texting him.

He got up and went to the door of the interrogation room.

"Hey! Don't leave me just sitting here for hours! I'm a surgeon!"

Keenan turned back. "I know lots of surgeons. Good men and women, good surgeons. And you know what? They don't behave as if they're superior to others. They like helping people, curing them, making them better. I even know a few who are lamenting on a Saturday night that they don't have dates. News flash, guy. You're not that special."

"Why you—"

Keenan didn't hear the rest; he let the door clang shut and strode into the observation room to see why Stacey had been beckoning him.

"What's up?"

"Jean thinks a woman who called in about being approached by strange people is the real deal. She was offended that anyone would think that she would accept a heart without it being in her hospital with her doctors, or that she consider taking a heart if it was from a questionable source. I think we should join Jean. Fred is going to stay here; he may go in eventually, when Dr. Lawrence is really getting impatient," Stacey said.

"If that works for you," Fred told him.

"I don't think we were getting anything out of him anyway," Keenan said, "but he did give me an idea."

"Oh?"

"Tell you on the way. It was a long night, but it's going to be a longer day."

They headed out. "Curious?" Keenan said as he drove.

"What's that? And what's your plan?"

He glanced her way. "Oh, I guess most areas are like this. We're on our way to a mansion, which is near the alley where Jess Marlborough, her friends and her pimp spent their days working. Mansions, hovels. All within a stone's throw."

"Any big area is going to have those with money and those without."

"Right. But it makes me think. This area just isn't that big. Anyway, let's see what this woman has told Jean and find out how viable the information might be!"

They were a large highway away from the down-and-out region where Jess Marlborough had plied her trade—six lanes and then several blocks before they reached an area of impressive single-family homes—with single families still living in them, in contrast to the many old mansions that now housed four or more apartments.

They parked behind Jean's unmarked sedan and headed up the walk.

Detective Jean Channing met them at the door.

"I don't know how much this can help us, but Mrs. Kendrick—Anita Kendrick—called after seeing the news from last night. A few weeks back, she was approached by a woman in a coffee shop. The woman wanted to let her know that she didn't have to wait and die. For the right price, she could receive a good, young heart almost immediately. Come in, come in, she's a lovely woman," Jean told them. "Through here. She's in what she calls her small parlor."

They went in, walking through the foyer, a large parlor with a huge hearth and through a door to a smaller sitting area. Anita Kendrick was sitting on her sofa, drinking tea. Chairs were grouped close, and a table sat near her perch and bore medications and water bottles, and anything the woman might need seemed within easy reach. She didn't rise to greet them.

"Forgive me. Some days I am stronger than others. I'm feeling a bit tired," she told them from her chair. "Please, sit, join us."

"You were approached by someone suggesting they could get you a healthy heart transplant?" Stacey asked, after she and Keenan had introduced themselves.

"I just didn't—well, I couldn't believe that it was serious! I was in the coffee shop. My niece was with me that day. She'd helped me out—they do have transportation from the medical center, but Elinor is so sweet, and I love seeing her, and she's happy to take me. But after my appointment—it was a good day—we stopped for a snack at the café. And while Elinor was at the counter, this woman came up, and of course, I was polite, thinking she needed help, and she told me she could get me a heart. I shouldn't die—'a woman of my class'—and hearts were available! I mean, she might have followed me from the cardiologist, but how she would know...?"

"What did you do?"

"Well, I stared at her. I thought it was a joke. I said that I was on a list—a just list, a good list. And she actually said that some people deserved to be in the world, and others just didn't. I still thought it was a come-on to get money in some way, so, I said that I was calling the police. And then, naturally, she ran away. And I didn't think anything of it—even when those poor women were being butchered—because I couldn't believe anyone could be killing to steal organs!" She was truly indignant.

Anita smiled at them. "I'm in my late sixties; I'd love to have more years. But I've had a beautiful life. I lost my husband last year. We didn't have our own children, but we adored our nieces and nephews, traveled the world and took them with us sometimes. I'd never take a single breath of life from another human being. This is so horrible!"

"Thank you for helping us, Mrs. Kendrick," Stacey told her. "What's your prognosis? Is there—"

"A chance?" Anita asked, smiling. "While there's breath, there's a chance. I don't give up. I just wish there was more I could give you."

"If we showed you pictures, do you think you might recognize the woman?"

"Maybe. But she was quite odd. Now that I think about it, I think that she was wearing a wig and glasses. I am certainly more than happy to try."

Keenan produced his phone, flipping through his apps quickly. He found the dossiers he had on Cindy Hardy, Sandra Smith and Agnes Merkle.

He thought about the others, the other women who were connected, in one way or another. Jess's friends, Nan, Candy, Betty, Tiffany and Gia. Tania Holt.

And Peggy Bronsen, the aide who had come running from Congressman Smith's office, worried about what her boss might be doing.

He would draw them all up next, if need be.

He showed the first three pictures to the woman. She studied the three of them carefully once, and then again.

"Maybe…"

Her voice trailed.

"Maybe?" he, Stacey and Jean Channing all spoke at the same time.

Their hostess looked up, smiling. "I could be wrong. I told you she was wearing a wig and glasses. But the nose…and her chin. I think…it might have been this woman. No, I don't just think. Yes, this is her, the woman who approached me."

She pointed. The picture she'd picked out was of Sandra Smith, the congressman's wife.

Keenan stood quickly, ready to head out.

"Wait, please!" Anita Kendrick pleaded. "Don't leave me—I mean, until you have her."

"Keenan, go," Stacey said. She looked at Anita Kendrick. "Is that all right with you? I was top as a marksman—or woman— in my academy class. And Jean has been a detective for years—"

"And years," Jean put in dryly.

"Yes, fine, I just thought that you were all going. And my housekeeper went shopping and hasn't come back yet. She's due soon. I just don't... I don't want to be alone. Just in case someone knows somehow that I called the police. Of course, you have the man, but that woman... I won't feel safe until you have her, too."

"We'll have the woman," Keenan assured her.

He headed to the door telling Stacey to call Jackson and find out just where this suspect was and say she should still be under watch.

Stacey followed him. "I'll lock up behind you. Still want to be safe," she said. She pulled her phone out of her pocket. "On it. Go."

"Thanks."

"Yes, sir. Keenan, maybe...maybe this will break the whole enterprise."

"At least," he told her, "we'll get it crumbling toward the ground."

He heard the door lock and hurried to his car.

CHAPTER SEVENTEEN

Was it possible? And if so, why? And if Sandra Smith really was the person who had approached Mrs. Kendrick, was Congressman Smith involved, too? He was the one who had known both Jess Marlborough and Billie Bingham. They'd suspected him from the beginning. But…

Stacey dialed Jackson, filling him in on where they were and what they had learned from Anita Kendrick.

He told her he'd talked to the agents watching the congressman's house just an hour ago; he'd check in with them again and let them know that Keenan was on his way.

Keenan would be bringing Sandra Smith in, even if they only had twenty-four hours before they'd have to charge her. And if Anita Kendrick would agree to view an identification lineup the next day, Sandra would be put under arrest. And pray God, she wouldn't make bail.

Stacey's call completed, she pocketed her phone again and started back to the smaller sitting room.

She paused, a strange dizzy sensation seizing her. She stopped.

The fireplace.

Every damned house they'd been in had a hearth. Her apartment had a hearth.

She was wide awake, but she was suddenly experiencing the dream. Fog seemed to fill the parlor area, dense and rich.

It wasn't real, she told herself. It was the way her dream-visions came, because they weren't clear. But she felt as if she was experiencing her dream; she was on the outside looking in, now, removed from the action, but seeing far too much.

Not the killer in the flesh there before her. But near. She could feel his mind, as if she were on a phone, or somehow hearing what played in the gray mass of his thoughts.

He was ecstatic.

She still couldn't see his face—but she could feel his mind!

Yes, for him…the time had come.

Stacey stood very still, trying to remember details of her dream and compare them to the present.

This didn't seem right. There was the hearth; there was the mist. But in her dream, the room had been smaller.

Yet, the killer was there. Somewhere, in or around the house. She could sense him. *Feel him.*

They were all in danger. She had to move quickly and quietly. She didn't even dare another phone call.

She hurried on, carefully, back to Mrs. Kendrick's smaller parlor, but paused outside the door and carefully looked in.

Neither Jean Channing nor Anita Kendrick was there. No, she was wrong. Anita Kendrick was there.

Lying on the floor.

Still desperately trying for silence, Stacey strode swiftly to her, then knelt down.

The woman had a pulse. Weak, but there. She needed medical help. Fast.

Stacey went for her phone: she needed help fast, too.

But she heard something—near. A strangled gasp, as if someone was trying to cry out but could not.

Stacey drew her gun, looking carefully out into the larger room, surveying it in whole, before walking through.

Someone else had come into the house. They hadn't come through the big parlor; she would have seen them.

There was a back door, of course. Whoever had come in must have slipped through the back. Maybe he'd even done so while Keenan was still there. Maybe this exit had been planned.

And even though she lay on the floor now, Anita Kendrick might have been in on it, might have known.

She might have wanted a new heart that badly.

The promise of life was a sweet one.

Whoever had come in, whoever now had Jean Channing, might have just arrived, too.

And now, they had to have moved to the back of the house. To the dining room and kitchen or office or bedrooms, whatever lay to the left side of the house.

Stacey stood very still, and she heard the desperate, strangled gasping sound again. She couldn't use her phone; she'd be heard.

She had her Glock, and she *was* a crack shot.

Take him down, fast, and then get help for Anita Kendrick.

Carefully, not making a sound, she started to move through the small parlor—to the door that lay beyond.

Which was it? What had happened?

Was Anita Kendrick a liar, the best of the actors they'd yet seen? Did she want a heart so badly that she'd make up an encounter to lure law enforcement so that the killer could manage his deed? Kill her—or kill Jean. Or both.

Only one of them could be the killer's Mary Kelly.

It would be her: Mary Kelly had been the youngest victim. She was the youngest one here.

Her movement was silent and careful. Her weapon was ready.

The door swung open and she took aim.

But she stood dead-still, waiting.

Because the killer was there, holding Jean before them, the business end of a scalpel against her throat.

And Jean was about to die.

Keenan's phone rang before he had driven more than a few blocks.

The caller ID showed it was Jackson, and he answered it quickly.

"You'll be able to get Mrs. Sandra Smith, but not her husband. Sandra is shopping—she does that a lot. But our people following the two of them lost Smith. He was with his wife not an hour ago, going in and out of stores. She went into a dressing room, he went to see what she was trying on, and he apparently disappeared from there."

"Wait, they lost Colin Smith?"

"Yes, and don't start swearing. It happens. The agents couldn't go into a dressing room. She's at that shop she likes so much. There must be a delivery door beyond the dressing rooms. Smith is gone. His wife is still there, though. The agents could see her as we talked."

"All right, but, Jackson, I'm not going to go in and take her. Have them bring her in—and make sure she's held for the next twenty-four hours."

"Where are you going?"

"Back. I don't like the fact that Smith has disappeared."

"We have Henry Lawrence. I thought you believed that we were looking for a woman."

"We are, and it may well be Sandra Smith. But he's a loose end. And Jean Channing and Stacey are back at the Kendrick house."

"You want back up?"

"I don't want bells and whistles. I'm going back quietly. Just in case. Maybe…"

"Maybe what?"

"Maybe she's a liar. Maybe Anita Kendrick did want a heart, and the killer gave her a way to get one."

"But we have Dr. Lawrence in custody."

"And maybe he does the transplants, but not the killing," Keenan said. "Whatever, I'm going back. Yes, can you get out here, but quietly. No announcement that you've arrived."

"I'll be there myself," Jackson promised.

He ended the call and swerved his car around.

He didn't have dreams that warned of evil things that might happen.

He had intuition.

And right now, he knew that something was wrong.

Dead-wrong.

He parked down the street from the house and slipped out, wondering if he should go and break the door down and just get in, or if he'd be risking someone's life.

There was no reason to believe that Colin Smith was here, and he didn't know if the man was involved. Maybe he just wanted to run out on his wife. Possibly understandable.

Instinct told him there was something happening, and he was furious with himself.

Stacey had been targeted. She'd been targeted when she'd received the piece of kidney, maybe long before. She might have been paying for her father's prowess at investigation.

He crept toward the house and came around to the side, hoping to look into the small sitting room through a window.

The windows were open, and the first room he looked into was the dining room. No one.

He crept down the length of the house.

The next room he recognized as the sitting room.

He twisted and strained to see the whole of it.

And he knew then that he'd been wrong. Wrong about Anita Kendrick. She lay on the floor at the side of the table, closest to the window.

He could see no blood. But the woman wasn't moving: she appeared to be broken and gone. The design of the windows obstructed a good view, but he thought that he saw a red spot smearing the top of her snow-white hair.

Had the woman been as innocent as she seemed? Or had she jumped in here to save those doing the transplants, not against the deaths of others—lesser, throwaway people—but desperate to save her own life?

He called Jackson back and reported.

"She needs medical help," Jackson said. "Now. It's our duty."

"Give me five minutes. Stacey and Jean are in there."

"You know that five minutes can be life or death."

"I'm trying to save three lives."

"Go."

The killer was in there somewhere. But how could he have known that they would come? Or had he sent his accomplice out to set a meeting with Mrs. Kendrick, knowing that she was honest and a woman possessing ethics? She would report what had happened to the police, and through that call, he and Stacey would come?

But the woman had pointed out Sandra Smith—and Sandra Smith was still shopping.

He realized they'd have to unravel the truth bit by bit, later.

Right now, he had to get in that house.

Without the killer knowing.

And he had to pray that the man wasn't going to kill swiftly, slashing another victim's throat with power and ferocity, and bringing an almost-instant death.

"You really are an idiot!" Stacey said.

Colin Smith arched a brow; he drew the blade closer against Jean's neck, drawing a line of blood.

"I'm an idiot?"

"I have a Glock trained on you."

"Shoot him! Shoot the bastard!" Jean insisted.

There was terror in her eyes. But Jean was a good cop. She might be frightened as all hell, but she was dedicated to taking down men like Colin Smith.

And she meant it: Stacey should shoot him rather than give in to him.

"I'm an idiot?" he repeated. "I'm the one holding all the cards."

"You're holding me, jerk," Jean said. "And nothing else. This place will be surrounded by cops any minute."

"You could have gotten away with it all," Stacey told him. "We have Dr. Lawrence in custody. He could have taken the fall for this. Now you will get caught because Henry Lawrence can hardy kill anyone while sitting in his jail cell."

"You know, I was supposed to keep the organs. But I guess that won't matter anymore. Anyway, drop the gun, or I kill her."

"If I drop the gun, you'll kill us both."

"Pull the trigger!" Jean said. "You're right—he'll kill us both. And then he'll go on to kill again and again. He does have power. Henry Lawrence is in jail, keeping his mouth shut, because he believes that we can't prove anything, and that Smith will get him out. If this bastard can't get him out—or if it gets dicey—he'll see that Henry Lawrence has an accident in jail, or that he gets a quick shiv from another inmate!"

Stacey couldn't let Jean die. The woman was a good detective and a good human being. And no matter how brave her words, the terror in her eyes was real.

"Drop the gun. I'll let her go," Smith said.

"Did you kill Mrs. Kendrick?" Stacey asked.

"Hope so," he said casually. "Just thumped the old bat on the head. Don't worry, she didn't see me. I made sure. Now, you want to talk about idiots… She could have had a new heart! I mean, this whole thing works on desperation for life at all costs, right? And if you're rich, you can buy life. That old bitch looked as if she was being offered poison instead of life."

"There are moral people in the world," Stacey said. She wasn't sure why but she didn't know if Anita Kendrick would survive now.

She prayed that she did. Even if the woman only had a few more months because of heart disease, Stacey hoped that she would survive. She was the kind of human being who gave others hope for humanity.

"So, let's see if I have this right. Billie Bingham and Henry Lawrence met at McCarron's trial, all those years ago. They talked about what a wonderful business this would be. Billie was a beautiful young woman. She figured she could make some start-up capital by running her escort service. Is that how she brought you into it? And to think we thought it was your wife!"

Smith let out a snickering sound. Stacey didn't want to amuse him: it caused him to laugh, and the deadly sharp blade of the scalpel jiggled on Jean's neck.

"My wife! My darling wife. Well, don't kid yourself. She made use of Billie's escorts, too—she didn't just hire women, you know."

"What a perfect family—enjoying the same recreational activities!" Stacey said.

"We both enjoy money," Colin Smith said. "And politics. You can make it work. Money helps in politics, politics helps in making money."

"Wow."

"Capitalism. It's the American way."

"As you see it. I see the American way as being a people who are born equal, with the same unalienable rights to life, liberty and the pursuit of happiness."

"An idealist! See where that gets you!" Smith snorted.

The blade against Jean's throat had moved a few times too many.

Stacey had to get him to let her go.

How? Well, at least she was keeping him talking. Keenan would call soon enough—they'd have the man's wife. And when they did, he'd call her, or he'd return…

"Put the knife down, and then I'll put the gun down. I'm not letting you out of here."

"Fine. Watch me kill her. If I go down, I'm taking you both with me."

"Oh, you will go down. Keenan has gone to get your wife, you know."

He grinned. "Yeah, I do know. I knew that you would walk him to the door and lock it—and that Jean, here, believed the old lady. I knew the old bitch would need something, and that Detective Channing here would go to the kitchen for it. Had to clock the old woman since she wouldn't play the game. But… I'm damned good at this."

"But you wanted a grand finale, right? A Mary Kelly killing. How the hell are you going to do that here and now? Keenan is coming back. The FBI and other police officers will soon be swarming this house."

He smiled. "You're going to walk outside with me. Out back. A florist's van is waiting. We're going to hop in that van. When you do, I let Detective Channing go."

"I don't think so. Because I still don't see how. I'm not putting my gun down until you let Jean go."

"I'll just slice a little deeper…"

Jean couldn't help it; she let out a cry of pain.

Stacey winced inwardly. *Shoot him. Shoot him*, she told herself.

No. No matter how fast the bullet moved, he just needed to jerk and Jean was dead.

"Who else is involved in this?" Stacey asked.

He laughed softly. "Well, yes, there are others. But for obtaining the right victims—we had a pretty good thing going—a bizarre ménage à trois, if you will. Billie, me and my beautiful, darling witch of a wife. We found the clients and the victims. Henry Lawrence did the transplants. He liked money, and he was never the man you thought he was. But enough of this. Shoot me, or let this woman live. Your choice. Otherwise, I'm out of time. Put the gun down. Hey, you'll have some hope! I'm not slicing you up here. There's a charming little building where I keep an empty loft for…storage." He grinned. "Not in my own name, of course. You'll have a chance… We'll see if your heroic agency can do something fast enough. I really had wanted to take my time with you. Really. Chop, chop, slice, slice, get all gooey and sticky with your blood…but I'm afraid that it's time to get away. Still, you'll have a chance."

"They have your wife."

"Yes, God bless them! I'll be heading off to a South American beach without her! Oh, I won't be alone, but I won't be with that virago! So, you tell me, how do we do this? I've been a politician, Special Agent Hanson. I play for keeps. I'm sick enough, you know, not to care if I die with a blast to my head if I get to watch Detective Channing's blood spurt everywhere as I do. It's all or nothing for me, now."

"I guess you're not winning the next election."

"No problem. People whining, whining, whining. One wants to control climate change, another is crying over bears in caves, another wants more drilling rights… Politics! Hey, it was fun when I needed to be in it, and now…all or nothing."

He'd grown deadly serious.

"Wait!"

"For what? She and I die—or you try to save her."

"Why did you target me?"

"You—and your father. There were whispers in the court-room about PI Hanson having a daughter who warned her dad he was going to be killed. Henry Lawrence heard that. Funny thing is, he told us that McCarron never knew that he had killed Vargas. Of course Vargas knew. That Henry Lawrence is an-other delightfully sick man—he enjoyed watching Vargas die!"

He laughed.

She couldn't make him laugh. The ring around Jean's neck was growing brighter.

"Didn't you brilliant people figure that out yet? Henry Lawrence killed them! Oh, not that McCarron wasn't guilty of a dozen murders—just not those murders! Lawrence hated Vargas; he'd been approached by McCarron because McCarron needed to buy a liver or something for a cousin of his, and Vargas had said that he had to match all the criteria, that organs were precious. Lawrence was up for it. All he had to do was get rid of Vargas."

She felt sick. Emotions raced through her despite the desperation of the situation.

"You've been killing people...since that trial?" she asked.

"Only a few at first. And of course, I wasn't in on it at first. Billie came to me, and then to our other accomplices!" He smiled cruelly. "Let's see how noble you really are. Your life... or her life? Detective Jean Channing—well, she's had a good run of it!"

Stacey had played for time.

And time was up.

"Shoot him!" Jean insisted. Then she screamed, "Watch out!"

There was someone behind Stacey.

And now, it was all or nothing. She fired a shot and spun around, just as something cracked down hard on her head.

Keenan fired several shots, breaking the storm windows at Anita Kendrick's house.

He'd seen the woman hurrying to help Colin Smith, and he'd known then that, while he couldn't see Stacey or Jean, he had to get to them.

He leaped through the window and rushed to the next room.

Jean lay on the floor.

He swore, leaning down to her. She opened her eyes. "Out the back. Go!"

"Jean—"

"She wouldn't let the bastard kill me. There's a van out back. Go."

"Help is on the way."

"Go!"

He raced on through the house, reaching the back door just in time to see a van driving away. It was an off-white color, dirty, but with designs beneath the dirt with splashy colors and a lot of green.

The license plate was covered by vines that escaped from the back door. He couldn't see the numbers, but the vines suggested a florist's or gardener's van.

He pulled out his phone and called Jackson. He was already running, back to the front of the house and the street, desperate to reach his own car to follow the van. As he slid into the driver's seat, he was asking Jackson to get an APB out on the van. In seconds, he was speeding in the direction the van had gone. He could still see it down the long, straight street. He had to get to it.

Before it reached its destination. A room somewhere with a hearth. A burning fire.

And a killer.

She woke slowly, feeling a stabbing pain in her head.

She'd been clocked hard from the rear, but she had gotten her shot off. She knew that she hadn't hit Jean. She just hoped that she had caused Colin Smith to drop the detective.

They may have taken her, but there was a prayer that they'd left her.

She struggled to a sitting position.

She was on a table. A stainless-steel operating table. The room was dark; heavy shades covered the two windows. Through the gloom, she saw the room contained medical equipment. Another table held scalpels and saws. A fridge hummed in the corner. The killer was there. She felt him. Knew that he was coming for her.

"Ready?" Colin Smith asked.

He was standing across the room. His scalpel in his hand, and that hand raised so that the dim light caught the edge of the scalpel.

"Colin, stop messing around!" a woman hissed.

"Leave me alone," Smith muttered. "Bitch. You're all bitches."

"Get on with it!" the woman's voice said, cutting harshly through the misty smoke that filled the room.

"Just shut the hell up!" Colin Smith said. "This…this…this! Shut up! I have been waiting for this. Hey, it could have been you!" he reminded the woman who stood in the shadows. "Leave me alone. Let me do this."

He smiled, and he took a step toward Stacey. She tried to leap from the table.

She could not.

She hadn't realized that her hands and feet were tied, with nylon stockings, she saw.

It was a given that her gun was gone.

She could fight, but tied to the bed?

He came toward her then, smiling—knowing that she was fully aware of her position.

"Special, Special Agent! Here I come!" he told her.

Keenan had lost sight of the van somewhere around Lafayette Square. He should have been able to see it once he got to the corner, but it was as though it had disappeared. Police cars were already swarming the area, but no one had called in that they'd seen the van.

Desperate, Keenan abandoned his car and was running, seeking anywhere a van might have slipped into a parking garage. It must have got off the streets.

He saw a garage in a derelict old building—one not old

enough to be historic, but old enough to be extensively restored, or bulldozed to the ground.

He headed toward the building at a run. He looked up bleakly at the many stories in the building. He had to be fast.

He realized that someone was running next to him.

His great-grandfather, along with Philip Barton Key II.

They flanked him, and he glanced from one to another.

"Fifth floor!" Bram told him.

"We think," Philip Barton Key II said. "We noticed things like cartons containing heavy curtains, and then there was a work vehicle that arrived with soundproofing materials."

"And there was a box labeled 507," Bram told him.

"Thank you!"

He kept moving as fast as he could.

He had to be on time.

Her dreams were warnings, right? They were dreams that warned of what had to be stopped, and he had to stop this, now.

Stacey lashed out at Smith as he came toward her, landing a hard blow to his jaw that sent him staggering backwards.

And rebounding with a fury, wrenching at the stockings that held her.

Nylon was strong. It jerked her back to the bed.

She saw his face, saw his intention.

And saw the knife.

Then, there was a shuddering sound, a massive explosion, it seemed to Stacey.

The door burst open.

Colin Smith looked in that direction.

Keenan had arrived. Miraculously, he had arrived.

The woman jumped out of the shadows at last. She had a gun; it was aimed at Keenan.

The woman was Cindy Hardy.

She rushed at him. Keenan fired.

Cindy Hardy went down, falling onto Keenan, causing him to stagger back.

Colin Smith let out a roar of fury. He raised the scalpel high, ready to thrust it deep into Stacey's chest.

She was desperate. She surged up the best she could, head-butting the man with all her strength.

He screamed, thrown backward, just an inch...

But it was enough.

Another shot thundered.

And Smith went down, the scalpel still in his hands, crashing into the bed, barely an inch from Stacey's side.

She looked at Keenan. He rushed to her, ripping at the ties that bound her.

She saw his eyes, and she smiled.

"Dreams are good!" she told him.

"Dreams are good," he agreed.

Keenan helped Stacey up. She was shaking. And it was all right, she told herself.

She'd been strong, tough, all the right things when she'd needed to be.

And now it was okay to shake.

"Jean?" she whispered.

"At the hospital. But she's going to make it," he told her. "Thanks to you. Stacey, are you all right? Did he cut you?"

"I haven't a scratch on me," she said, and smiled. "I've got the best partner ever."

"No," he told her softly. "I have the best partner ever."

EPILOGUE

"It's terrifying to even try to comprehend just how long the killing was going on," Jackson said, leaning back in his office chair. Keenan had to agree. The entire plot had been insidious, horrific, and devised by people who should have been the pillars of the community.

Three days had passed since Stacey had escaped being Colin Smith's final event.

Colin Smith and Cindy Hardy were dead.

Dr. Henry Lawrence, hearing that news, and aware that he wasn't getting out and there would be no congressman there to fight for him and see to any kind of a release, began to talk.

It had all begun years before.

Not immediately after McCarron's trial: it had taken a few years to set up and get going.

Lawrence still claimed that he'd never killed anyone. Billie and he had first gotten into it, then Billie had noted that Congressman Colin Smith had certain sadistic tendencies. He'd been brought in—along with his long-suffering wife. Sandra refused to get her hands dirty with the killings, but she helped recruit clients, such as when she'd approached Mrs. Kendrick.

Then, when Cindy Hardy had started such a ruckus over her husband, Billie had found a way to lure her into the business side of things. Billie's charm worked for many things, it seemed. And Cindy had obviously felt the money made up for what had happened previously with her husband.

Between Congressman Smith and Dr. Lawrence, the group had enough wealthy contacts to have a stream of clients. Billie would often find the female victims, recruiting them as potential escorts. Cindy Hardy had used herself as bait to trap victims, too, chatting up business travelers to see if anyone would miss them after they were attacked outside the bar or hotel.

"And, by the way," Keenan said, turning to Stacey, "your upstairs neighbor, Marty, wasn't being paranoid. Lawrence hired a few thugs to keep an eye on your apartment. Lawrence and Smith had decided you were a threat. It just took them a while to decide when to strike."

She looked at Jackson and grimaced. "Keenan saved my life."

"She saved her own life," Keenan said. "Don't cross her. The woman has a hell of a headbutt."

"We all save each other. That's what we do here," Jackson said.

He went on to try to explain more details, though many were still to be figured out.

Sandra Smith was the one who filled in much of what they were missing. She knew she was going to jail, though she claimed she never killed anyone, either.

She had been the one to approach Anita Kendrick. She had watched the woman and knew that she was ridiculously—in her mind—ethical. They hoped she would call the police about the offer they'd made her. Colin would get his chance to kill Stacey. However, it was Henry Lawrence who had wanted her dead.

He was uneasy about her. He knew how close Stacey's father had come to discovering the truth about Dr. Vargas's death all those years ago.

He had relished the idea of sending her a piece of kidney.

The Yankee Ripper plot had been Sandra's invention. She had convinced Colin that Billie was getting out of control. She would be part of it all. She'd been told that there were officers getting a little too close on a few of their missing persons, and they had to throw the law off somehow. Billie had been willing: she had killed the woman in her basement.

She'd had no clue that when she met with Smith, she would be the next victim.

The details in the case, and the follow-up, would be endless.

But, Jackson told them that morning, it was over for the two of them.

"You're on vacation. Go somewhere. Get far away from here. You two were key in solving more murders than we may ever really know. Hopefully all the victims can find some peace now. Go! Get out of here."

Keenan looked at Stacey.

"I… I just started. Are you sure?" she asked the assistant director.

"Get out of here," he told her, smiling.

Keenan stood and took her hand, and they left the office.

"So, where are we going?" she asked.

"Hawaii? Um, Europe? What's your pleasure?"

"A stop-off, first," she said.

"Just tell me where."

In Lafayette Square, they found Philip Barton Key II and Bram Wallace by the fountain. A mime was entertaining a group of schoolchildren, and the two were watching both the mime and the delight of the children with smiles on their faces.

"We came to thank you," Stacey said. "Without you—"

She broke off, noticing that the two weren't alone.

Tim Dougherty, one of the ghosts from Dr. Lawrence's woods, had managed to get himself to Lafayette Square.

"Hello!" he said, peeking around Bram's ghostly form.

"Hey!" Stacey said.

He looked at Keenan. "Hitchhiked," he told him. "Your boss is a great guy. Came up with him, his wife, Raina—the dog lady—and the dogs! It was a bit crowded, but…"

"Good. Glad you're here. Happier?" Keenan asked.

He nodded.

"And your friends?" Stacey asked.

"They went on," Tim said. "It was…well, I think it was beautiful. There was a light…and they went on. I guess I want to stay a bit. I found these guys. I have purpose. We're, uh, going to fight for justice."

"A rookie," Bram muttered, "but what can you do."

Keenan laughed. "Rookies can be the best!" he said.

They stayed a while longer, chatting, the ghosts wanting to make sure that Stacey was okay, and both Stacey and Keenan wanting to make sure they knew how grateful they were.

"We played such a small part," Philip said.

"A small part that saved time and probably my life," Stacey told him.

"See! I want to be part of that," Tim said.

When they left Lafayette Square, they headed for Stacey's apartment.

Keenan was mulling the question, but decided to ask Stacey again. "Where to? The beautiful beaches of Hawaii? The majesty of the mountains? Europe? Italy, Germany? Ah, Iceland is supposed to be amazing."

She didn't answer.

A quick look showed she was relaxed in her seat, eyes closed. He thought that she was sleeping. He prayed that her dreams were over.

She made a little moaning sound.

"Stacey, Stacey! Wake up, I'm here."

Her eyes opened. She stared at him. He pulled over to the side of the road, wanting to touch her, hold her, and give her his full attention.

"You were dreaming," he said.

She smiled. "I was."

"And?"

"We were in a room. It had a gorgeous balcony. We watched the sun from the balcony, streaming down. Then you walked over to me, and we closed the curtains…"

"And then?"

"Oh, well, then we stripped one another naked, kissed and touched and did amazing things, and had the most incredible sex ever."

He laughed softly and begin to drive.

"So, where do you think we should go?" she asked.

"Don't care, as long as it has a room with a gorgeous balcony, sun streaming in, curtains to draw and that delicious bed where we can be together. Hey—I may know the place. Jon and Kylie are in Scotland. He sent me a text this morning, said we were welcome to join them there. Did your room with the balcony resemble a castle in any way?"

"A castle?"

"Yeah."

"Oh, definitely. It could have been a castle. Scotland sounds great."

He drove in silence, smiling.

Suddenly Stacey said, "I think I love you."

He glanced her way, his smile broadening.

"I know I love you," he told her. "Best rookie ever."

She took his hand.

"Best partner—ever!"

★ ★ ★ ★ ★